Damned Cold

Kevin Lee Swaim

PUBLISHED BY: PICADILLO PUBLISHING
COVER DESIGN BY: THE COVER COLLECTION
EDITING BY: CLIO EDITING
PROOFREADING BY: DONNA RICH
ISBN: 978-0692622186

10 9 8 7 6 5 4 3 2 1
FIRST EDITION
PRINTED IN THE UNITED STATES OF AMERICA

Also by Kevin Lee Swaim

Project Strikeforce

Project StrikeForce

The Chimera Strain

Project StrikeForce: Exodus

StrikeForce Reborn

Sam Harlan, Vampire Hunter

Come What May

Hard Times

Damned Cold

Deal with the Devil

DEDICATION

To my wife, MaryAnn.

Chapter One

They say a watched pot never boils. I disagree. I once owned a diner, and I can assure you a pot boils whether anyone watches the damned thing or not.

I stood at the kitchen sink, thinking about watched pots and my recently developed urge to smash a pot against someone's face.

Anyone's face.

Before I fled my old life, I had rarely felt anger. Not *real* anger. Not that kind that makes you want to hurt people, to make them bleed and cower in fear and piss themselves. No, *this* anger was new and fresh and terrifying.

I was scrubbing a skillet, still contemplating watched pots, when the phone finally rang. I glanced back to the kitchen table, where Sister Callie Calahane was quietly reading the book I had given her for Christmas.

She raised an eyebrow, her emerald eyes wary.

I held up my soap-covered hands and nodded down the hall. "Can you?"

She closed her copy of *The Epic of Gilgamesh* and hurried to grab the phone before the answering machine picked up.

I went back to scrubbing the cast-iron skillet, then rinsed it off, turned on the stove, and put the skillet on to dry. While the skillet warmed, I listened as Callie spoke quietly with whatever lost soul had called for our help.

Her end of the conversation was as clear as if she were standing next to me, even though she was fifty feet away. People who knew about such things called it the change—the result of my first kill, the vampire essence burning through my body, enhancing my senses, giving me great strength and resilience.

They neglected to mention it also brought a soul-crushing,

mind-numbing hunger. My meals were full of bloody rare steak, and the grease and blood that drained down the back of my throat never quite satiated the hunger.

And, apparently, it gifted me with a bottomless pit of rage.

Just fantastic.

I could barely discern the man's voice on the other end of the call. Callie answered, her voice warming by degrees. "Yes," she said. "We will be there. Yes, Father. Of course. Let me write it down."

There was a scratch-scratch of the pencil as she hurriedly scribbled information on a pad of paper, then cleared her throat. "Thank you, Father. See you soon."

She hung up and returned to the kitchen, a pad of paper in her hand. Callie was a young woman in her mid-twenties, tall, with striking auburn hair and wearing jeans and a dark flannel shirt. She constantly reminded me she was a sister, not a nun, and she had followed me home from Peoria after I had murdered my daughter.

Her twin sister, Katie, had helped me during my first vampire hunt, until a vampire named Pearl had ripped her guts out.

The death of Katie Calahane lay between us during every moment and every conversation. The death of my daughter, and my wife, and my kin, Jack Harlan, lay there too. Their deaths cast a long shadow, and Callie dealt with it better than I did.

"That was Father Jameson," she said.

"What does he want?" Father Jameson was a priest from St. Louis. I had last seen him in the basement of the Cathedral Basilica when he helped me up the concrete stairs and into Jack's truck. I mentally counted up the weeks and winced.

Fourteen weeks. It has only been fourteen weeks.

Callie absently thumbed the pad of paper. "A woman is missing."

I laughed before I could stop myself, a grating sound that carried no humor. "There always is."

Callie frowned. "Sam—"

I turned away, afraid to speak, and took a seat at the kitchen table, trying to avoid her gaze. "Tell me about it."

"The Father received a call from a priest in Bement," Callie said, taking the seat across from me, watching me intently.

"A vampire?"

She shrugged. "The priest isn't sure. It's not like the Church prepares them…"

It was a sore subject with Callie. And, now that I was in the family business, it didn't sit well with me, either. "What's Jameson want us to do?"

"He would like us to look into it."

"I'll bet he would. Why doesn't he go himself?"

"He's there now," she said.

I tried and failed to hide my surprise. "He is?"

She nodded. "I told him we would help."

"Of course you did." I was still avoiding her gaze, but from the corner of my eye, I saw her lips quiver.

"We need to talk about it."

I shook my head. "Talk is overrated."

"It's not your fault. You did everything you could." The growing sense of frustration in her voice belied the pity in her eyes.

"Tell that to Lori Glick," I said, shoving away from the table. The oak chair screeched against the wooden floor, and I was up and walking before Callie could answer.

I made my way down the basement stairs, past the freezer full of paper-wrapped beef, and swung the door to the armory open with a clang. The armory was a forty-foot-long, thirty-foot-wide concrete room, with a domed ceiling I couldn't reach with a stepladder. A dizzying array of weapons lined the walls, with knives and swords and guns hanging from pegs. A wooden bench full of gunsmithing tools occupied the center of the room, and gray carpet tiles covered the floor.

Industrial metal shelves full of ammunition stood neatly arranged to my left. Beside them was a Rubbermaid container full of wooden stakes. At the far end of the room, near the door that led to the garage, sat an old-fashioned black steel safe as tall as a man and nearly as wide.

Inside the safe was a fortune in gold, silver, and paper currency, a gift from my great-great-great-grandfather, Jack Harlan. The money, the armory, and the house and land in Toledo were his legacies—mine to use as I saw fit.

I *had* wanted to hunt vampires.

Until it all went so wrong.

The change had already healed my broken finger and ribs. The bruises and contusions had disappeared—gone as if they never existed. My side still ached, as did my back, my finger, and wrist, but my body was in some semblance of working order.

If I could just get my mind right.

I removed the Kimber .45 from my Galco shoulder holster, checking the magazine for silver bullets. It was a gift from Mary Kate Glick, originally intended for Jack, and its substantial weight felt good in my hand. Two extra magazines rested in leather pouches under my right arm, and I checked those as well, then holstered the Kimber.

It was my new nervous tic, like checking every room in the house for misplaced items and craning my neck to listen for unexpected noises.

Footsteps approached from the basement. Callie entered the armory and watched as I removed a plastic ammo can and filled it with boxes of silver ammunition, and then she grabbed several boxes of silver twelve-gauge shotgun shells from the metal shelves and handed them to me. I grunted and filled the ammo can to the brim, shut it, and looked up to her.

She had removed the modified Remington 870 from the wall, a heavy shotgun with a pistol grip and collapsible stock that she had claimed as her own after Jack's death. She was now proficient enough with it that I no longer worried she might accidentally shoot me.

I had spent most of November and the early part of December practicing with the Kimber. After countless hours, it was now an extension of my arm. It had to be. The weapons were beautiful, well-maintained tools of our new trade, but more than that, our lives depended on them.

That thought depressed the hell out of me.

Callie set her Remington on the bench and said, "I've got the directions."

"How far?"

"Bement is in Central Illinois. About three hundred miles, give or take."

I grunted. "Anything nearby?"

"It's east of Decatur," Callie said.

I could almost hear her unspoken words. *The place where Katie died.*

I bit my lip. "We won't make it until after dark."

She watched me, her face a careful blank. "I want to stop in Peoria if you don't mind."

"You want to see—"

"Father Lewinheim."

It was the least I could do for her. "I'm sure he'll be glad to see *you*."

"Sam—"

"What am I supposed to tell him?"

Her eyes were full of empathy. "You don't have to seek his approval, Sam. He won't judge."

"He ought to," I said. "He damned well *ought* to."

* * *

It was only a short walk through the tunnel to the machine shed, a heated building with a concrete floor and a mechanic's lift in the far right bay. A Camaro, an F-150 pickup truck, and even a vintage Indian motorcycle occupied the garage, but the Chevrolet Cheyenne had been Jack's main vehicle. I had repaired it as best I could after a vampire had slammed me into the side and crushed the passenger door.

The truck wouldn't win any awards, but it was powerful and functional, and that's all I cared about.

Pegboards full of tools draped the walls. Rolling tool chests sat underneath. I placed Callie's Remington inside the middle drawer of the four-foot-long black Craftsman toolbox against the back wall. The plastic ammo cases went in the top, along with several wooden stakes and an ancient Army Colt M1911, a duplicate of the one I had lost in October. The silver Bowie knife joined them. It was fourteen inches long and would be awkward driving with it strapped to my hip.

I grabbed the toolbox, picked it up, and made my way to the back of Jack's truck. The toolbox weighed in at several hundred pounds, but I easily manhandled it into the truck's bed before shutting the tailgate and topper.

Callie stood watch, dressed in a thick brown jacket and faded jeans. Her eyes swept over me, appraising. "Are you going to keep wearing that?" she asked.

I glanced down at my black leather trench coat. "It suits me."

"It's cold. Wouldn't you prefer something warmer?"

"Don't need it," I said. "I don't *get* cold. Not anymore."

The corner of her eyes tightened. There was worry there, but there was also something else. I had a sneaking suspicion that it wasn't just empathy, but that she was carefully charting the progression of my bodily changes.

Jack had become something far from human, and Callie had

to know it would happen to me. I hadn't asked her about it because I really didn't want to know the answer, but if push came to shove, I was hoping she would kill me before I turned into a monster.

"Will you need something to eat?" Callie asked.

I nodded. We had taken to carrying a paper bag full of beef jerky wherever we went.

There was no telling when the hunger would strike.

Callie left, and I climbed into the truck and pushed the remote button hanging from the truck's visor. The door rumbled sideways behind me with a squeal of metal. I thought about replacing the home-brewed contraption Jack had built. The shed had enough overhead space for a roll-up door. Then I realized I would have to find someone I trusted to do the work.

It was probably the reason Jack had built it himself.

Callie returned with a heavy canvas duffel bag slung over her shoulder and a paper bag in her hand. She turned off the lights in the shed and got in the truck, stuffing the bag full of beef jerky behind the seat and the duffel in the floorboard.

I hit the button to close the shed door and backed down the lane. A light dusting of snow covered the gravel lane, just enough to make the rear tires slide. The temperature was hovering in the upper twenties. It wasn't terribly cold, but wasn't warm enough to melt the snowfall from the day before.

A few miles of gravel roads and soon we were heading east on US-30. The truck ate up mile after mile of interstate, passing rolling fields empty of corn and soybeans, the bleak, dreary landscape broken only by lonely stands of trees, rest areas, and the occasional blip of a town.

The sun was setting when we cruised into Peoria. The winter solstice was barely a week behind us, and the sky now darkened before peak afternoon rush hour traffic. We parked the truck down the block from the rectory and got out. The air was thick with the smell of bitter car exhaust and the rank, fishy odor from the Illinois River to the south.

An old warhorse of a nun sat behind a wooden desk inside the rectory, reading a book. She wore a brown dress with a matching headdress, and when she glanced up, her mouth puckered like she had sucked on a lemon. Her eyes narrowed and her breath caught in her throat.

I gulped. I had seen that nun handle a massive semiautomatic pistol, and the look on her face suggested she had no problem pulling it again.

Then the nun saw Callie and her expression warmed from subarctic to something almost resembling warmth.

Almost.

"Sister Beulah," Callie said, stepping forward. "It's so good to see you."

The old nun tilted her head ever so slightly. "Sister Callie. Still with the Harlan."

"Good to see you too, Sister," I said. Well, that's what I *meant* to say, but the words that came from my mouth were, "Frighten any children today?"

Callie's mouth dropped.

I didn't blame her. I looked from her to Sister Beulah. The old nun's brown eyes darkened, literally darkened, and there was a whooshing in the room like the air pressure had dropped.

"*What* did you say?" the nun demanded.

I was trying to stammer out an apology, but the unexpected surge of anger came back. The blood rushed to my face and made the tips of my ears burn. "Don't worry, Sister. It's okay to look down your nose at me. I'm *just* a Harlan."

A buzzing ran up my spine and the tension in the room increased. I felt like a very small insect that Sister Beulah was about to smite, and I knew in that instant that the old nun was no longer *just* a woman, the same way I was no longer *just* a man. Whatever Sister Beulah was, it was interwoven with things like faith, and power, and God's judgment.

The nun spoke softly, but her words hammered me to the hard linoleum. "Hold your tongue in the House of the Lord, boy."

"Sister!" Callie cried out, raising her hands. "We're not here to cause trouble. We just want to speak with Father Lewinheim!"

I was sprawled on the floor, panting for breath. It felt like an invisible boulder had landed on me. I strained against it, but it was useless. I couldn't lift a finger.

And I didn't *want* to.

I'd felt God's presence before, and it wasn't the warm, fuzzy love of a creator who sacrificed his son for our salvation. It was a mind-clawing terror that made my bladder burn and my sphincter tighten. I would give anything, do anything, to make it go away. Tears ran down my face, and I choked out a contrite, "Sorry. I'm *sorry.*"

And, like that, it evaporated, gone as if it had never existed. The nun stood there, her hands on her matronly hips and her piercing eyes focused on me with laser-like intensity.

I stood and tried to apologize, but Sister Beulah turned her attention to Callie. "The boy shall not pass."

Callie was watching with a horrified expression. "But Father Lewinheim—"

"The Guardian decides who shall pass," Sister Beulah said, "and I say the boy *stays*. For now."

* * *

I watched the traffic pass by outside while I waited for Callie to return. Sister Beulah sat at her desk, but I kept my eyes focused on the window.

Me? Scared?

Sure I wasn't.

The only sound in the room was the rumble of the cars passing outside and the occasional whisper of paper as the Sister flipped a page in her book. Finally, after what seemed an eternity, the door to the hallway opened and Callie entered. "Father Lewinheim says to let him pass."

Sister Beulah closed her book and stared at me for an uncomfortably long time, then grunted and said, "Be on your best behavior, Harlan. Your *best* behavior."

I didn't gulp. Nor did I race from the room. "Yes, Sister."

Callie nodded her approval, then led me through the hallway and up the stairs to Lewinheim's door. "He wants to speak with you. Alone."

"Why?"

She shrugged. "He's already spoken with me."

I knocked softly and waited until the old man's voice beckoned me in.

The smell of the elderly and the infirm was heavy in the small room. A neatly made bed pressed against the far wall, a stuffed-to-the-brim bookcase against the other. Lewinheim sat on his recliner in the center of the room. He looked tired. His face was a maze of wrinkles and age spots, and the thin ring of white hair on his head was almost gone.

He raised a weathered hand and motioned for me to come

closer. "Samuel."

I nodded. "Father."

The old man eyed me critically. "You've changed."

"How so?"

The old man motioned to the chair at his desk. "Sit. Please."

I grabbed the chair and approached him, sitting as close as I dared. "What did Callie tell you?"

Lewinheim offered a small smile. "You've been busy. Tell me about … Halloween."

"There's not much to tell," I finally said. "There was a vampire. I killed it. People died."

"Yes," the old man said, nodding his head. "The Sheriff was there?"

"Henry helped clean up," I acknowledged.

"You don't trust him," the old priest noted.

I barked out a laugh. "Not in the slightest. He's been … helpful, but he's an ancient vampire. Sometimes our interests align. He seems to like me, but I don't know if that matters."

The old man closed his eyes. "Well spoken. He fights against his nature, but he's *still* unbelievably dangerous."

I nodded, even though Lewinheim couldn't see me.

Henry Hastings was the right-hand man of the Ancients, the twelve oldest vampires on earth. In his role of Sheriff, he kept the vampire world hidden from the public and maintained the status quo. Henry had helped with Jack in Tangier and with Ignacio Santiago in Marshalltown, but he *was* a thousand-year-old vampire.

"What else did Callie tell you?"

The old man opened his eyes and squinted at me. "I would rather hear it in your words."

"There was a vampire. He was after this family—"

"They were scourged," the old man said.

I nodded. "We didn't know. The vampire … got into their heads. The mother and daughter were willing, I think. There was another daughter. Olivia. I saved her, but the rest of the family…" I swallowed hard. "Only the father survived. He's…"

I paused, waiting for the tightness in my chest to ease, then continued. "The father's been committed to the state. They say he's suffering from dementia. There was another family. The Glicks. The father and daughter were murdered by the vampire. I thought I had saved their son…"

As I spoke, I realized how inadequate it sounded. The Mendozas were dead, the Glick family torn apart.

I heard a growling sound and realized it was coming from me.

"You cannot blame yourself," Lewinheim said. "You tried."

"I tried—" The words caught in my throat. "I tried and failed. Miserably. I almost got myself killed. I almost got Callie killed. I didn't think—"

"It would be so difficult?" Lewinheim asked. "You didn't expect to make decisions that were a matter of life or death? You thought you could take Jack's place and exact some form of revenge for your family?"

I felt the anger rising again. "I sound like an idiot."

Lewinheim shook his head. "You are no idiot. You are a troubled young man who thought his grief would somehow make him perfect."

I rocked back in the chair. "I'm not Jack. I have no idea what I'm doing."

Lewinheim sat quietly, his sad gray eyes full of empathy. "I know what it is like to fight against evil, Samuel. You ask a question I've pondered since Jack's death. I wonder if *I* made a difference. I wonder if the lives lost due to my actions were part of God's will. I wonder if I did the *right* thing."

We stared at each other in silence, until I finally asked, "What's the answer?"

"After many years of prayer, I've come to the conclusion that there is no *right* answer," Lewinheim said. "Only *faith*."

* * *

Callie had joined us in Lewinheim's room. I offered her my seat, at which she rolled her eyes. Lewinheim watched us with great interest, and it was starting to creep me out. "Father? Why do you keep looking at me like that?"

Lewinheim shrugged. "You know about the change. You know the effects are … profound."

Callie turned to stare at me, her face full of concern.

My stomach sank. "What aren't you telling me?" I asked. It felt like I was moving through a fog. "There's more, isn't there?"

"What more?" Callie asked. She turned back to Lewinheim. "Father? What don't we know?"

Lewinheim glanced down at the floor. "You've experienced the hunger, but yes, there is more."

"Why didn't Jack tell me?" I asked.

Lewinheim raised his head and said, "He probably would have told you—"

"What else?" Callie asked. "What else will Sam endure?"

The Father's hand trembled as he wiped at his forehead, and I noticed the old man's hands were covered in even more liver spots than before. "Increased emotions, Callie. He will feel intense anger, greater than he has ever known."

I realized I was holding my breath. "What else?"

"Fear, of course. Disgust. Sadness. Surprise." The old man paused. "It's not *all* bad. You will also feel great happiness."

I shook my head. "I don't see *that* happening."

"There's more," Callie said, "isn't there? I could always tell when you weren't completely honest."

The old priest's head jerked and his lips twitched. Finally, he said, "He will have … strong appetites."

Strong appetites? "That doesn't sound that bad. I'm getting used to the hunger."

The priest glanced from Callie to me. "Appetites, Sam. Longings."

Callie blinked.

I managed to say, "Uh—"

"You mean … sexual urges," Callie said.

The Father nodded. "It's difficult for me to speak of. Jack mentioned it, but only briefly and never in detail. I didn't pry, of course. I preferred not to hear the salacious details."

Callie's eyes found mine, eyes that were so much like her sister's. "Have you been having feelings like that?"

"I'm not comfortable talking about this," I said. "Not with you." I hitched my thumb at Lewinheim. "Not with him, either. No offense, Father."

"I'm a sister," Callie said patiently, "not a robot. I understand how sex works."

"Callie," I said, "I don't care if you were Jesus Christ himself, I'm *not* discussing it."

"Sam!" Callie said, clearly upset by my blasphemy.

"Leave the boy alone," Lewinheim said. "He hasn't recovered from losing his wife. He doesn't want to speak of it."

Callie bit her lip. "I respect you, Sam, but I also *live* with you."

"Damn it!" I barked. "Of all the things to be worried about, that's what bothers you? Not the vampires? Not that we could die at any moment? Or that we keep making mistakes?"

"Calm down," Lewinheim said. His tired old eyes blinked furiously. "This is the anger I was talking about."

I growled in frustration. "Father, people depended on me. They trusted me. I promised them I would keep them safe and I ... *didn't*."

Callie started to speak, but I fixed her with a stare and said, "C'mon, Callie. You know it's true. I tried my best, but it wasn't good enough. I almost got you killed in Marshalltown. You saved us, not me."

"That's *not* true," Callie said. Her eyes were full of emotion. "You did your best. I know you blame yourself, but if not for you, Santiago would be alive, and Olivia would have received the gift. Juan and Franco and Elias would still be dead. Colden, too."

I wanted to scream at her. I wanted to scream at the Father. Instead, I just laughed until I felt tears streaming down my face. "Yeah. Maybe. But what about Duane and Carrie Glick? What about Angie Bent? Twenty-four years old and her head torn from her body like so much useless meat. Carrie wasn't even seventeen, for God's sake. Seventeen!"

I stood and paced around the room. I wanted to move, to walk or run, to do something physical to relieve the tension boiling inside me.

Callie and Father Lewinheim just watched in silence.

I must have made two circuits of the Father's small room before taking my seat again. "Father? I know God exists." I nodded at Callie. "I've seen His wrath. What I don't understand is why He allows evil to exist. Why do vampires get to roam this earth?" My voice rose, sounding almost panicked. "Why doesn't He *do* something about it!"

The Father shook his head sadly. "Sam, you may not take comfort in my words, but I *do* understand. I was like you, a long time ago. I wanted to do the right thing. The Christian thing. Without Jack's help, I would have died." He paused, his breath rattling around in his chest. "I asked many of the same questions. My faith almost deserted me. I was full of anger. I wondered how God could leave us to the monsters. Then I realized..."

Callie turned to the Father, her mouth open. "What did you realize?"

The old man turned his gaze upon me. "That perhaps God *had* done something. Perhaps God had sent me Jack Harlan."

* * *

Callie was speaking quietly with Lewinheim, but I wasn't listening. I was leaning back in the old chair, and although I tried to focus on their conversation, a part of me wondered if the Father was right. I wondered if God had led Jack to a young Edmund Lewinheim, and if fate was a real thing, manipulated by a powerful divinity. Was I part of it?

Did God allow Stacie and Lilly to die so that I might do His bidding?

I was so caught up in my thoughts that I almost missed Lewinheim's comment about Father Jameson. "What was that?"

Lewinheim glanced up in surprise. "I was telling Callie about my first meeting with Patrick. He was quite skeptical of vampires. You know that many in the Church are kept unaware of their existence—"

"I don't understand that," I said. "I was underneath the Cathedral Basilica in St. Louis. They've practically got a dungeon under there."

Callie started to speak, but the old man hushed her. "You have to understand, Samuel. The modern age has washed away much of the Church's ancient ways, but there are still things the Church must do. Functions the Church must perform. Patrick was … training."

"For what?" I asked.

"You have seen much since September," Lewinheim said. "There is much you have *not* seen. How much do you know about demons?"

"Demons?" I asked. "You're kidding."

The old man frowned. "Patrick was a young man and strong in his faith. He was training as an exorcist."

I looked to Callie for confirmation, but she just bit her lip. I wasn't ready to let it go. "You're serious. Exorcism? Like in that movie?"

"A shameful spectacle," the old man said through pursed lips. "An exaggeration of certain aspects and a glamorization of others.

Demons exist. They are *very* real."

I was rendered speechless. Just when it seemed I had come to grips with the dangers lurking around every corner, a fresh new monstrosity exposed itself. I looked from Lewinheim to Callie, but I couldn't even formulate a basic question.

"Demons are those angels God tested and found wanting," Callie said. "They were cast out from God's presence."

"Demons are real," I finally managed. "They exist? They walk the earth?"

"Not in the physical sense," Callie said. "They are spirits of intellect. They think and reason and try to prove to God how fallible humans are. They possess people so that they might experience a physical body, and so they might tempt mankind away from God's love."

"And Jameson was training to exorcise them?"

Lewinheim nodded. "Anyone can exorcise a demon if they have a sufficient amount of faith. The stronger the faith, the easier the exorcism. The young train with older priests so they might be prepared, so that their faith won't waver. Demons are cowards."

"How does that work?" I asked. "How can the Church acknowledge demons and exorcisms, but vampires are kept quiet?"

"No one knows where vampires come from," Lewinheim said. "They are not fallen angels. They are … something else. Demons are as interested in vampires as they are in humanity. Nothing would suit the demons' purpose better than to use the knowledge of vampires to corrupt humanity's faith in God."

"So how did Jameson wind up fighting vampires?" I asked.

Lewinheim sighed heavily, then raised a coffee mug from the small table next to his recliner and took a sip. "Patrick's success came at a high price. The eighties were a difficult time. The Church had almost abandoned exorcisms after a … series of accidental deaths. That movie did not help. As the older priests retired, there were so very few who still believed. Patrick's work was in demand, and it led to—"

"He burned out," I finished for him.

Lewinheim took another sip from his mug. "His faith was still strong, but he suffered from stress."

"Post-traumatic stress disorder," Callie said quietly.

Lewinheim nodded. "It wasn't called that, but yes, he had panic attacks. Nightmares. He had seizures. I thought he might lose his mind if he continued. Demons are infinite. They have forever to tempt humanity. Our lives are but a flicker of a candle to them."

I guessed what was coming next. "Someone was attacked by a vampire. Someone he knew."

"Yes," Lewinheim said. "A parishioner was attacked and left for dead. Father Frank Ford, a dear friend of mine, was called in to try and cleanse the woman. He asked Patrick for help." The old man's eyes filled with tears, and he wiped at them with the back of his hand. "The woman turned and slaughtered Frank before he could finish the ceremony. Patrick managed to stab her with Frank's crucifix. It was made of silver, you see, and set fire to the woman. She burned, and Patrick saw for himself what so few of us knew. He came to me, then, and I taught him as best I could. I introduced him to Jack. It was so long ago…"

"Father?" Callie asked. "Are you okay?"

Lewinheim blinked. "I … don't know where the years went. I remember the look on Patrick's face. He didn't want to believe, but he saw it with his own eyes. I remember it as if it were yesterday. Where have all the years gone?"

The old man was tired. I caught Callie's eye and nodded at the door. "We have to go, Father. We have a job to do."

Callie leaned in and hugged the old man. "Thank you, Father. For everything."

"Of course, my girl. Be safe." Lewinheim turned to me. "Be good, Samuel. Don't lose your faith. I believe God works through us. Through you."

Before I could stop myself, I said, "God needs to start pulling His weight."

Chapter Two

We made our way down the stairs and to the vestibule where Sister Beulah waited. She glanced up from her desk and nodded at Callie before fixing me with an icy glare.

I stopped and bowed my head. "Thanks for letting me pass, Sister. I'm sorry about earlier."

Sister Beulah harrumphed, but she relaxed a bit and said, "Be on your way, Harlan, and keep Callie safe."

I nodded. "As if my life depended on it."

There was steel in the old nun's eyes. "It just might, boy. It just might."

Callie grabbed my arm and hustled me out through the front door. "Come, Sam. We're running late."

We were crossing the street when I finally asked, "What's up with Sister Beulah?"

Callie glanced down the now-darkened street and pointed to a gap in the heavy traffic. We hurried across the street, and Callie said, "Sister Beulah protects the rectory. I thought you knew that."

In fact, I had not known that. "Why does she keep giving me the stink eye?"

Callie was opening the passenger door when she finally spoke. "The Sister can … look into people."

I slid behind the wheel, digesting that. "She sees something in me she doesn't like. Doesn't that concern you? Because it's freaking me the hell out."

"Language, Sam," Callie said sharply.

"Sorry," I mumbled. "Heck. It's freaking me the heck out."

Callie spoke slowly, as if to a child. "You're a good man, Sam Harlan. You'll get through these changes. Jack survived them. You will, too."

I stuck the key in the ignition and fired up the Chevy. "Do I have to remind you what happened to Jack?"

Before Callie could speak, I threw the truck into reverse, backed out of the parking space, and headed for I-74.

We had crossed the Illinois River and were headed up a hill when I heard Callie finally murmur, "I haven't forgotten."

I didn't have a comeback, so I focused on brooding while I drove. We headed east to Bloomington, then south to Decatur. Small town after small town whizzed by, little Podunk out-of-the-way places that were little more than a gas station, a small school, a few houses, and a fast-food joint if they were lucky.

We roared through the darkness. The empty fields outside were an endless sea of grayish black with no evidence of the snow we had left in Iowa. I took the I-72 exit on the north side of Decatur, and we were almost past the edge of the city when I said, "Do you want to see where Katie died?"

Callie had been staring into the darkness, but she turned and frowned. "What did you say?"

"Warren's house is just a few miles south of here," I said, "along the lake. That's where Pearl killed her."

Callie shuddered and turned to stare out the window at an oil rig slowly pumping away in the middle of a nearby cornfield. "No," she finally said. "I don't want to see where Katie died. No more than you want to go back to Arcanum."

I sighed. She was right.

What's done is done.

We reached Monticello, a small community halfway between the cities of Decatur and Champaign, around seven. I took the first exit, drove over the Sangamon Creek and past the sewage treatment plant, and stopped at a four-way light next to the Super Pantry gas station.

"Father Jameson is meeting us at Hardee's," Callie said, pointing at the garish building to our right.

The light turned, and I made the right and then a sharp left into the parking lot and parked near the back, well away from the few cars in the lot. "Is Jameson inside?" I asked.

"Yes," Callie said. "He said there's nowhere to get coffee in Bement."

"Every town should have a good coffee joint," I grumbled, then pointed to the restaurant. "When this becomes your best coffee bet, it spells doom."

Callie offered a rare smile, and it warmed me to my toes. I immediately felt guilty. It wasn't that I didn't like Callie as a person, but I still had mixed feelings about her sister.

Sometimes when we were preparing to go to sleep for the night, me with my Kimber in Jack's old room and Callie with her Bible in the spare bedroom she had claimed as her own, I could almost imagine she was Katie.

Then I would blame myself for letting her sister die at the hands of Pearl Mills. And, after that, I would feel even worse as I remembered how I had loved my wife, Stacie, and how my feelings for Katie had risen before Stacie was even dead.

Completely dead, anyway.

I shivered, even though the cold air no longer bothered me.

* * *

Father Jameson sat with another priest at a corner booth. They were the only customers in the place. Normally I have found the greasy smell repellent, but it made my stomach growl with a hunger that went all the way to my core. I motioned for Callie to join them as I made my way to the counter and placed my order.

I paid the plump woman in the red shirt and took my bags and my large coffee and headed to join them. Father Jameson looked exactly as I remembered—a medium-sized man in his late fifties, with broad shoulders, short sandy-blond hair, and wrinkles around his hazel eyes deep enough that they wouldn't be considered laugh lines anymore.

The man next to him was six inches shorter than me and in his late twenties. He had close-cropped black hair, brown eyes that looked abnormally large thanks to his black horn-rimmed glasses, and a neatly trimmed goatee that matched my own. Jameson wore jeans and a dress shirt while the young man was dressed completely in black.

Both wore the white priest's collar. Neither looked thrilled to see me.

"Samuel," Jameson said, starting to rise from the orange booth.

I waved him back down and sat across from him, next to Callie. "Father." I opened one of the paper bags and yanked out a hamburger, one-half pound of beef on a thick bun. I bit into it and barely chewed, then swallowed and took another bite.

They watched me eat. Callie displayed no emotion, but the young man watched me with skepticism. Jameson frowned and started to speak, but I glared at him until he stopped. I continued until the hamburger was gone, then drank half my coffee in one long swig.

The hamburger tasted good, much better than it had any right to. There was a part deep inside of me that wanted the hamburger to be less well-done and more bloody, but I tamped that part down and withdrew another hamburger. I took a big bite, chewed a little, then tipped the hamburger to the other priest. "Who's the kid?"

The young man started to speak but Jameson raised a hand and stopped him. "This is Ethan Mosley. He's the priest at Saint Michael in Bement and the one who called for help."

"Uh-huh," I said, then slurped more coffee to wash down the burger. "The kid calls you and you call me."

Jameson had a pained look on his face. "I'm sorry about Jack."

"You heard," I said. "Why am I not surprised?"

"I talked to Edmund shortly after," Jameson said. "He told me what happened."

"Uh-huh," I repeated. "Lewinheim's a good man. But that's not what you need, is it? You don't need a *good* man."

Father Mosley shook his head. "I'm afraid we've made a mistake." He turned to Jameson and said, "He's no older than me. Surely there is someone else."

"You should be thanking God that he sent you Samuel," Callie said, her soft voice carrying the hint of anger. "If the situation is as you fear, you'll be *begging* for his help."

Jameson's face softened. "I tried to warn you, Samuel. I told you what Jack might become."

I polished off the second hamburger and belched. "You did, Father. You surely did."

I drained the last of the coffee. It was bitter but not disagreeable. The change had messed with my sense of taste; a fact I had realized since September. I opened the second bag and took the last hamburger, then shoved the bag to Callie. She removed a chicken sandwich and fries and nodded gratefully.

The two priests waited for us to finish. Mosley started to

speak, but Callie would take another bite of her chicken sandwich and glare at him just as I had.

Finally, I asked, "What makes you think you have a problem?"

Father Mosley glanced at Father Jameson. "Are you sure about this?"

Jameson ignored him, leaning forward and putting his hands on the table. "A woman is missing."

Before he could continue, I said, "Somebody's *always* missing."

I saw Callie out of the corner of my eye. She didn't speak, but I could tell she was waiting for me to continue. I sighed. "Tell me about it."

"Her name is Dorothy Hamm," Jameson said. He eased back against the seat. "She's been missing for two days. Her daughter contacted Ethan. No one has seen her. Neither friends nor family. Her sister doesn't seem concerned, but the daughter is quite distraught."

"The sister isn't worried, but the daughter is," I said. I thought about it for a second. "What makes you think it's … you know…?"

There was a flicker of something on Father Mosley's face. Fear, maybe, or disgust.

"I felt something unholy," Mosley said. "Something that goes against God."

I bit back an urge to laugh in the young man's face. "Lots of that going 'round, I'm afraid. How do you know it's the thing I deal with?"

Mosley's face reddened. "I've felt it before. I was a priest in Chicago. A young boy was taken from outside my church. I saw the thing that did it. I *felt* the thing that did it."

"You try and stop it?" I asked.

Mosley wiped his palms against his shirt, unable to meet my eyes. "I didn't know what it was. I didn't know about … about *them*. I cried out in the Lord's name, but it just laughed at me and then…"

"You did your best," Jameson said.

"I couldn't help the boy," Mosley said, the color draining from his face. "His name was Toby Davis. He was only ten years old." He looked away. "Nobody has seen the boy since. His parents were devastated. They'll never know what happened to him. It was because of that boy that I found Father Jameson and learned the truth." His haunted eyes finally met mine. "I can't even tell the boy's parents the truth."

"Are you of the blood?" I asked.

"The what?" Mosley asked.

Jameson licked his lips. "Ethan is not of the blood, nor does he know about it."

"What does that mean?" Mosley asked. "Of the blood? What blood?"

Before Jameson could stop me, I said, "It's a lineage dating back, well, a long time. The Sister here is of the blood, and I suspect the Father here is, too. It grants you a little more … protection. Without it, you don't stand a chance."

"I couldn't have stopped it?" Mosley asked Jameson.

"You're lucky it didn't rip your damned fool head from your body," I muttered.

The priests winced. Callie crossed herself and said, "We will help look for this woman."

Jameson nodded gratefully, but Mosley gave no sign that he had much faith in us. An anger rose inside me, first at the young priest for not understanding what he faced, and then for not being grateful that we were willing to help.

I recognized the anger for what it was and mentally counted to three. "Like the Sister said—we'll take a look. We'll see if it's the thing we do, but if it's not, you're on your own."

* * *

We followed Father Jameson's blue Nissan through Monticello and south on US-105 to Bement. The town was small and Christmas lights still adorned many of the houses. A cold front had moved in from the west, and the warmth of the farm ground was now heavy with fog, but it thinned out by the time we crossed the railroad tracks in the center of town.

We followed Jameson a few blocks south, turned left by the library, and then left again before coming to a stop in the parking lot of the Catholic church. Jameson and Mosley got out and made their way past a rusted-out Ford Taurus.

"Sam?" Callie asked.

I took a deep breath. "Give me a second."

Callie nodded in the dim light. I closed my eyes, stretching out with that part of me that was now changed, feeling for the oily black darkness that indicated *vampire*. I could hear Callie's breathing like the sound of a far-off train, and the whoosh-whooshing of the blood in my veins. Even the smell of our bodies was thick in the air, hints of skin, and soap, and sweat—smells so faint I would never have noticed them before.

I concentrated harder, pushing all that aside. I focused on my own breathing, slow and rhythmic. I let my concerns and anger and hunger fade away until only the darkness within me was left. I embraced it, reaching out, looking for a matching darkness around me.

The darkness was empty.

I opened my eyes and nodded at Callie. "If there's anything nearby, I can't feel it."

"Let's go inside," Callie said. "They're waiting for us."

We got out of the truck and headed for the back of the church. The Kimber slapped against my armpit, a reassuring weight I found gratifying. If I'd learned anything over the past several months, it was to be cautious.

And to keep my friends close, but the Kimber closer.

Father Mosley's office was a large room filled with wall-to-wall bookcases, a massive desk, and a comfortable-looking couch against the north wall. The priests had removed their coats, and Father Mosley sat behind the desk across from a young woman who turned to look at me with concern.

"Dawn," Father Mosley said, "this is our friend."

I stood there awkwardly while the girl inspected me. Her eyes flickered to Callie, then back to me. She probably wasn't more than a handful of years younger than me, but she had an innocence about her. She wore gray sweatpants, a heavy blue flannel shirt, worn sneakers, and a heavy brown Carhartt jacket that matched the color of her short, mousy hair. She wasn't pretty, but she certainly wasn't ugly, either, with a few pounds of extra weight that filled her out nicely.

In fact, the extra weight did all kinds of things to her chest and hips that I suddenly found intriguing.

Christ. Lewinheim was right.

I calmed myself and focused on the task at hand. "My name is Sam. I'm here to help."

Jameson nodded approvingly from the couch against the

north wall.

The girl finally offered the barest hint of a smile. "I'm Dawn McKie."

"Glad to meet you, Dawn." I approached her until I could lean gently against the oak desk, ignoring everyone else in the room. I spoke slowly and confidently so I wouldn't spook her. I also made sure my trench coat hung loosely but didn't gape. The last thing I needed was her seeing the Kimber. "Father Moseley tells me you believe your mother is missing. What makes you think that?"

"Mom wouldn't leave without telling me," Dawn said. "She *has* to be missing. Where else could she be? Nobody is taking this seriously. Not my husband. Not my aunt. It's like nobody cares."

I felt for the young woman. "Tell me about your mother. What does she do?"

Dawn wiped at her eyes. "She's a teacher at the grade school."

"Really?" I asked. "What grade?"

"Second," Dawn said. "She's great. Everyone loves her."

"What about your father?" I asked.

"He died when I was nineteen," Dawn said as tears streamed from her eyes. "Six years ago. It was a heart attack."

"I'm sorry to hear that," I said. "Does your mom have anyone in her life?"

Dawn squinted at me. "You mean like a boyfriend? No, just me and my aunt."

"Your aunt?" I asked. "Is she your mom's sister?"

"Yes," Dawn said. "Aunt Jodie works at the school, too."

"She's a teacher?" I asked.

"No. She's a secretary. Aunt Jodie and Uncle Gene are my mom's only friends."

"Are you married?"

"Yes," she said. "My husband's name is Jay."

"Any kids?"

"Not yet," Dawn said. "We can't afford it. Soon, though."

"You and your husband visit your mom?"

She nodded. "We go to her house every Friday for supper. Aunt Jodie and Uncle Gene stop by every Sunday afternoon."

I smiled. "Sounds like your mom loves her family. When was the last time you saw her?"

"Friday night," Dawn said. "Like I said, Jay and I went for supper."

"Anything unusual?"

Dawn shook her head. "Not that I remember. We were talking about our Christmas gifts. Mom bought us a vacuum cleaner and gave us a gift certificate to Kohl's for new pots and pans." She sniffed and wiped at her eyes again. "I asked if she was trying to tell me something. Like, I needed to cook and clean more. Jay was laughing. We were *all* laughing…"

Callie had stepped close behind me as I questioned Dawn. "You haven't heard from your mom since Friday?"

Dawn turned to Callie in surprise. "Who are you?"

"Sister Callie Calahane," I said. "She's with me."

Dawn hesitated before shaking her head and tucking a loose strand of brown hair behind her ear. "No, I haven't heard from Mom since Friday. I tried calling Saturday, but she never answered. I didn't think anything of it. She goes shopping sometimes…"

"Shopping after Christmas," I said. "Really?"

Dawn offered a meek smile. "That's when they have the best sales."

"Your mom shops a lot?" I asked.

She nodded. "She goes to Decatur or Champaign with Aunt Jodie *all* the time. They mostly walk around and look."

"So you went there Sunday, but she wasn't home," I said. "What about your aunt? You said she goes to your mom's house every Sunday?"

Dawn nodded. "Mom fixes supper for my aunt and uncle and they…" She cast a sidelong glance at Father Mosley. "They have a few glasses of wine and play dice games."

"Did you talk with your aunt?" I asked. "When was the last time *she* spoke with your mom?"

Dawn frowned. "Christmas night. After Jay and I left."

Christmas was the previous Thursday. Dawn's aunt had spoken to her on Christmas night, and Dawn had been the last person to see her on Friday. "Does your mom take any trips?"

"Trips?" Dawn asked, an edge to her voice. "Teachers don't make very much. She's got a little left over from my father's life insurance, but she can't afford trips and she would *never* leave without telling me she where she was going."

"Sorry," I said. "Just trying to piece it together. What about friends or neighbors? She speak with any of them?"

"Not really," Dawn said. "She's … quiet. I think if it weren't for Aunt Jodie, Mom wouldn't have anybody besides me in her life."

"Has there been anybody new around?" I asked. Dawn's eyes were brown, with rich swirls of amber, and her pupils were slightly dilated. I focused on them until everything else in the room faded away, taking note of her breathing.

"Not that I've noticed," Dawn said. "Why do you ask?"

Her pupils didn't change. Nor did her breath. If her mind had been messed with, it wasn't the same thing I had experienced before. "Just thinking out loud," I said. "You can never be too careful. No homeless drifters in town?"

Dawn smiled and cast a sidelong glance at Father Mosley. "He's never been here before, has he? We don't have things like that here. This is a small town and we … don't like outsiders. A stranger stands out like a sore thumb."

Father Mosley cleared his throat. "She's right, Mr. Harlan. Very little happens here."

Father Jameson leaned forward on the couch and nodded his agreement.

No strangers—none that she remembered, anyway. "Anything weird happen lately?" I asked. "Any missing time?"

Dawn leaned back in the chair, her face puzzled. "Missing time? You mean, like, time got away from me or something?"

"Or something," I said. "Any episodes where you can't remember how you got somewhere? Maybe you found it was time for supper with no recollection of what happened in the afternoon?"

She shook her head and turned to Father Mosley. "What does this have to do with Mom? I don't understand what he's asking. I thought you said you could help."

"Have you gone to the police?" I asked.

Dawn frowned. "What?"

"The police," I said. "Have you talked to them?"

"I talked to Bob," Dawn said, "but he didn't take it seriously. He said to give it a few days, and if Mom wasn't back by then, I should file a missing person report."

"Bob Gary is our town police officer," Mosley offered.

I squinted at him. "Uh-huh. Nobody but Dawn seems to miss Dorothy, and no one filed a missing person report. Nobody saw her leave, and nobody knows where she went. She doesn't have many friends and her neighbors aren't particularly close to her."

Dawn's face reddened. "What are you saying?"

"I'm saying you should have demanded to file a police report," I said. "I'm not sure what's happened to your mom, but when someone goes missing, you go to the police."

Dawn turned to me and glared, her jaw clenched, then the waterworks started again as she choked back sobs.

Damn it.

It wasn't Dawn's fault, and I didn't know why I was taking it out on her.

Probably more of what Lewinheim warned me about.

It might not be anything more than a mom taking a vacation without telling her daughter. Dorothy could be in Vegas, playing the slots, or maybe she'd found a man her daughter didn't know about. Either way, Dawn was clearly struggling with her mom's disappearance. "Look, I'm going to talk to your Aunt Jodie, if that's okay. Can you give me her address?"

Father Mosley spoke up. "I know where she lives. I can introduce you to her."

Dawn's sobs were becoming louder. "You really—really think I should file a police report?"

Behind Dawn, Father Jameson shook his head.

"Let me talk to your aunt," I said, "and I'll get back to you." I patted her awkwardly on the arm. "Everything will be okay."

Dawn sniffled, rubbing her nose with the sleeve of her coat. "You think so?"

I honestly had no idea. If a vampire *had* taken her mom, the last thing I needed was Dawn filing a police report while I was hunting it. That way led to nothing but trouble for everyone involved. "Yes, I'm sure of it." I gave her the biggest, fakest smile I could muster. "Go home. We'll have this straightened out in no time."

* * *

Father Jameson, Callie, and I spoke quietly in the front of the church while Mosley comforted Dawn in the rear office.

"You really think this is something more than an old woman who ran off?" I asked.

Jameson frowned. "Dorothy *isn't* an old woman, and yes, I believe that Ethan felt a vampire's presence."

I walked down the aisle, passing rows of oaken pews, my boots scuffing the worn red carpet. The smell of incense lingered in the air, almost masking a musty smell that made me want to sneeze. I stopped halfway to the front door and said, "I'm not seeing it. Dawn doesn't have any of the signs."

"Sam—" Callie began.

"You believe there's a vampire here?" I asked Callie.

She pursed her lips, then nodded. "I do."

I turned to stare at the wooden Jesus hanging from the cross behind the podium. "We're supposed to trust Mosley's feelings? Excuse me, but Father Mosley's feelings don't seem that reliable."

"Why do you remain unconvinced?" Jameson asked. "Ethan is a good man and a good priest. Trust his instincts."

"Trust?" I said, whirling to face the priest. "Sorry, Father, but I'm all out of trust."

"Sam?" Callie said softly. "I know things have been hard, but you have to trust *somebody*."

"With all that I've seen?" I asked. "With all that *we've* seen? I *won't* make the same mistakes. People won't die because I trusted the wrong person."

Jameson nodded slowly. "You've had a rough time of it, Samuel. It's hardened your heart." He raised his hand to shush me before I could speak. "I'm not saying you throw caution to the wind, but surely you must see this young woman is struggling with the loss of her mother. If it is as you say it is, and there is nothing more to it, what can it hurt to look deeper?"

The Father had a point. My anger evaporated as I took a seat and grabbed the back of the pew in front of me, squeezing the oak until my fingers hurt. "I said I'd speak with the aunt, and I will."

Father Mosley emerged from the office. "Dawn is going home. It's late, but I think there's still time to speak with Mrs. Rexford."

"Maybe that will explain everything," I said. "This is probably just making a mountain out of a molehill."

Mosley frowned. "You don't believe me, do you?"

"Doesn't matter," I said. "Jameson believes you. Callie believes you. That's enough."

Mosley gave me a look usually reserved for the gum found on the bottom of a shoe. "You're a strange man."

"I'm something you're not used to dealing with," I said.

"And what would *that* be?" Mosley asked, raising an eyebrow.

I shrugged and said, "A killer."

Chapter Three

The Rexfords' home was the last on the east side of town, past the towering grain elevators. I pulled the Chevy in behind Mosley, who was driving Jameson's Nissan. Neatly trimmed hedgerows lined the Rexfords' property until giving way to the barren corn and soybean fields beyond.

The house was an older two-story that was closer to rustic farmhouse than Victorian or Queen Anne. While similar to the other houses around it, the Rexfords' was in much better repair. The darkness made it hard to tell whether it was white or robin's-egg blue, but there was no mistaking the gaily decorated front porch.

Christmas lights still twinkled around the porch's railings and posts. Tufts of green vines snaked between them, punctuated by streamers of silver that danced merrily in the breeze. A massive wreath of twigs and vines hung from the front door. Giant pine cones were almost buried in the decoration, but I could smell the sweet and spicy hints of holly and pine.

It was an odor that I always equated with the candles my dad used to burn during the holidays, but here the scent was almost a physical thing that scratched at the back of my throat.

I followed Mosley and Callie up the wooden steps and whispered, "That's a little overpowering, isn't it?"

Callie turned up her nose and murmured, "It *is* strong."

"Mrs. Rexford likes to celebrate Christmas," Mosley said. "She's taken down most of her lawn ornaments for the season, but she will leave *these* until March."

I smiled. "People are the same no matter where you go. Father? This is your show. They know you."

Mosley nodded, took a deep breath, and rang the doorbell.

There was the sound of footsteps within, then the door

opened and a man in his late fifties or early sixties peered out. He was a little shorter than me, with the beginnings of a pot belly, and gray hair thin enough that you could see scalp. A pair of wire-rimmed reading glasses rested on the end of his nose, and he was dressed casually in a red-and-green sweater over a button-up shirt with khaki pants that ended well above his leather slippers.

"Father Mosley?" the man asked. The light above the door blazed to life and the man opened the door wider staring at us. "What are you doing here?"

"Sorry to bother you, Gene," Mosley said. "Do you have a moment?"

There was a moment of hesitation before the man nodded and beckoned us in. "Sure, Father. Of course."

He led us through a hallway into a large dining room, motioning for us to sit at the table. The room was lined with wooden shelves filled with candles and ceramic figurines of children kissing, holding hands, or lazing about next to signs that declared they had gone fishing. There were so many that I could barely see the peach wallpaper behind them.

We took the offered chairs, and Father Mosley pointed to us and said, "These are my friends, Callie and Sam. Is Jodie here? This would be easier to explain if she were here, too."

The man's brow furrowed, but before he could speak, a woman entered the room and said, "Father Mosley?"

She was approximately the same age as the man but wore a black sweatshirt and matching sweatpants. Her hair was brown, with frosted highlights, and while she wasn't fat by any means, she *was* pleasingly plump. Her cheekbones were soft, her eyes a vibrant brown, and she bore an uncanny resemblance to Dawn.

"Jodie," Mosley said. "I've brought some friends. We'd like to speak with you, if you don't mind."

Jodie Rexford smiled warmly. "Of course, Father. What's this about?"

"Dawn says her mom is missing," Mosley said.

"Dawn?" Jodie said, frowning. "I can't believe she came to you." Her eyes flickered to Callie and then lingered on me before returning to Mosley. "Who are your friends?"

"This is Sam and Callie. They're—" Mosley hesitated but recovered so quickly it was almost unnoticeable. "Private investigators."

"Private investigators?" Jodie asked, her eyes widening. "Like on television?"

I had spent the last six weeks reading Internet articles about a vast array of things unknown to me, including learning about private investigators so that I could lie convincingly if needed. "We mostly investigate insurance claims," I said, putting on my warmest smile. "Cheating spouses. Things like that."

Jodie shook her head. "I'm sorry to tell you this, but Dorothy is on vacation."

"Really?" Mosley asked. "Dawn is under the impression that she's missing."

"Why on earth would she think that?" Jodie asked. "Dorothy has left before."

"She has?" I asked.

Jodie's eyes focused on me and her expression darkened. "I'm sorry…"

"Sam Harlan," I offered.

"I'm sorry, Mr. Harlan," Jodie continued, "but I don't know you." She waved at Callie. "Or you. This is a family matter."

"I don't take it personally," I said. "I'm sure it's nothing, but Dorothy's daughter is pretty freaked out. Perhaps if you spoke to her and reassured her that her mother has left before—"

"Dawn told us her mother *hasn't* left before," Callie said. "She thinks this is out of character."

Gene Rexford cleared his throat. "Dawn doesn't like to think about her mother having a … gentleman caller."

Gene's pained expression indicated he didn't like to think of it, either. "I'm sure this can be cleared up if you just speak with your niece," I said. "Surely you don't want her spending the rest of her holiday thinking her mother ran away?"

Jodie nodded. "I'll speak with her. She's just going to have to accept that Dorothy has her own life."

"Great," I said. "You tell her where her mother went and when she'll return and everything will be good."

An expression crossed Jodie's face so quickly that I almost missed it. Her pupils dilated just a fraction, and the corners of her eyes tightened. She didn't like me pushing the issue, but it went beyond that. There was anger there, and a touch of fear.

"Of course," Jodie said. She stood and nodded her head again. "Thank you for coming. I'll take care of everything. Dawn won't bother you again."

Gene stood and offered Mosley his hand. "Thanks, Ethan. We appreciate it." He smiled blandly and offered me his hand. "Mr. Harlan."

I took his hand and shook it, and when I did, a shiver ran up my spine and the skin on my scalp tried to crawl its way off my head.

What the hell?

I released Gene's hand and the sensation disappeared as quickly as it began. While I was busy trying to figure out if I had imagined it, Callie stood, smiled politely at Jodie, and stepped around the table, stopping next to me and waiting for me to move. I hesitated, rubbing my fingers together and thinking maybe it was a static discharge from the Rexfords' carpet, then noticed Callie's raised eyebrow. I gave her a small shake of my head and followed Mosley out of the house.

The Rexfords smiled and held the door for us as we left, but I caught the suspicious glance between them, then we were on the front porch in the crisp December air. Gene closed the door behind us and the smell of pine from the door wreath once again overpowered my senses.

* * *

Callie cleared her throat as we passed the grain elevator. "What do you think?"

"I think," I said slowly, "that Dorothy Hamm is shacked up with a man and Dawn doesn't want to acknowledge it."

"There's more to it than that," Callie said. "They say Dorothy has done this before, but that contradicts Dawn's story."

I stopped at the stop sign as Father Mosley turned left onto US-105. "I don't know what to say. I didn't feel *anything* like a vampire. The Rexfords spoke without hesitation. It wasn't like the Mendozas."

I followed Mosley south and turned left into the gravel parking space south of the church. The streetlight on the corner lit Callie's yearning face. She was looking for anything that might help Dawn, but I still had no proof of a vampire. "I'm not saying Mosley didn't feel something, but there was no sense of mind tampering."

"There *is* something going on," Callie said. "Something unusual. I can tell when you're hiding something."

"They *were* a little suspicious," I admitted. "And pissed, in case you didn't notice. Two strangers show up with a priest and give them the third degree based on Dawn's ramblings? Hell, I'd be pissed, too."

Callie winced. "That's *all* you sensed?"

"Well…"

"What?" Callie demanded.

"Nothing like a vampire," I said. "I just felt … a creepy-crawly feeling. Kinda weird, actually."

"Your skin crawled?" Callie asked. She frowned and I could almost see her mental gears spinning. "That *could* be a sign of the supernatural."

"It *could*," I admitted, "or it could be nothing. Damn it, Callie, I said I would talk to the aunt and I did."

Callie squinted at me. "You're not going to help."

"In point of fact," I said, "I *would* help. *If* it was a vampire." I opened the truck door. "Coming?"

Callie sighed and got out, slamming the truck door with just a little too much force. Father Mosley stood next to the Nissan, tapping his foot. We followed him into the church office.

Jameson jumped from the couch and wiped his hands against his jeans. "How did it go?"

Mosley started to speak, then turned to me. "I'd like your assessment."

"I really don't have one," I said.

"You're just going to turn that poor girl away?" Mosley demanded.

I didn't answer, but motioned for everyone to take a seat. "Callie knows the signs. If you really want someone's opinion, ask for hers."

Mosley and Jameson turned their attention to Callie, who sat up straight in her chair, her jaw clenched so tightly that the tendons in her neck stood out like cords. "There were no signs of vampiric influence," she finally said.

"So that's it?" Mosley asked, his face screwing up in anger. "You spoke to Dawn's aunt for five minutes and then you wash your hands of it?"

Jameson was watching me intently. He didn't appear happy about our conclusion. I was about to speak, to tell the priest that we were returning to Iowa, but my mind flashed back to that spark of unease I'd felt at the Rexfords' house.

The crawling sensation against my scalp had unnerved me more than I had let on to Callie.

Everyone was waiting for me to speak. I started to say that we *were* going to wash our hands of it, but changed my mind and said, "We'll stay the night and talk to Dawn again tomorrow. *After* we get some sleep."

Jameson smiled. There was a thoughtfulness behind his eyes like he was seeing more of me than I was of him. Callie squinted at me, but she finally nodded to Mosley. "If there's anything to be found, Sam *will* find it."

I bit my lip. I wasn't sure which concerned me more, my sudden change of heart or Callie's unwavering confidence. "It's getting late," I said. "We need to find a place to stay for the night."

"There's nowhere to stay in Bement," Jameson said. He stood and handed me a sheet of paper. "We booked a room at the Best Western in Monticello. It's on the north side, out by the interstate. The directions are on the back of your reservation."

I took the paper, glanced at it, then looked up. "Only one room?"

"The hotel was booked," Jameson said with a pained look. "This was the only room available. As it is, I'll be sleeping here on the couch."

Moseley cleared his throat. "I would have offered my apartment, but it's smaller than this office."

I glanced at Callie. Before the change, I would never have noticed the hint of rose in her cheeks. "It's fine. We'll work it out."

I almost missed the tremble in Callie's hand.

* * *

I wheeled the Chevy into the surprisingly packed hotel parking lot. "Whoa," I said.

"People are visiting their family for the new year," Callie observed.

There was a touch of something in her voice, but I let it go. The building was newish, and the lobby only looked five or ten years out of date instead of the twenty I expected. We checked in at the front desk, posing as brother and sister, then made our way to the room on the southeast side. Most of the rooms were dark, the occupants already fast asleep. Except for the hum of the heaters turning on and off, the building was quiet.

Callie carried our duffel bag into the room and tossed it on the bed, then curled up her nose and asked, "Why do hotels *always* smell moldy?"

I smiled, then scanned the room. There was a chair and a small couch that wasn't much bigger than a loveseat. A short black lacquered dresser sat against the east wall, and a door on the north led to the hard-tiled bathroom. "Why do hotels always have the same beige wallpaper?" I asked.

Callie snorted. She opened the duffel bag and tossed me my ditty bag. Mine contained a safety razor, deodorant, shampoo, toothpaste, and a toothbrush. Callie's contained whatever toiletries she deemed necessary for travel. The duffel bag held a change of clothes for each of us, but nestled under the clothes was a large silver cross that Callie placed on the floor in front of the door. She mumbled a few words, then nodded with satisfaction.

I took the opportunity to remove my coat and shoulder holster, placing them on the carpet in front of the couch. "I'll take the floor."

"The Christian thing to do," Callie said with a smile, "would be to offer you the bed while I slept on the floor, but I'm going to let you make the sacrifice."

She grabbed some clothes from the duffel bag and went to the bathroom, closing the door behind her, and returned soon after with her hair pulled back in a ponytail and dressed in oversized sweatpants and a heavy flannel shirt.

I scrounged around inside the duffel bag until I found my own sweatpants and shirt, and took my ditty bag to the bathroom to brush my teeth and change.

When I returned, Callie was already in bed. She looked young. Vulnerable. Her red hair practically blazed against the white pillow and her creamy white skin caused a sudden surge of something deep in me, something *more* than affection.

Is that ... desire?

I pushed it deep inside. Callie was a woman religious. I couldn't allow such thoughts to enter my head. After what Lewinheim said in Peoria, I couldn't *ever* allow those thoughts to take root.

Callie caught me staring. "What?"

"You look like Katie," I said.

I stepped past the bed and noticed she had placed a pillow on the floor, along with a spare blanket from the closet. I dumped my boots and jeans and heavy denim shirt on the floor between the couch and the bed and stretched out on the carpet, grabbing the cold, lumpy pillow and working it between my hands.

Callie rolled to her side and watched as I tried to get comfortable.

I caught her staring and asked, "What?"

"Do you want to talk about it?"

"We'll know more tomorrow."

She shook her head. "I meant, do you want to talk about Katie?"

Did I want to talk about Katie?

We'd mentioned her only briefly since moving to Iowa. Perhaps it was time to give it a shot. "After what happened," I started, then my voice caught in my throat. "After everything, I needed time to get it right in my head."

Callie finally asked, "And now?"

"When I saw my wife dead on the kitchen floor, I felt so … powerless. Things like that aren't supposed to happen. Not in the real world. I was scared. Then when Silas took Lilly, I couldn't think of anything except getting her back."

"Your entire worldview was shattered," Callie said.

"That's—that's one way to describe it. Then Stacie almost killed me. I was confused. Then we saved Katie from Timm, and…"

"Sam—"

"It wasn't love, Callie. Not like I felt for my wife. It wasn't lust, either. I'm reasonably sure I know the difference. It was kinship. We were going through the same thing. I wanted to save Lilly, and she wanted to save you."

I'd been infected by a vampire, my wife Stacie, and Callie had promised to help me if I saved Katie from the vampire Larz Timm. Jack and I killed Timm and rescued Katie, but when Callie performed the cleansing ceremony, the vampire essence infecting me latched onto Callie's soul and threatened to kill her.

Callie was at death's door, her body in a coma. Katie joined me in trying to save my daughter, but also because killing Silas would free her sister.

If only Katie had lived.

In the dark nights since moving to Iowa, I had spent many hours drinking and thinking about what *could* have been and what *should* have been.

"She *should* have left me," Callie said, her voice rough with emotion. "She should have left me for *dead*."

"It wasn't your fault," I tried to explain. "She was willing to do anything to save you. If Pearl hadn't ... if I had ... I *tried* to save her. I wasn't strong enough."

"If only I had been with her, I might have—"

"*You'd* be dead," I said. "She tried, Callie. She called upon her faith, but it wasn't enough."

"My faith was *always* stronger than hers," Callie said, wiping at the tears that ran down her cheeks. "She never gave herself to God. Not like I did. That's why you and her..."

"You think Katie's lack of faith got her killed?" I asked. "Wait, you think something happened between us?"

"I didn't mean—"

"We were desperate people in a terrible situation," I said. "I was in shock, mourning for my wife, and she was ... Timm *abused* her. *Fed* from her. When we saved her from Timm, of course she was bound to feel something for me."

"That's what I'm trying to tell you," Callie insisted. "If Katie had truly given herself to God, she couldn't have ... been ... with you."

"*Nothing* happened between us. We held each other and comforted each other." Her eyes widened and I felt a brief stab of anger. "My God, Callie. All this time you thought we'd slept together?"

Callie started to speak, stopped herself, then snapped out, "It was none of my business."

Then why do you sound like a jealous lover?

I paused before I could say anything I might regret, only continuing when I'd taken a few deep breaths. "Nothing happened. Nothing intimate, at least. I swear it." I rolled over on the carpet, stuffing the pillow under my head. "Any physical attraction I *might* have felt for Katie was ... it was just from all the craziness going on. The problem is..."

"What?" Callie asked.

"You look like her. Sometimes I see you out of the corner of my eye, and I can almost imagine you *are* Katie."

There was a long silence before Callie spoke in a voice barely above a whisper. "You're attracted to me?"

I sighed. "I'm a man, Callie, and you are a beautiful woman. Of course, I feel urges. Lately, those urges have been…"

"This is what Father Lewinheim spoke of."

"The hunger scares me. You've seen how bad it gets. Lewinheim says I'm going to feel other emotions. I'm not saying I was a saint before I married, but I didn't chase every pretty woman within sight. The idea of losing control scares the hell out of me."

"Language," Callie said, but without her normal amount of reproach. "You can control yourself. You're a good man, Sam Harlan."

"Maybe," I said, more to myself than to her. "There's something else. I'm angry. All the time. There's a fire in the pit of my gut. Sometimes I just want to smash the hell out of everything, like everything's gone red around the edges and I'm gonna lose control."

"But you haven't."

"Not yet." I wanted to tell her that even thinking about it started the burning again in my belly.

There was an uncomfortable silence that stretched on until I heard a rustling and then the sound of a paper bag plopping down on the carpet next to me.

"Speaking of the hunger, I thought you might need this."

I opened the bag and withdrew a piece of beef jerky, salivating so much that spit drooled down the corner of my mouth. I tore into the jerky, ripping shreds off with my teeth and wolfing it down. It was greasy, and smoky, and salty, and my body shuddered at the flavor. I swallowed and tore more off until the piece was gone, then I grabbed another. The hunger finally began to subside, and with it, the anger. "Thanks, Callie."

"Things have changed," Callie said. "No matter what trials and tribulations we encounter, I firmly believe we are doing the Lord's work."

"The Lord's work? You still believe that?"

"I do," she said firmly. "But, Sam? No one ever said it would be easy."

I was still uncomfortable with the idea that a loving God would allow vampires to exist. No amount of 'the Lord works in mysterious ways' made it easier to accept. Callie believed. She had faith. I only knew that vampires had cost me everything. "You know what our problem is? We've been running a marathon and there's no finish line. We need pie time."

"Pie time?"

"Yeah, that's what the farmers in the diner used to call it. Time to relax and eat a piece of pie. Things always look different after you've had a piece of pie."

Callie sighed. "I wish you could have your old life back."

"I can't think like that anymore. Wishing for what will never exist doesn't get the job done."

There was a click as Callie turned off the light, and then she said, "Sam?"

"Yeah?"

"Thanks for agreeing to stay. It means a lot."

"It's nothing."

"No, it's not. You could've left. I would have gone with you."

I thought back to the weird sensation I'd had at the Rexfords' house. It could have been my imagination, but it wouldn't hurt for us to check it out. "Maybe it's nothing, Callie, but after what happened in Marshalltown, I'm not taking any chances."

There was a long silence broken only by the gentle sounds of our breathing. "Good night, Sam."

I stared at the ceiling until my eyes finally adjusted to the dim light from the clock radio next to the bed. I thought about God, and vampires, and all that had happened since the night Silas had turned my world upside down. I thought about how I had been forced to kill my wife. Even worse, I had stabbed my little girl through the heart with a silver knife.

Those thoughts kept me awake as Callie gave in to exhaustion, her breathing slow and steady, and then I drifted off to a merciful sleep.

* * *

I dreamed of death and suffering, then I looked up to a velvet black sky. I stood in a field of hard dirt and the remains of papery dry corn stalks. The smell of smoke tickled at the back of my throat and every breath filled my lungs with fire.

There was scratching near my feet, but I was too afraid to look down. There were no landmarks, no way to orient myself, just a field that went on forever, row after endless row of silage stretching to the horizon.

"Hello?" I called out.

Again there came a scratch-scratching from below.

I cleared my throat. "Is there anybody there?"

The scratching intensified, becoming louder and closer, but I still couldn't bring myself to look down. "What do you want?"

Pressure built behind my eyes and was soon the worst headache imaginable. A thought wormed its way into my head, full of malice.

I want you dead.

In the distance, a girl's voice screamed for me to wake and then the dream ended and my eyes snapped open. There was an overwhelming smell of trees, and dirt, and dried leaves. But, beneath it all, there was the coppery stench of blood.

The hotel door room stood open and a towering figure loomed over me. I tried to stand, but the figure grabbed me by the neck and started choking the life from me.

Shit, shit, shit!

I struggled for air, trying to scream for Callie, but all that came out was a dry croak.

The thing held me in an iron grip, and I realized it was a *thing* and not a man, then it lifted me with inhuman strength and shook me like a rag doll.

The thing's arms were thicker than a man's but made up of hard rods. I grabbed them and squeezed, desperate to pry the thing's fingers from my throat, but to no effect.

I kicked approximately where the thing's crotch would be and my foot slammed into something hard and unyielding. The thing holding me didn't notice, it just kept choking the life from me.

"Sam?" Callie asked sleepily.

I tried to call out to her, but I didn't have any air left. Stars swam before my eyes, even though the room was dark, but Callie must have sensed something was wrong because she turned on the light, allowing me to finally get a good look at my attacker.

It stood almost seven feet tall and was made of sticks and branches arranged in a humanoid shape. There were eyeballs, honest-to-God eyeballs with wide rectangular pupils, in the abomination's face. The thing glared at me and I could sense the hostility oozing from it.

"Sam?" Callie hissed. "What is that thing?"

The thing's head swiveled to inspect her. The pressure let up for a moment and I took in a breath and choked out, "Run!"

The stick man's head swiveled back to me and its eyes bored into mine. There was a palpable sense of hate coming from it.

It meant to kill me.

I'm not going down without a fight!

Fire rushed through my veins and I grabbed the thing's fingers, long twigs bound together with mud and vines, and used my rage-fueled strength to snap off one of them. The finger wiggled and squirmed in my hand. I dropped it, and it hit the hotel room's carpet and fell apart into a pile of dead wood and moldy earth.

The thing went crazy and redoubled its efforts to choke the life from me. It squeezed me with the force of a dozen men and I found myself desperate for air once again. My eyes felt like they were going to burst and there was an ocean of noise in my ears.

My vision was going black when Callie jumped on the thing's back.

Its head swiveled around to stare at her and the pressure eased again, and then Callie screamed, "Its chest, Sam. Go for its chest!"

I released my grip on the thing's arms and plunged my hands into its chest. If not for the change, I wouldn't have made a dent, but with its help, my fingers burst through the twigs, bark, and mud until I felt something soft and squishy.

The thing went mad. Its head jerked around and slammed into my face.

It was like being smashed by a tree limb. Sharp, stinging pains erupted across my face with every blow.

The squishy thing between my fingers pulsed rhythmically. I squeezed as hard as I could, with all my enhanced strength, until I felt it burst.

The creature collapsed to the floor like someone had flipped a switch. I rubbed at my throat where it had choked me, and when I finally glanced down, there was nothing but a large pile of branches and tree limbs.

Callie was staring at my hands. I held them up and found them covered in crimson. Then I recognized the thing I had been squeezing was a heart.

I gasped and shook my hands, trying to fling the blood and remains of tissue from my fingers, then wiped them furiously at the soft cotton of my sweatpants.

"What *was* that thing?" Callie asked in a hushed tone.

I shook my head, staggered to the bathroom, and flipped on the light. My bruised and bloody face stared back at me in the mirror. There were scrapes and scratches on my face, and my eyes were tinged with red. I leaned closer to the mirror and realized several blood vessels in my eyeballs had burst.

From the other room, I heard the hotel door slam shut and the lock click into place.

"Sam?" Callie said from the other room. "Are you okay?"

"That thing almost killed us," I said. My voice was hoarse and shaky.

"What happened?"

I ran water in the bathroom sink, then stuck my hands under the cold water. Rivulets of blood stained the white porcelain sink, and I brushed at the bloody stains, grabbing for the towel hanging from the towel rack next to the mirror. "I don't know, Callie, but it sure as hell *wasn't* a vampire."

Chapter Four

I pawed through the muddy branches on the carpet, trying not to get blood on my hands. The eyes were too large and too weird-looking to be human. I suspected that the heart wasn't human, either. "I think this came from a goat."

Callie watched my inspection. Her face was pale and her throat quivered. "A goat?" She looked like she might vomit, but held it together as I continued searching the remains. "Is there anything else in there?"

I touched the heart and found it cool, but not cold, and firmer than I expected. "Just a heart. And the eyes."

"Do you think this was the vampire?"

"I hope not," I said. "I'm pretty sure this thing was held together with magic. Can vampires *do* magic?"

I poked at the eyeballs. They were large and gelatin-like and squelched when I poked at them.

Callie gulped and said, "There's nothing in the church records about vampires performing magic."

"Well, this stick man was trying to kill us. We need to leave. It's not safe here."

"Where will we go?"

The smell wafting up from the stick man's remains made me want to vomit, but damned if I would do it in front of Callie. I swallowed a few times until my stomach settled down. "Let's head back to the church. Maybe Jameson knows what the hell this thing is."

* * *

We wrapped the branches and organs in an extra bedsheet from the closet. I dressed quickly in the bathroom, making sure the Kimber was still loaded and ready for action, then carried the bedsheet outside and threw it in the back of my truck.

The vehicles in the hotel's south parking lot were empty. A line of trees stood thirty yards to the south, but there didn't appear to be anyone watching from them. Light spilled between the drapes of a few hotel rooms. Otherwise, the hotel was quiet.

Whoever had sent the stick man after us hadn't stayed around to watch.

Or they didn't want to get their hands dirty.

The door opened and Callie exited the hotel room carrying our duffel bag over her shoulder.

I nodded as she approached. "Get in the truck."

Her eyes scanned the tree line. "We're leaving?"

I snorted. "Hell yeah."

"Shouldn't we check out first?"

"That's the first thing that comes to your mind?" I asked. "We're sitting ducks out here."

"You think someone might try to kill us while we're checking out?"

"Fine," I said. "If it gets us out of here, but you go where I go. There's no way I'm leaving you in this parking lot by yourself."

We drove around to the north side of the hotel, got out, and entered through the front entrance. A sleepy-looking woman in her late twenties sat at the counter, typing away on her phone. She glanced up, her eyes dully appraising, then asked, "Can I help you?"

"We'd like to check out," I said.

"We have a policy," the woman said, straightening her red blouse. "If you stay longer than two hours, you have to pay for the entire night. You understand that, right?"

"That's okay," I said. "The room was already paid for." I removed the pair of plastic key cards from my trench coat and shoved them across the granite countertop.

The woman reached for the key cards and her eyes tracked across my face, taking notice of the scrapes and spots that were already scabbing over, and then came to rest upon Callie. "I don't know…"

"We didn't like the room," Callie said.

The woman frowned, her expression doubtful. "If there's

something—"

"Please," I said. "We just want to go."

The woman sighed. "Fine. But if there's any damage to the room, we'll be billing it to the credit card on file."

"Fair enough." I figured that Jameson or Mosley had used their credit card to book the room. I wasn't concerned. Surely the Catholic church could afford it.

* * *

The shakes hit as we crossed the hill next to the Bement Cemetery. The town was a maze of lights a mile to the south. I had a moment to think how pretty it looked, like fireflies glowing in the night, and then my hands started trembling so badly that it was a struggle to keep the truck from roaring off the road and into the steep ditch to the west.

"Sam?"

I blinked. Callie was staring at me with wide-eyed concern. She grabbed the wheel and steadied the truck, steering us back between the lines.

"I'm okay," I said, focusing on my hands until they stopped shaking, allowing me to regain control of the truck. "I'm just a little…"

"Upset?" Callie asked.

I swallowed hard. There was no sense lying to her. She seemed to know more about my emotional state than I did. "I'm scared, Callie. Really, *really* scared. Maybe it's a side effect of the change." I chewed on my lip. "We almost died tonight."

Callie nodded. "I know. I'm scared, too."

I glanced her way. She didn't look scared. She appeared … calm. "If I hadn't been able to stop it—"

"But you did."

"Barely, Callie. *Barely.* I … can't protect you. I can barely protect myself." I hesitated, then the words rushed out. "You might be safer if you weren't here. I can't bear to think of anything happening to you. I'm terrified I'm going to get you killed."

I slowed the truck and made the bend into Bement, following US-105 through town until we reached the church, pulling the truck into the gravel parking lot and turning off the engine.

We sat there in the dark. "We're *all* going to die," she finally said in a voice as hard as iron. "If it's God's will that I die fighting evil, then so be it."

* * *

I knocked softly on the church's office door. There was movement inside and a crash as something fell to the floor, then Jameson opened the door and peeked out. "Sam? Callie?"

I nodded and said, "Father. Can we come in?"

Jameson's face went pale. He threw the door wide and ushered us in. Barefoot, the priest wore black sweatpants and a worn undershirt. He waved us to the chairs next to the desk and folded the red wool blanket he'd been sleeping with and placed it neatly on the tiny pillow at the end of the couch. "What happened? Are either of you hurt?"

A mustard-colored ceramic lamp on the table next to the couch provided the only light in the room. I stared at it for a moment, then stood and flipped on the switch to the overhead fluorescent lights, feeling an instant sensation of relief as they blazed on.

It was the feeling you get when the light vanquishes the evil things in the dark, but I could only wish that was true.

"We were attacked," Callie said.

Jameson frowned, his face full of concern. "By a vampire?"

"No," I said, taking the seat nearest the door. "That's the weird thing."

"If not a vampire—"

"It was magic," Callie said. "Witchcraft."

"Witchcraft?" Jameson sat down heavily on the couch. "Tell me what happened."

I ran through a quick description of the events at the hotel. Jameson listened intently, then said, "That's a golem. You were attacked by a golem."

My jaw dropped. "You mean the thing from *Lord of the Rings*?"

Jameson shook his head. "No. Not Gollum. A *golem*. They're creatures of magic, animated by a gifted magician and infused with their will."

I rocked back in my chair. "Magic. Why does it have to be magic?"

Jameson looked like someone had stuffed a lemon in his mouth. "Golems have existed since mankind first learned to harness magic. There is a long history in the Jewish tradition of the creation and uses of golems. The Talmud—"

"I don't care about Jewish tradition," I said. "Tell me how they're made."

"In Jewish tradition," Callie spoke up, "golems are made from clay or earth. But with magic? They can be made from almost anything."

I swiveled to look at her. "How do you know so much about them?"

"The Church records are actually quite extensive—"

"Callie," Jameson said, shaking his head.

"He *needs* to know," Callie said, her green eyes blazing with a sudden ferocity. "He's already involved. Keeping him in the dark will only put him in more danger."

"What are you talking about?" I asked.

"The nature of magic," Callie said before Jameson could stop her. "The Church's official position is that magic does not exist. That any display of magic or witchcraft is a demonic trick, played on humanity by demons to corrupt them and lead them from God's will."

"Like Lewinheim was talking about," I said, the conversation suddenly making sense. "But that can't be true. I saw my great-uncle perform magic. It wasn't demonic." Something else occurred to me. "And Jack said *anyone* could learn magic."

Jameson sighed heavily and leaned back against the couch. "The unofficial position of the Church is that magic does exist, but that to involve oneself in it can lead to demonic possession."

"Jack was right?" I said. "I could learn magic?"

"It's best you don't try," Jameson said. "Magic manipulates the very forces of creation. That … infringes upon the Lord's will."

"That's a problem?" I asked.

"Of *course,* that's a problem," Jameson said, his voice growing louder. "*Nothing* should infringe upon the Lord's will. Playing with magic dances close to a fine line that opens one to the demonic."

"Let me guess," I said. "That's bad?"

Jameson sagged against the couch, his gaze turning to the floor, and ran his hand through his shaggy hair. When he finally glanced up, his eyes were full of emotion—anger, definitely, but fear as well.

"Demons are no joke," he said wearily. "They exert their will in an eternal battle against God. Against His will. Against His judgment. They will stop at nothing to prove that He made a terrible mistake."

"What mistake?" I asked.

"Creation," Jameson said simply. "They will stop at nothing to prove to God that *creation* was a mistake."

I chewed at my lip while absorbing that information. "Okay, avoid magic. Got it."

"That might prove difficult," Callie said. "Someone used magic. The golem is proof of that."

"Yeah," I said. "About that. The eyes and the heart. What was that about?"

"I'm not sure about the eyes," Jameson said, raising his head. "The heart gave it life. You were lucky. If you hadn't crushed it, the golem would have killed you."

I finally asked the question that had been gnawing at me. "Why send that thing after us? We haven't *done* anything."

Callie nodded. "Sam has a point. We only just arrived. Why try and kill us?"

"You must represent a threat," Jameson said slowly. "Something you did, or something you might do, threatens someone."

"Why?" I asked. "Who?"

Jameson shook his head. "I have no idea."

"You think it has something to do with Dorothy's disappearance?" I asked. "Or is it because Mosley felt a vampire?"

"Now you believe Ethan?" Jameson asked, raising an eyebrow.

"I have no idea what to believe," I said. "I do know one thing. Someone tried to kill us, and that just galls me." My hand reflexively slipped to the Kimber in its shoulder holster. "I don't like being galled."

We spent the rest of the night on the church's floor. Callie lay next to me, her head laying on her soft coat, her body covered with another wool blanket Jameson had scrounged from the church's closet.

I rolled my trench coat into a ball and used it as a pillow, but held on to the Kimber.

The night passed slowly. Every time I was on the verge of sleep, my eyes would snap open, half expecting to find the stick man standing over me, trying to crush my windpipe. The desktop computer on Mosley's desk cast shadows that danced across the ceiling and kept jerking me awake.

I finally fell into a fitful sleep. My dreams were full of anger and menace, and I'll leave it at that.

The rustling of fabric and quiet footsteps finally woke me. Jameson was fiddling with an ancient Bunn coffeemaker in the corner.

I peeked over to find Callie still asleep. She was strikingly beautiful, even with messy hair and wearing an old pair of sweatpants. She looked so young and vulnerable, and I vowed to keep a repeat of the previous night from ever happening again.

I will do anything to protect her.

The glow-in-the-dark dial of my Timex read five in the morning, and I groaned softly.

"Sorry to wake you," Jamison said. He finished pouring water into the coffeemaker, then inserted the carafe and pressed the button.

"That's okay, Father." The smell of fresh-brewed coffee filled the room and my hunger began to rise. I stretched my arms and tried to work out the kinks, then staggered to my feet and did the same with my back. Twisting from side to side made everything ache. "Where is the bathroom?"

Jamison smiled and pointed to the door that led deeper into the church. "There's a toilet and sink down the hall."

I carefully shut the door behind me so that I wouldn't wake Callie. After finding my way to the bathroom, I flipped on the light. There was a mirror over the old porcelain sink, and the face staring back at me was gaunt and hollow-eyed. I'd lost ten pounds of fat in the months since Silas had kidnapped my daughter. My hazel eyes were haunted and my hair was wild and unkempt. I rubbed at my goatee. It was on the verge of unmanageable, and the rest of my face was covered in stubble.

I looked like the kind of man I used to avoid, thinking him dangerous or unstable.

Now I was the dangerous one.

The scratches on my face were healing quickly, the scabs almost ready to fall away, and the bruising had already gone through the purple and yellow stages and was a barely visible brown.

I splashed cool water on my face and wiped it clean with some paper towels from the wall dispenser before returning to the office. Callie was perched on the edge of the couch, talking softly to Jameson and drinking from a coffee cup.

There was a steaming mug of coffee waiting for me on the edge of the desk and I gratefully accepted it. It was black, without cream or sugar, but the bitter flavor warmed me and I mumbled something appreciative to Jameson.

He nodded, then gave me an appraising look. "What will you do?"

"I'm going to speak to Jodie and Gene," I said. "The simplest explanation is usually the correct explanation. They sent the stick man or they were involved, somehow."

Jameson started to protest, but Callie nodded in agreement.

There was a rattling outside. The Kimber appeared in my hand as if by magic, an instinct now ingrained in me, but I lowered it when Father Mosley opened the door.

His eyes widened when he saw us, and he blanched when they slid to the Kimber. "What happened?"

I broke it down for him—the hotel, the stick man, and how I'd managed to stop it before it could murder us. I explained how we'd left the hotel and spent the night in the church, but he winced when I said we were going to speak to the Rexfords.

"You really think they sent that thing?" he scoffed. "I've known them for years."

"Are you willing to bet your life on it?" I asked. "Are you willing to bet Dorothy Hamm's life on it?"

"But why attack you?" Mosley continued as if I hadn't spoken. "You only expressed concern for Dorothy. There's no reason—"

"Maybe they weren't as close as they seemed," I said. "Or maybe they don't want anyone looking into her disappearance. Or maybe it's not them." I turned to Callie. "I won't have a repeat of Marshalltown. I'm going to speak to the Rexfords and I'll get answers." The anger boiled over inside and my lips pulled back in a snarl. "One way or another."

* * *

Mosley hung up the phone and shoved it across his desk. "I told them you urgently need to speak with them about Dorothy. They agreed to meet."

I stopped speaking to Callie and turned my attention to the young priest. "When?"

Mosley checked his watch. "They said they would be available after eight thirty, so twenty minutes from now."

"Good," I said.

"Samuel," Jameson said, his voice full of apprehension. "What do you plan on saying to them?"

"I'm going to push them a little," I conceded. "I tried beating around the bush a few months ago. It didn't go well."

Callie winced. "He has a point, Father. I know he sounds gruff…"

Jameson sighed heavily. "They're just people. Not monsters. You can't beat them into submission."

The hell I can't. "I'll be careful, Father. Don't worry." I pointed at Callie. "Besides, I'll have my babysitter with me."

Mosley watched our exchange with alarm. "Please, Mr. Harlan, these people—"

"They lied to me," I growled. "I can *feel* it." I stood and headed for the door. "Coming, Sister?"

I left before anyone could speak and made my way to the truck, rummaging through the toolbox in the back until I found what I was looking for, then climbed into the front and started the engine. Callie exited the church. The sun hadn't warmed the earth yet, and the temperature was well below freezing. She hugged her jacket against her for warmth and joined me in the truck.

I held up my hand before she could speak. "Take this," I said, offering her a snub-nosed revolver. It was loaded with silver ammunition, and Callie had been practicing with it regularly.

She frowned, then took the Smith and Wesson .38 and stuffed it in her jacket pocket.

I waited for her to speak, but she remained silent. Finally, I asked, "Not going to argue?"

"No," Callie said.

"Going to give me grief?"

"No."

I grunted. "Going to say more than one syllable?"

She turned and frowned at me. "You're right. We can't make the kind of mistakes we made with Santiago."

I snorted. "I'm starting to understand how Jack got to be such a hard-ass."

That brought a smile to Callie's lips. "Please be nice to the Rexfords. It won't cost anything to give them the benefit of the doubt."

"I can't guarantee anything, but I'll try. Scout's honor," I said, holding up two fingers. I turned the key and the truck's engine roared to life. I let it run for thirty seconds, not daring to look at Callie, then threw the truck in reverse.

Bement is a small town, and it was only a couple of minutes before we were heading east on Bodman street. In the daylight, the grain elevators weren't a menacing presence but a cheerful wall of white concrete that stretched to the sky. We passed them and I realized I'd been holding my breath.

What a weird town.

Like the grain elevators, the Rexfords' house looked different in the daylight. It was warm and festive, and the paint appeared fresh. The lawn was well groomed and not a single dead leaf from the oak and maple trees disturbed that sense of order. A vine-covered gazebo sat next to the house, looking like something out of a Rockwell painting.

If Marshalltown had taught me anything, it was that looks could be deceiving.

I parked behind their tiny green Toyota Prius. "Tree huggers."

Callie looked puzzled. "What?"

I pointed at the Prius. "I haven't seen a lot of those around here. What kind of people in a farm town drive a Prius?"

"People who like small cars?" Callie said, rolling her eyes. "Or maybe they're concerned about the cost of gas. The Chevy must burn ten times as much gas as that thing."

I snorted. It was true, though. After I had inherited Jack's estate, I found that while the engine was original to the truck, anything that could be replaced *had* been replaced with high-performance aftermarket parts that I felt every time I hit the pedal.

Like everything Jack had owned, the truck was hard, powerful, and functional.

We made our way up the front steps. Gene Rexford opened the door before Callie could ring the doorbell. I almost missed how his eyes flickered across my face, taking note of the scratches and scrapes, before glancing away.

He knows something.

"Please," Gene said. "Come in."

I turned to Callie and raised an eyebrow. The smell of pine emanating from the door wreath was so thick I could almost taste it. I bit back the taste. Callie's nose twitched, but she shrugged and followed Gene inside the house, down the hall, and into the dining room, where Jodie Rexford waited.

They were dressed much like the night before, except in lighter colors. Both wore a lot of tan, and Jodie's blouse was a print of green and brown leaves. She cradled a cup of coffee in her hands, nervously wiping the lip with her thumb. "Father Mosley said you needed to speak with us," she said. Her voice was neutral, but her thumb wiped faster.

"Yes," I said. Callie and I took the seats across from them, and again I noticed the ceramic figurines of boys and girls lining the shelves.

She must have a fortune tied up in those stupid things.

There was an uncomfortable silence until Gene cleared his throat. "Would you like some coffee?"

"No, thanks," I said.

Callie turned to look at me, clearly confused by my silence. I let Gene and Jodie stew a few more seconds until I said, "We don't have any new information about your sister, but we did have an interesting development last night."

"Oh?" Gene said. A fine bead of sweat ran down his forehead. "What kind of development?"

"The kind where we were attacked," I said.

"Attacked?" Jodie said. Her eyes widened and she sat up straight in her chair. "That couldn't have anything to do with Dorothy." She took a drink from her cup, unable to meet my gaze. "Are you okay?"

I glanced over to Callie. "We're fine," I said pleasantly. "That's funny. You didn't ask *how* we were attacked."

Jodie's mouth opened, her jaw working, until she finally stammered out, "You—you're right. How rude of me. *How* were you attacked?"

I thought about playing along, not giving them anything too specific. Perhaps I could get more information from them, but after Marshalltown, I wasn't in the mood. "A magic stick man tried to kill us."

Jodie grabbed her husband's hand and squeezed it tightly. "I don't understand."

Gene shook his head. "Mr. Harlan? We don't know what that means."

"I think you do," I said. "I think you know *exactly* what it means."

Jodie chewed at her lip and then said curtly, "We really don't."

I saw Callie frowning, and my anger came rushing back. I slammed my fist against the dining room table, cracking the oak from side to side.

The sound was as loud as a gunshot, and the figurines on the shelves around the room came to life, gasping at the sound and shrinking back against the wall while covering their mouths in shock.

There was a tickle against the back of my neck, the feeling of something brushing against the fine hairs.

Magic.

My hand moved before I could think, darting under the trench coat. Jodie's hands were moving as well, but the Kimber cleared the holster and time seemed to slow.

Jodie and Gene's eyes widened, and they rocked back in their chairs. Jodie started to speak, but I held the Kimber pointed at her chest.

"Don't," I said quietly.

I expected Callie to admonish me, but she stared at the figurines in shock, then said, "Sam will do it. He can shoot before you finish."

There was anger in Jodie's face, along with a haughty pride, but Gene placed his hand on Jodie's shoulder. "Dear? Please don't."

"Yeah," I said. "Don't, or whatever you're about to do will be the *last* thing you do on this earth. How about we talk, instead, and avoid any unnecessary complications?"

"You brandish a weapon in my house," Jodie said through gritted teeth, "and you think there *won't* be complications?"

"Please," Gene urged. "Tell him. He might be able to help."

The muscles in Jodie's jaw were clenched tight, but she blinked hard and sat back in her chair.

I didn't holster the Kimber.

"Sam *can* help," Callie said. "If you are in trouble, he *will* help."

I would?

I didn't come to Bement to fight witches. I came for a

vampire, but maybe the two were linked. There was only one way to find out. "The stick man," I said. "Tell me about it. Then tell me what *really* happened to your sister."

Jodie slumped forward in her chair. When she did, the little boys and girls on the wall assumed their original position, becoming inanimate ceramic figurines once again.

Now that's creepy.

Jodie hung her head, deflated. "What do you want to know?"

"The stick man," I said. "Did you send it?"

"Goddess, no," Jodie said, glancing up in shock. "I would *never* do such a thing."

"So," I said. "You *are* a witch." I could actually *feel* it, now that I knew what I was looking for. She exuded something akin to a scent. The disturbing thing was that I didn't smell it, but sensed it with that part of me where the vampire essence coiled and slithered about.

And, it wasn't just Jodie. Gene Rexford exuded the same thing, but to a lesser degree. He appeared to be a bland middle-aged man, but I held no illusions. Neither of them were people. They were something a lot more dangerous.

Witches.

Chapter Five

J odie bit her lip, but her eyes never left mine. "We are not evil, Mr. Harlan. We worship the Goddess—"

"Save it," I said. "You're witches. You use magic. I know. I've *seen* it before. I've *felt* it before."

Jodie leaned forward and Gene put his hand on her shoulder to pull her back, but she shrugged it off. "I'm sure you have."

Her eyes shifted, becoming swirling pools of amber that threatened to suck me in. There was something in those eyes that scared the hell out of me. "What's that supposed to mean?" I asked.

Jodie continued to watch me with those creepy eyes. "I don't know *what* you are, Mr. Harlan, but you're not human. Not anymore."

"Don't forget who has a forty-five full of silver bullets pointed at your chest," I said. "Tell me about the stick man."

"It wasn't us," Gene said. Jodie turned her glare upon him, but he shook his head. "Just tell him."

"You were attacked by a creature made of sticks?" Jodie finally asked, her eyes returning to normal. "Was there anything else?"

"Like what?" I asked.

Jodie shook her head. "I'm sorry, Mr. Harlan. It's too dangerous. Leave this place. Go back to wherever you came from." She turned to Callie. "It's safer for the *both* of you."

"We can take care of ourselves," Callie said. "You practice witchcraft. It gives you the sight. Look upon us and behold the truth."

I had no idea what Callie was talking about, and I was about to demand an explanation when Jodie closed her eyes.

When she opened them, they were a rheumy white, like they were covered in a thin layer of cream. She stared at me for a moment, then her face went pale. "So much death. Dear Goddess, so much death."

I turned to Callie and raised an eyebrow, but Callie just shook her head.

Jodie turned her gaze upon Callie and her face blanched, her mouth forming an *O*. "Glory be upon Him," she whispered. She blinked and her eyes returned to their normal shade of brown. "Perhaps you *can* help," she said.

What was that all about?

"What did you see?" I demanded.

Jodie sighed heavily. "Nothing I could explain to you. The stick man that attacked you. What else did you find?"

"There was a heart," I said. "And two eyeballs."

"A heart to beat," Jodie said, "and eyes to see. He was watching you."

"*Who* was watching us?" I demanded.

"The man who took her sister," Gene said angrily. "Carlton Meriwether."

"Who the hell," I asked, "is Carlton Meriwether?"

"The one who set the stick man upon you," Jodie said, her face turning red. "*He's* the one who took Dorothy."

"Let's start from the beginning," I suggested, holstering the Kimber.

Jodie visibly relaxed and the cloud of magic dissipated, like a passing storm cloud on a spring day. "He lives in Monticello," she said. "His family is Chicago old money. They used to vacation downstate during the summer along with the other wealthy families. He lives on the north side of town."

"Okay," I said, my frustration rising, "now *really* tell me about him."

"He's powerful," Gene said, raising his hand to shush Jodie. "He's the most powerful witch we've ever met, and we've met a few. Being near him is like standing next to a waterfall. It's … hypnotizing. Carlton is no good. He delights in pain like it's a drug." Gene shook his head and I could almost smell the fear rising from him. "Meriwether is … there's something *wrong* with him."

"Why did he take your sister?" Callie asked.

"I don't know," Jodie said. "It doesn't make sense. We've known each other our entire lives. It comes with being a practitioner in such a small community."

A lightbulb went off in my head. "Dorothy is a witch, too."

Jodie nodded. "Our family is gifted. Even Dawn, although we've kept it from her. Dorothy is strong, almost as strong as me. I don't know why Carlton took her or what he plans to do with her, but it can't be good." She took a choking breath and her eyes grew watery. "I'm scared, Mr. Harlan. I'm afraid of what he might do to her."

"What does he stand to gain?" I asked.

"I don't know," Jodie said. "Unless…"

"Unless?"

Jodie shuddered. "Unless he means to feed on her."

I cast a sidelong glance to Callie, who looked as confused as I felt. "Can he do that?"

"Emotions have power," Jodie said. "If he evoked enough terror, he could feed on it, especially given how strong Dorothy is. But it doesn't make any sense. Carlton is already wildly powerful."

"Why attack us?" I asked.

"He must be watching you," Jodie said. "He must think we contacted you. You're a threat to him."

"I wonder what makes him think that," Callie said.

Jodie leaned forward and said to me, "You reek of death, Mr. Harlan. I sensed it last night, but once I looked upon you with my sight, I saw how dangerous you are. I don't know what bargains you've made, but it has *marked* you."

She turned to Callie, and the tone of her voice was full of something bordering on awe. "You are … something else. I've never seen anything like it. You are bathed in a power that makes me feel small. You are pure, like a newborn baby."

Callie said, "Mrs. Rexford—"

"Whatever you are doing with him," Jodie said, nodding at me, "I strongly urge you to reconsider."

"She'll keep that in mind," I said dryly. "Look, I don't know what's going on. I don't know if I can trust you. I believe Dorothy is missing, and I believe you think this Meriwether fellow is behind it." Jodie and Gene turned to look at each other, and they both started to speak. I raised my hand and silenced them. "Save it. I'm not a charity worker, and frankly, I don't do missing women, but Meriwether attacked us, and that I won't abide."

* * *

The houses in Monticello were variations of clapboard-style bungalows, farmhouses, and one-story ranches common to the Midwest, but the homes along State Street were elegant Victorians and colonials that spoke to an earlier time of wealth and influence.

Carlton Meriwether's home was all that but turned up to eleven. I wasn't an expert, but it was probably at least ten thousand square feet—perhaps even more—a two-story brick monstrosity that sprawled across the better part of two acres of tastefully maintained lawn. Even though the grass had gone dormant for the winter and was faded shades of green and brown, it was obvious that Meriwether spent a significant amount of money maintaining it.

I turned into his driveway, between a pair of thick brick pillars, and followed it to the circle drive in front of the house. "The guy sure likes his brick," I said as I turned off the engine. "Doesn't come cheap, either, I'm guessing."

Callie snorted. "I don't know much about housing costs, but this seems … extravagant."

"Kinda screams pretentious," I said.

Callie sighed. "I've never understood people's fascination with material belongings. Even before I took my vows, I never wanted physical things."

"Some people are just assholes."

Callie gave me a disapproving look. "Please, will you stop using such language?"

"I sure as he—heck will," I said.

That earned me a rare smile. "The Lord understands the occasional slip."

"Then he must understand the heck out of me," I muttered under my breath. I ran my hand under my trench coat and checked for the reassuring weight of the Kimber. Satisfied that it was still firmly in its holster, I opened the door, got out, and made my way up the steps to the front door.

Callie followed me up the steps. "What will you say to him?"

"Relax. I'm not going to shoot him or anything." I raised an eyebrow and muttered under my breath, "Unless he deserves it."

"Sam—"

"I'm just going to ask some questions," I said, ringing the doorbell. "I won't have to drop a body. Probably."

The door was made from a dark wood, heavy and massive, with stained glass on each side. There was a rustling from within, and the door opened to reveal a man in his early forties dressed in a Teenage Mutant Ninja Turtles t-shirt that was a size too small, green sweatpants, and plastic flip-flops. His wide face was plastered with a delighted grin.

"Hey," the man said, his mouth drooping at the corner. "Are you here to play?"

"Carlton Meriwether?" I asked.

The man's face lit up. "Hah, you thought I was Daddy! That's funny." His grin faded and he wiped at his messy black hair. "You want to see Daddy?"

The man spoke with a lisp, and the innocent twinkle in his light blue eyes made me glance at Callie. There was clearly something wrong with the man.

Callie came to my rescue. "What's your name?" she asked slowly as if speaking to a child.

"Nicky," the man said. He showed a mouthful of teeth. "Will you play Ninja Turtles with me? I *love* playing Ninja Turtles."

I hesitated, unsure of what to do.

Callie said, "We need to speak to your father, Nicky. Maybe after that we can play Ninja Turtles."

"Nobody *ever* comes to see me," Nicky groused, his face falling. "Nobody ever wants to play Ninja Turtles."

He turned and took off down the hallway, leaving the front door standing wide open. "Daddy! Somebody wants to see you and they won't play Ninja Turtles with me until you talk to them."

We stood awkwardly on the front steps. From inside, we heard an older man's voice say, "Nicholas? Did you leave the door open again?"

"I don't 'member," Nicky hollered, shrugging his shoulders.

There was a sigh and the older man said patiently, "Please don't leave the front door standing open. It's cold outside. If you leave the door open, it makes it cold *inside*."

"You *told me that* already," Nicky said.

"I'm sorry," the older man said. "I'm just trying to help you remember. Now go play."

Nicky stomped off, then the older man stepped into the hallway. He looked like Nicky, except twenty years older. His hair was a close-cropped black threaded with silver, but where Nicky's eyes were innocent, the man's blue eyes brimmed with intelligence. He wore a tasteful pair of brown slacks and a long-sleeved black shirt, in sharp contrast to Nicky's sloppy clothes, and a pair of burgundy leather slippers. He stopped in front of the open door and smiled neutrally. "May I help you?"

"Are you Carlton Meriwether?" I asked.

"Yes, I'm Carlton Meriwether."

There was a long pause. I didn't know what to expect, but I certainly didn't think the man who'd attacked us would stand there without a hint of recognition. I glanced to Callie, who shrugged, then I said, "Jodie and Gene Rexford sent us."

I half expected the man to blast us with magic, but he just shook his head and frowned. "I'm sorry you were dragged into this, Mr....?"

"Harlan," I said. "Sam Harlan."

"I'm sorry, Mr. Harlan. I'm afraid they are quite mistaken. I have no idea what happened to Dorothy, and I can't fathom why they would accuse me."

"You admit knowing about her disappearance?" Callie asked.

"Of course," Meriwether said. "Please, come in. We can talk about it inside, where it's not so chilly." He ushered us into the house and led us down the wood-paneled hallway and into a living room the size of a basketball court. The ceiling was at least twenty feet above us, and the walls were covered in paintings of wooden bridges and rural farms. A massive fireplace big enough for a grown man to lie down in occupied the north wall. A cheery fire roared away, and the fireplace mantel was covered in scented candles.

All in all, it didn't seem like the lair of a man who would send a golem to attack us.

I could sense that Callie was confused as well, but we took seats on the fancy white couch in front of the fireplace, and Meriwether took the seat on the couch across from us.

"What did Jodie accuse me of this time?" Meriwether said.

I ignored his request. "How do you know her?"

Meriwether smiled. "You want me to admit to being a witch. I will readily admit it. I am, indeed, a witch."

Out of the corner of my eye. I saw Callie's jaw drop. The encounter was completely different than I expected. "You're a witch?"

"Of course," Meriwether said. "I would never speak of such a thing to the public, but you are a practitioner yourself, aren't you?"

"Uhm," I said. "Not exactly."

"Really?" Meriwether asked. "I assumed based upon the feeling I got when you crossed my threshold—"

"It's complicated," I said. "You can sense what we are?"

Meriwether frowned. "Gazing upon someone with the sight without their permission is gauche."

"How do you know the Rexfords?" Callie asked.

"It's a small community," Meriwether said. "Practitioners tend to congregate together."

"Socially?" I asked.

Meriwether threw his head back and laughed. "Monticello was quite a haven for the well-to-do in the early part of last century. The wealthy and powerful families who summered here were quite a motley collection. Some of them, like my own family, were gifted. They used to throw elaborate parties ... that would have been quite scandalous if word ever got out."

In a moment of clarity, I said, "You mean sex parties."

"I believe they called them orgies," Meriwether said with an embarrassed smile. "Sexual energy is one of the oldest known ways to focus power. Witches have cavorted with each other since mankind discovered magic."

"That's how you know the Rexfords?" Callie asked.

Meriwether cleared his throat. "As the century wore on, the families ostracized certain members for their ... proclivities. They were sent to live here. Permanently."

I was curious, in spite of myself. "Proclivities?"

Meriwether leaned back against the couch. "Those who didn't fit neatly into that era's social conventions. Some were socially awkward, but some were gay. Or bisexual. Or enjoyed multiple partners. My father found himself banished here because he enjoyed the company of both men and women. He had a minor talent. When he found there were other witches living here, he gathered them together and they ... well, let us say they threw some *remarkable* parties."

He rubbed at his eyes. "The Hamm family were gifted. They were farmers, mostly. Hedge witches. There were a few here, and in other small towns like Cerro Gordo and Bement."

"*That's* how you know them," I said.

"Yes," Meriwether admitted. "Our families were aware of each other. As a young man, I sowed my wild oats when I was home for the summer after my freshman year in college. Dorothy and I dated that summer, but I ended things before I went back for the fall semester. I met my wife shortly after and haven't really spoken to Dorothy since."

I said, "But—"

Meriwether held up his hand and said, "We've spoken in passing. The witches occasionally meet to discuss the art, perhaps a few hours every year…"

"They think you kidnapped Dorothy because of a fling you had forty years ago?" I asked.

"You make me sound ancient," Meriwether said with a smile, "but I have no idea why they accuse me. We do disagree about the art—"

"Disagree?" Callie asked.

Meriwether shrugged. "They worship magic. They view it with a mythic amount of awe and wonder. I tend to take a more prosaic approach."

"What's the difference?" I asked.

"Magic is a manipulation of primordial energies," Meriwether said. "The Hamms worship it. For me, it was more like learning to construct a brick wall. Some brick, some mortar … I realize that sounds inelegant, but magic isn't the answer to every problem. My father used magic to seduce men and woman, sometimes sexually, and sometimes for financial purposes. When I inherited the family business, I found I could charm people."

"What's your business?" Callie asked.

"I own the Meriwether Insurance Agency. Well, that's one of my concerns. I also own the Best Western hotel and a winery a few miles north of here."

"The Best Western?" I asked.

"Yes," Meriwether said. "I believe you were there last night."

A knot formed in my gut. "How do you know that?"

Meriwether laughed, a rich and musical sound that echoed against the wood paneling. "You checked out in the middle of the night. Sarah, the desk clerk, called the general manager, who called me. They gave me your name. It's a small town, Mr. Harlan. Very little goes on without everyone knowing. Why did you leave, if I might ask? I take great pride in my hotel."

"We were attacked."

His smile evaporated and he leaned forward with sudden interest. "What?"

"By a stick man," I said. "A golem, I think it's called."

"A full-sized golem?" he asked. "That's not possible. Do you know how much magical energy that would take?"

I had no idea. "A lot?"

Meriwether began fidgeting, rubbing his hands together. "Animating a full-sized golem requires more energy than I possess. I simply can't believe—"

"It was real," I said. "It was made of sticks and twigs, with eyeballs and a heart."

"You have to understand," Meriwether said, his voice growing louder, "I'm not strong enough to animate a toothpick, let alone a golem. My talents lend themselves to simple charms. I can influence someone into purchasing a more expensive insurance policy if they are so inclined."

"You're saying you couldn't have created the golem," Callie said.

Meriwether shook his head. "You've met Nicholas. My wife became very ill during her pregnancy. I tried to use magic to heal her, but I simply didn't possess the capability. She died giving birth and Nicholas suffered traumatic brain injuries. I realized then how little magic could accomplish. Like I said, my meager talent can barely sway someone that's already leaning in my direction."

I didn't know what to make of Meriwether. He sounded sensible, honest, and forthright. The more he spoke, the less I could picture him setting the stick man on us. "If you didn't animate the golem, who did?"

Meriwether frowned, his jaw clenching. "Someone strong. Someone who wanted to make sure you didn't interfere."

"Interfere with what?" I asked.

His eyes flitted around the room. "With whatever plans a person who can animate a golem might have, obviously."

"Could Jodie or Gene animate a golem?"

He squinted at me and I saw his hands shaking. He placed them next to his side. "I'd rather not say."

"Why not?" Callie asked.

"Because if they *could*," Meriwether said, "it might make them angry. And if they could animate a golem, there's no way I can protect myself." He stood and motioned toward the hallway. "I don't want to be rude, but I think it's time you leave. It's nothing personal, you understand. I have Nicholas. He needs me."

"I understand," I said, motioning for Callie to stand. "I know what a father will do to protect his child."

Relief washed over Meriwether's face. "I'm sorry I couldn't be of more assistance. I strongly urge you to leave, before someone tries to harm you again."

"I can take care of myself," I said. "What about you?"

Meriwether led us down the hall. "Maybe it's time Nicholas and I took a vacation. Somewhere warmer, perhaps. I hear Florida is nice this time of year."

Nicky appeared behind Meriwether. "Are you leaving? We didn't get to play Ninja Turtles!"

Meriwether turned to his son and his expression softened. "They don't have time to play, Nicholas."

We reached the front door and Meriwether opened it for us. He turned to Nicky and said, "I'll play with you."

Nicky stomped his sandal against the hardwood floor. "I wanna play with *them!*"

Callie gave the man-child a warm smile. "Next time, Nicky. Would that be okay?"

Nicky's face fell, but he nodded. "Yeah, okay. We can play *next* time."

I smiled at him, remembering how much Lilly used to love Dora the Explorer. "We'll play Ninja Turtles with you. I promise."

"I *love* Ninja Turtles," Nicky said, turning to his father. "See, they *wanna* play with me. Can they come back soon? Can they?"

Meriwether smiled in return, but it never made it to his eyes. "We'll have to see, Nicholas. We'll just have to see."

* * *

As we passed the Shopko on the south side of Monticello, Callie asked, "What did you think of Meriwether?"

"He seemed awfully damned normal for a witch. The Rexfords made him out to be a monster. He didn't strike me as anything but a concerned father. A bit pretentious, maybe…"

Callie sighed. "I agree. What does that mean?"

"It means," I said, "the Rexfords lied to us."

Callie stared out the window. The sun had knocked the winter chill back to something approaching comfortable. We passed a few vehicles on the road, mostly dirty farm trucks and the occasional sedan driven by solid-looking men and women. "The one thing the change didn't give me was a magic lie detector. We don't even know if Dorothy is alive."

A thought occurred to me and I grabbed my cell phone and punched in a number.

"Who are you calling?" Callie asked.

"Someone who can tell us if Dorothy is still alive."

The phone rang and then a voice on the other end said, "I told you not to call me."

"I need some help, Billy."

Billy Two-Feather Davenport, a Meskwaki from Tama who had helped us in Marshalltown, sighed. "When you call, it ends up biting me in the ass."

"That's the spirit," I said. "There's a missing woman."

"There's *always* a missing woman," Billy said. "That's none of my business."

"Still going to meetings?" I asked.

There was a long pause. "That's a dirty thing to do."

"I take it that's a yes?"

"Yes," Billy said. "I just got my thirty-day chip."

"Only thirty days?"

"I … had a bad time around Thanksgiving."

"Ah. Is that an Indian thing?"

"No, jackass, that's a lonely alcoholic thing. Why did you call?"

"The missing woman. Her name is Dorothy Hamm. I need to know if she's still alive."

"A spirit walk isn't a phone book, Sam. I can't just step through the veil and call her."

I'd seen Billy do amazing things in Marshalltown. I also knew that he was more powerful than he let on. "It's important, Billy."

"I'll give it a try," Billy said, then hung up the phone.

Callie raised an eyebrow. "Will he help?"

"I think," I said.

My belly rumbled and Callie frowned. "Hungry?"

"I wish I could say no."

She rummaged around behind the seat for the paper sack of jerky and passed it to me. I took out a piece, tore the plastic corner open with my teeth and popped the desiccated meat in my mouth. It wasn't as good as a rare steak or hamburger, but it quieted the hunger. "If the Rexfords lied, then what happened to Dorothy?" I asked between bites.

"Do you think they did something to her?"

"Does Jodie seem the type to hurt her own sister?"

"She seems proud," Callie mused, "and perhaps a bit arrogant."

"I'll give you that, but I don't sense that she'd hurt her own sister."

We had made it to Bement, and I turned left on Bodman and headed east.

Callie finally said, "We must be careful. We don't understand their motivations."

I tended to agree. My hometown of Arcanum was much like Bement, and I knew the kind of small-town intrigue and backbiting that could lurk under every corner.

All we need is to get involved in family politics.

Chapter Six

Gene led us past the living room and into their kitchen. I resisted the urge to sigh in relief. The idea of sitting at their dining room table with all the creepy dolls made my skin crawl.

Their kitchen was small, with a plain maple table that barely offered enough room for the chairs around it. Jodie was waiting for us, and she stood when we entered. "Did you find my sister?" she asked. I didn't speak, and her face fell. "You didn't find her."

I grunted. "I don't know what you were expecting—"

Jodie started to speak, but Gene cleared his throat. "Have a seat," he said, motioning to the table. "I think my wife wants to offer you an apology."

"For *what?*" Jodie asked, glaring at her husband.

"For assuming that Mr. Harlan and his friend would miraculously find Dorothy," Gene said. "Please, have a seat."

We took seats at the table while Jodie looked flustered. Finally, she spat out, "You saw him, didn't you? You spoke with Carlton?"

"We did," I said. "He admitted to being a witch. He said he doesn't know where your sister is."

"That's ridiculous," she said. "If you knew him like I know him, you would understand. Carlton is a liar."

"We don't have any proof of that," I said.

"Mrs. Rexford?" Callie asked. "We aren't … qualified to resolve disputes—"

"But—"

"—and that's what this looks like," I finished. "

Gene leaned back in his chair and asked, "What did Carlton say to you?"

I hesitated. "He told us Jodie hasn't liked him since he dated her sister. He said he doesn't have enough magic to animate a toothpick. All he cares about is his son."

"Nicky?" Jodie asked in disbelief. "Nicky is ... a bad seed."

"Come on. He's mentally handicapped," I said. "He's just a child trapped in a man's body."

Jodie squinted at me. "Carlton spun a yarn and you bought it."

"He didn't seem—"

"Like the Devil?" Jodie said. "Did he tell you about his talent?"

"He said it was charms ... that he could barely influence someone—"

"He told you his talent was charming people *while* he was charming you." Her voice was full of disgust.

I gave Callie a sidelong glance. She was frowning and I could tell she was as disturbed by the conversation as I was.

Meriwether had sounded so reasonable. Had he charmed us?

"There must be *something* you can do to help find Dorothy," Gene said. "I'm sure you can help." He glanced down at the table as if he was too embarrassed to speak.

"What?" I asked.

Jodie rolled her eyes. "Tell him."

Gene coughed uncomfortably into his hand. "What do you know of the Tarot?"

"The cards?" I asked, trying not to laugh. "That doesn't work, does it?"

"Sam," Callie said. "The Tarot isn't—"

"It's *real*," Jodie said, nodding at her husband. "Gene's readings have been all over the place lately, but one card keeps coming up. Death."

"That sounds ... ominous," I said.

Gene shook his head. "Death represents change, and my readings have continually shown that card in play. There have been a few other cards, including the reversed Magician."

It was like he was speaking in another language. "The what?"

"You are the reversed Magician. I believe *you* are a manipulator."

I felt my anger rising. "I'm not some ... some manipulator—"

"It's not what you think," Gene said hastily. "It means that

76

you are the main driver behind our fates."

"Whose fates?" I asked, trying to contain my disbelief.

"Ours," Jodie said. "And Dorothy's."

Gene said, "There's also the Hermit—"

Jodie raised her hand and shushed him. "The important thing is that you are vital to finding my sister."

* * *

"What are you going to do next?" Mosley asked.

We were sitting in Mosley's office as I recounted how I'd met with Meriwether and given Jodie my findings. Jameson was sitting on the couch, and I'd taken Mosley's seat at his desk. Callie and Mosley sat across from me, waiting for me to answer. I sighed. "What else can I do? I told you, I don't do missing women."

Mosley started to protest. "But—"

"I only talked to Meriwether because I thought he might have sent the golem to kill us," I said.

Jameson raised his hand. "We understand," he said, even though it looked like Mosley didn't understand at all. "But you can't just abandon Dorothy."

"Abandon her?" I asked. "I'm here for a vampire, remember?"

"You also want to find out who attacked us," Callie pointed out.

"Yeah, well, for all I know it was the Rexfords."

Callie frowned. "Why attack us?"

"Maybe they're protecting the vampire," I said. "Or working for it. Or maybe it has nothing to do with a vampire. Maybe it's because we started poking around in their business. Maybe they don't *really* want us looking into Dorothy's disappearance."

"That … doesn't seem likely," Jameson said. He stood and paced the room. "I suspect they truly want Dorothy back."

I watched as the older priest paced back and forth. "You seem awfully upset."

Jameson turned to me and opened his mouth, paused for a moment, then finally said, "We should all be upset. A woman is missing. Ethan has sensed a vampire's presence. Witches are active in this community. None of this bodes well."

"Sounds like another day at the office," I murmured.

"Sam," Callie began.

"Don't Sam me," I said. "Bad stuff happens everywhere, every day, and there's nothing I can do about that. I *can* do something about vampires."

Jameson shook his head. "Magic is dangerous, Sam, perhaps even more dangerous than vampires."

"Hah. Nothing is more dangerous than vampires."

"They're playing with the Tarot," Jameson said. "Oracles like the Tarot and the I Ching aren't just toys. They can be ... deadly."

Callie turned to look at Jameson. "I know that you think—"

"I don't just think," Jameson said. "I *know*. Oracles don't tell the truth. They present possibilities. Which, by the way, are open to interpretation. Trying to assign meaning to them can cause the very event you're trying to avoid."

"So I'm not the Manipulator?" I asked. "Great. I don't really want to be the driver of fate."

Callie sighed. "Should we go back to the hotel?"

"What?" I asked. "Why?"

"Those trees to the south," she said. "They must have been watching us from there. Maybe they left a clue."

"A clue?" My stomach tightened. I took a deep breath and held it until the surge of anger faded. "We're not the police. We don't have any training. How are we supposed to find clues? And, if we do find a clue, what are we supposed to do with it?"

She turned to me and her eyes were shiny and hard. "Do you have any better ideas?"

She's got me there. Maybe she's the smart one and I'm just the dumb sidekick.

My stomach growled loud enough for everyone to hear. "Fine," I said. "We'll go back to the hotel, but I'm going to stop and get something to eat. Didn't I see a Subway in this town?"

Mosley nodded. "Right after the railroad tracks."

"Great." I nodded to Callie. "We get an early lunch, and then we go back to the hotel. Fathers, do you want to join us?"

Mosley started to nod, but Jameson shook his head. "No," Jameson said. "I think the four of us traipsing around makes too much of a display."

I thought about that, and how absurd we'd look parading through town, just a beautiful woman, a rough looking man, and two priests. It sounded more like a bad joke than a serious attempt to find an evil witch, a vampire, and a missing woman. "We'll be back when we find something," I said.

* * *

I placed my order with the pretty Indian woman at the counter who quickly made my two roast beef foot-longs. I paid for my sandwiches, coffee, and Callie's chicken salad, and we took seats near the front of the building. It was a newer franchise. The building looked a little rough on the outside, but the inside was clean and inviting and smelled of fresh-baked bread. I opened my sandwich and took a bite. I had the woman load the sandwich with extra roast beef, and it tasted delicious. I started to chew and had a moment where I longed for the beef to be rare, almost bloody, and quickly shook my head.

"What's wrong?" Callie asked. Her plastic fork was hovering over her chicken salad, but she was eying me intently.

I started to speak, but a man in his early sixties opened the door behind her, causing the bell to tinkled. The man had an orange, bottled tan and dyed blond hair. I put him in his early sixties, and he was a shade taller than me, but wore a suit just expensive enough to set him apart from the locals.

The woman on his arm was a different matter. She was starkly beautiful, with coal-black hair, deeply tanned skin, and a skirt short enough to be considered indecent. I put her in her early thirties, but the man said something and she laughed, and I saw crow's feet around her eyes and upped that to early forties. The woman glanced my way, smiled, then turned back to her companion.

I felt a sensation I hadn't expected. Just a glance from the woman had ignited my libido.

"*Sam*," Callie said, just loud enough to bring me back to my senses.

"Sorry."

"Why are you acting so … weird?"

I gulped down some of the coffee. It was hot, and that's about the only thing it had going for it. "Edmund said I'd be feeling things, and he's right. I'm angry."

"Everyone gets angry," Callie said. "It's only human."

I took a bite of my sandwich, chewed, and swallowed. "I'm hungry."

She smiled. "None of this is news to me, Sam."

"Yeah, I know, but it's happening even more since we've gotten here. What if I change? What if it doesn't take me hundreds and hundreds of vampire kills?" My voice dropped until I was whispering. "What if I just wake up and I'm a monster?"

She was starting to respond when the door opened again. This time, it was a man dressed in a police officer's black uniform and black coat. The man was a few years older than me and bigger than me, and his beefy face and build hinted at time spent doing manual labor or dedicated sessions in the gym. On his arm was a woman with a long black ponytail. They took their place in line, glaring at the couple in front of them.

Callie shook her head, then said, "I don't think you'll become a monster."

"But how do you know?"

She smiled. "You've been through ... so much, and you haven't given up yet. You chose to fight back. You have free will, but you chose to fight. That says something. I think we have plenty of time to figure out how to keep you from becoming a vampire."

I wanted to tell her I was plenty worried that we weren't going to figure out how to stop me from changing. I wanted to tell her that I was troubled by the witchcraft, and by the missing woman. I wanted to tell her that unless there was a vampire to fight, we had no business being in Bement, Illinois.

Instead, I took another bite and another, until I'd finished my first sandwich and moved on to my second. I washed it all down with more of the bad coffee, then asked, "What do you think of Jodie and Gene?"

She sipped her iced tea. "I think magic is a temptation most people aren't able to resist. Think about your life before the vampire attack. Wouldn't you have been tempted?"

"Tempted by what?"

"Power. People used to have faith in God, but as faith has waned, it's left an empty hole in them. They feel that God doesn't care. You still feel that way."

"Maybe," I said grudgingly. "I just don't get," I waved my hand around, "this."

"God cares, Sam. God loves. Just because we don't understand His will, doesn't mean He's not with us."

"Why can't He be with Dorothy Hamm?" After I'd said it, I realized how bitter it sounded. Before Callie could respond, I continued, "If God loves us, how can He let an innocent woman be taken."

"*If* that's what happened," Callie said. "The problem is that we see things through our eyes and not His. It's not that God doesn't intervene, but if He did, we wouldn't have free will."

I glanced up as I finished unwrapping my second sandwich. "You're saying that Dorothy deserves to be missing? That something she did brought this on?"

"Not at all. What I'm saying is that people make their own decisions. We are *all* responsible for our decisions, even if they impact others."

"You mean Jodie did something she shouldn't have, and that's why Dorothy is missing?"

"We don't know, Sam. That's also part of being human."

I started in on my sandwich. Callie continued to pick at her salad. Finally, I said, "Well, being human sucks."

She smiled at me. "It's hard when we don't have the answers. I heard Father Jameson and Father Lewinheim discuss the nature of free will."

"Yeah? How'd that go?"

"Several hours of extensive discussion led them to the same conclusion. Not quite in your words, exactly, but they agreed that sometimes it … sucks to be human. That's why we must hold tightly to our faith."

* * *

We finished eating and I threw our trash away while Callie used the restroom. When she returned, we exited the restaurant and headed for the truck. Behind us, the door opened and the man in the suit followed us out, along with the woman he seemed intent on displaying as his arm candy. I was opening the truck door when the man cleared his throat. I turned to him in time to have him stick out a business card in my direction.

"Del Doll," he said, "I own Del Doll Dodge in Monticello. I can't help but notice that you've got yourself quite a beauty here."

I glanced at the truck. "It gets me where I need to go."

"Well, lucky for you that we caught you here." He smiled his megawatt smile. "This is my wife, Lisa."

I didn't say anything, but I saw Callie frowning. I didn't take the card from his hand, nor did I speak.

"Pleasure to meet you," Lisa said in a voice that was low and sultry.

I offered them a perfunctory smile. "We have to be going—"

"I'm a little flush on new Dodge trucks," Del said. "A man that would hang on to a truck like this is the man who would appreciate the comfort and style of a new Ram or Silverado."

I almost laughed. If it were possible to sound like a late-night commercial, Del Doll had it locked up. "No thanks."

His smile never wavered. "I hear that all the time, but it never hurts to take one for a test drive. We've got the best finance officers of any dealership in the area. The sky's the limit."

The door to the Subway opened and the police officer came out. His badge was embossed with the name Gary, and he stopped within arm's reach of Del. "He doesn't seem interested, Del. Maybe you should turn off the salesman bullshit and let the man be on his way."

Lisa's smile faltered. She was giving the woman with Officer Gary an unpleasant look. "What do you have against the free market, Bobby?"

"If he's not interested, then he's not interested," Officer Gary said. He pointed to the sign in the Subway window. "No soliciting."

Del's smile finally dropped a notch. "No reason to get testy. We were just drumming up business."

"Your business is always plenty busy."

Del raised a hand. "Fine, fine. We'll be on our way." He motioned for his wife to follow and they got into a black Dodge Durango. He waved as they backed out and headed north.

I turned to the officer. "Thanks."

Officer Gary didn't speak. His gaze wasn't hostile, but it wasn't friendly, either. He spun on his heel and headed to the car with the Bement Police logo. The woman with him offered us a polite nod, and they were backing out and heading north.

I turned to Callie. "What the he—heck was that about?"

She looked baffled. "I have no idea. These small towns are ... strange."

"Sister, you got that right." We climbed in the truck and I backed it out and headed north to Monticello. "I hope we find something in those trees. I hope there's something that points to who is responsible."

I was passing the grocery store on the right, taking the small bend in the road, when Callie said, "If you can't find a vampire, what are you going to do?"

I grunted. "Someone tried to kill us. That's got me more than a little … miffed. I'd like to find the responsible party." I'd been thinking about it during the meal at Subway. "However, if we can't find anything, and I can't find Dorothy Hamm, and there's no vampire, I might have reached the end of what I can do. If nothing pans out, maybe it's time to call it a day and head home."

Callie turned to me and nodded. "I agree. I want to help Dawn find her mother, but free will only takes us so far. Good intentions aren't enough to help."

I laughed.

"What?" she asked.

"We finally agreed on something," I said. As I spoke, a red Ford pickup truck towing a plow turned onto US-105 heading south. We were only a mile north of the Bement Cemetery and the next nearest vehicle was a couple of miles in front of us. The plow was folded up, and the tips of the iron chisels gleamed silver in the December sun.

The Ford swerved into our lane and I had a moment of clarity where I saw the old man driving the truck, a shock of white hair on his head, his face tan and weathered and bearing a grim look of determination.

The old man's lips were moving and Callie was screaming and I was swerving, desperate to avoid the plow's chisels. The Ford swerved deeper into our lane before swerving back. The plow whipped around and the chisels caught the side of the Chevy. The metal shrieked and squealed and we went crashing off the road and into the ditch, slamming into the grassy earth.

My head slammed against the steering wheel and I didn't even have time to think before everything went black.

Chapter Seven

If you've never been knocked unconscious, you can't imagine the feeling. At first, it feels like you're floating on a warm cloud. Everything is peaceful. Quiet.

Then the pain comes. Sometimes it's your whole body. Sometimes it's an arm, or a leg, or your ribs.

But one thing's for certain—your head *will* hurt. And not just hurt. There're no words that accurately describes the agony in your brain.

I managed to open one eye, saw a gray patch of concrete, then rolled to my side and puked my guts out, spewing roast beef all over the floor. Every heave caused a new muscle group in my body to spasm, which prompted me to vomit again.

The roast beef was followed by bitter green bile, until nothing was left but spit. I was empty and hollowed out, my head pounding in time with my heartbeat. I lay there helplessly until the room stopped spinning.

I was at the bottom of a round concrete pit, twice as wide as I was tall, and nearly fifteen feet deep. There was a buzzing fluorescent light far above, and I could barely make out the strange Celtic-like runes etched into the walls.

Callie wasn't with me.

I staggered to my feet, which was a huge mistake, and went right back down again. I managed a few dry heaves, and after what seemed like an eternity, the churning and roiling in my stomach came to halt.

I was freezing.

Then I realized it was because my trench coat and shoulder holster were gone. Even my silver Bowie knife was missing.

"Hello?" I shouted, then immediately regretted it. My throat was raw and felt like it had been sandpapered.

I could hear voices far above, but I couldn't make out what they were saying. "Hello?" I tried again.

The old man who had driven the Ford truck into us leaned over the edge of the pit. He shook his head, then turned to speak to someone else.

"What's going on?" I yelled. "Where's Callie?"

The old man glanced down into the pit. "Why didn't you kill Meriwether?"

"Why do *you* want him dead?" I countered.

"You shoulda *killed* him," the old man said. "He almost murdered you. You were *supposed* to kill him!"

"This isn't just about Dorothy, is it?"

The old man scowled in frustration. "We would all be safer with him dead."

"Nothing indicated—"

"He's evil, boy. You shoulda done what you're good at."

"I'm not a killer," I said. "You don't point me like a loaded gun."

The old man pulled back from the edge and I lost sight of him. "Hey!" I yelled. "Come back."

The old man leaned back over the edge. "You got something to say?"

"I'm not a killer," I repeated. "That's *not* what I do."

The old man shook his head. "I know what you are, boy. You're a man of violence, and death follows you."

"Damn it," I shouted. "What do you want from me?"

He stared at me with a face as hard as stone. "We have your friend. You'll kill Carlton or you'll never see her again."

* * *

I stewed in my anger while I waited for the old man to return. He had Callie, and I was trapped at the bottom of the pit.

Every part of my body ached. The Chevy wasn't designed to crumple on impact like a modern car, and it didn't have airbags. We'd been wearing seat belts, but it hadn't afforded much protection. It felt like I'd taken a beating. Callie might feel even worse.

I longed to jump to the top of the pit and pull myself up and over, but the edge of the pit was impossibly high. I searched for cracks or bumps that I could use to pull myself up, but the bare walls were smooth and offered no purchase.

My anger flared again, so strong I almost fell to the floor.

I'll pummel the old man, smashing and breaking the bones in his face. I'll beat him until his brain swells. His agony will be exquisite. He will feel the way I did when Ignacio Santiago beat me in Marshalltown. He'll know the desperation and terrible finality as he fades away into the long dark night.

I jerked, coming back to my senses, horrified by my thoughts. I didn't kill humans. I killed vampires. That made me a good guy. Killing humans would only make me a murdering scumbag.

I can't let the change take control.

There was a scraping above and I heard two voices speaking quietly, then the old man appeared again at the top of the pit. "We're gonna talk, Mr. Harlan. Face to face. Don't you try anything stupid. We have your friend. If you try any funny business, she's dead. You understand?" The man's voice was rough, like he wasn't used to idle chitchat.

"Yes," I said, trying not to imagine my hands wrapped around his throat.

"Good. Lower it."

There was more scraping above, then an aluminum extension ladder appeared over the edge and slowly lowered into place. When it touched the bottom, I grabbed it and hauled myself up.

"Slowly, boy. Very slowly."

I bit my tongue. Literally. The pain focused me, and I climbed until I reached the top, then gingerly climbed over the edge into a room with walls made of yellowed plywood. The old man was tall, with broad shoulders that appeared even broader thanks to his insulated undershirt and navy-blue overalls. Short white hair peeked out from under a DEKALB baseball cap. His skin was tanned and leathered, and I placed him somewhere in his late sixties or early seventies.

He watched me the way one watches a snake, his green eyes taking in my every motion, but I realized the old man was not alone.

The police officer I'd seen in the Subway restaurant was standing next to the old man.

Worse, the cop watched me with hard black eyes, his hand near his service weapon. He squinted at me. "Make a move and your girlfriend dies. That's the deal. Got it?"

"Yeah," I said quietly. "I got it. And she's not my girlfriend."

"You care 'bout her," the old man said. "That's enough."

"Where are we?" I asked, finally breaking eye contact with the cop.

"Not far from where we ran you off the road," the cop said.

"Bobby, here," the old man said, "is Bement's police officer."

I turned back to the cop. "Your name is Bobby Gary?"

The cop scowled. "You got a problem with that?"

I don't know why I said it. Maybe it was the stress, or the disorientation from the crash, or the change playing havoc with my emotions. Maybe it was just plain dislike.

"No," I said. "It's like you have two first names. Bobby Gary. Heh."

There was a brief moment where I saw his fist moving, and then I felt the meaty crunch as Bobby Gary's fist smashed into my nose.

I gasped. My vision went black and my eyes teared up. I fell back toward the pit, but somebody grabbed me and then there was a sense of weightlessness before I crashed into something hard.

I gasped for air and wiped at my eyes. When I could finally see again, I found myself on the floor next to the plywood wall, my hand covered in blood from my nose.

Officer Gary was staring at me and rubbing his knuckles. "Keep it up, asshole, and what happens to your girlfriend is gonna be the least of your problems."

I wiped blood and snot from my nose and cleaned it off on my jeans. My anger had evaporated, and it wasn't because of the punch to the face.

There was a buzzing against the back of my neck. Officer Bobby Gary was a witch as well as a cop.

I'm in trouble.

* * *

They led me into a hallway. The walls were yellow plywood, the type used in new construction. I glanced up at the open rafters above and realized that I was in a machine shed not unlike my own back in Toledo.

We stopped in front of a massive wooden door and the old man withdrew a skeleton key that hung from a thick silver chain under his shirt. He turned the lock and pushed gently on the door.

Officer Gary gave my shoulder a shove just a little too hard to be considered gentle and said, "Be smart, asshole."

I turned to glare at him, but he was unmoved. I sighed and stepped through the door.

The room was the same as the room where I'd been kept, but this room had no pit. Callie sat in the middle, bound to an oak chair by black plastic zip ties. A pentagram was inscribed in the concrete, with symbols etched around the circumference.

I took a step forward and slammed into an invisible wall of force.

"Callie!" I shouted, trying to step forward.

It was hopeless. I was rooted in place.

"You can't reach her," the old man said. "She's warded."

Callie's head lolled to the side and a smear of dried blood trailed from her nose, over her lips, and down her chin.

My heart thudded in my chest. "What have you done to her?"

"She was knocked out in the crash," Officer Gary said. "She'll live. I checked her myself. She's gonna hurt something fierce when she wakes up, but she'll be fine."

"We're gonna keep her unconscious," the old man said from behind me.

He placed his hand on my shoulder and yanked me back. When he did, I felt the force holding me give way. I was finally able to take a step backward, then another, until I was free of whatever magic protected Callie. I spun around and glared at the old man and Officer Gary. "Why did you do this?"

"You are gonna kill Carlton for me," the old man said. "You're going to do it, or your friend will remain asleep."

My anger finally boiled over. I pointed at Officer Gary. "You think this goon will protect you?"

Officer Gary took a step back. His hand, which rested on the butt of his gun, twitched. "You better—"

"*Please*," I said. "*Threaten* me. Even with a splitting headache, I will take that gun away from you and beat you to death with it before you even move."

The old man's eyes narrowed. "You wouldn't."

I felt my lips curl into a smile. "I'm fast, faster than you can imagine. How good are you with magic? You think you can voodoo me before I kill him and move on to you?" My smile widened. "I'd break your fingers like popsicle sticks. Let Callie go or you're going to learn about regret, and not the sort you feel over picking the wrong flavored coffee or burning the toast, but the kind of regret you get when you're taking your last breath and wondering what you should have done differently with your life."

Although Officer Gary appeared defiant, there was a hint of fear in his eyes as he finally recognized that I might be more dangerous than they'd bargained for.

"I can't release her, boy," the old man said wearily. "Your friend is well and truly bound. You ain't gonna free her. She will stay in that chair until she dies."

I started to speak, but the old man pointed to the writing on the floor and said, "That is our coven's work. Nothing you can do will break it. Your friend has minor injuries, but she'll live, at least for three days. That's how long it takes to die from dehydration."

"What if I *make* you release her?" I growled, my hands rising in front of me.

The old man stood his ground. "You don't understand, boy. Only our coven working together can release the binding. You can threaten us, boy, but you can't bend our will. Not all of us. You got to kill Carlton, or your friend dies."

* * *

"Who are you?" I asked. "Why are you doing this?"

A door slammed and footsteps echoed, then Jodie Rexford entered. Her face was pale, her eyes full of concern. "By the Goddess, Randy, what have you done?"

"You stay out of this, girl. Something's got to be done."

"I apologize for this, Mr. Harlan. Randy forgot his place. I'm the leader of this coven."

Randy chewed at his lip, then said softly, "You get to be in charge because I *let* you be in charge. Your talent is strong, but you didn't get near as much as your momma, and you sure didn't get near as much as me."

Jodie sucked in her breath. "You can't treat me like a child. Not anymore."

"If you weren't family," the old man said quietly, "I'd tell you to get the Hell off my property."

"You're related?" I asked.

The old man turned to me and there was a buzzing against

the back of my neck. His eyes, already a vivid green, deepened as he stared at me. I tried to catch my breath, but it was like my lungs were empty.

"My niece doesn't have my talent," the old man said, every word carrying an electric sense of power, "and she doesn't got the stomach to do what needs to be done. I can see you, boy. I see the goodness in you. I see the other thing, too. I *hate* asking you to do this, but we're all in danger."

Bobby Gary was glancing between the two, clearly torn between the old farmer and Jodie Rexford. "I don't think this is—"

"Shut up," the old man said, his eyes never leaving Jodie.

"You put me in charge," Jodie said. "You don't get to pick and choose which decisions to follow. I may not have your talent, but I'm level-headed. That's why Janice supports me."

The old man took a deep breath, then relaxed. "That's a dirty thing to do, and you know it."

"Let's get out of here," Officer Gary said, "before the prisoner does something stupid."

"Prisoner?" Jodie asked, arching an eyebrow.

Before I could speak, the old man nodded. They led me from the machine shed to a run-down two-story farmhouse fifty feet to the north. Jodie's Prius was parked behind Officer Gary's patrol car. Next to them was the same Ford pickup that had run us off the road.

I paused for a moment and searched for my truck, but a shove from Officer Gary sent me stumbling forward. We reached the side door to the farmhouse and I hesitated at the steps.

The old man held out his hand, and there was an excruciating pain in my chest. Liquid fire poured through my heart. I screamed and dropped to my knees, collapsing onto the welcome mat at the bottom of the farmhouse stoop.

"*Randy*," Jodie hissed.

And, like that, the pain was gone, the fire a distant memory. The old man regarded me coolly. "Sorry 'bout that, boy. I don't like to hurt folk, but you got to learn who's in charge."

A woman appeared behind him. She was also in her late sixties, with vibrant blue eyes and steel-gray hair in a small bun. Her face was makeup-free, and she had deep creases around her eyes and mouth. Unlike the man, she wore a colorful red sweater and faded denim jeans. "Don't be cruel," she said to the man. "It isn't necessary."

The old man turned to the woman. "We're deep in the ditch, hon. We ain't got time for manners."

"Wait," I said quickly, holding up my hands. "I don't understand. Can't you just—"

From behind me, Jodie cleared her throat. "There's no time for this."

The woman shook her head. "There's always time for manners, Jodie." She beckoned me inside. "Come in, Mr. Harlan. Please."

"Well," I said. "Since you asked so nicely…"

The man held the door and I followed the woman inside and into a surprisingly well-maintained kitchen.

The ceiling was at least ten feet tall, the way old farmhouses used to be, but the walls were painted a bright white. The cabinets were white, the countertop was white, hell, everything in the room was blindingly, spotlessly white—everything except for the ancient oak table in the center of the room. It was scarred, and cracked, and weather-beaten, and looked like it belonged on the set of a western movie.

The old man pointed to one of the chairs. "Sit, boy."

I sat.

Everyone else took a seat, but before I could speak, the old woman said, "We haven't been introduced. I'm Janice Korman and this is my husband, Randy."

I blinked. "I would say it's nice to meet you…"

"These are trying times," Janice said, frowning. "Carlton has us all on edge."

"Your husband almost killed me," I blurted out. "You've got my friend held in some kind of magic … I don't know what. You think *you're* on edge?"

Randy Korman sat up straight and stomped a heavy boot against the floor. "Pay attention, boy," he said.

"We just want my sister back," Jodie said. "I'm sorry for all of this."

"It's too late for that," Randy said. "Things have gotten outta hand. We got to take measures."

Jodie's face darkened. "Randy—"

"Don't, girl. If your momma was still alive—"

"Well," Jodie said sharply, "she's not. *I'm* in charge. We're going to focus on getting Dorothy back."

"Then let Callie go," I said. "As a good faith measure."

Jodie opened her mouth to speak, but she paused, then said, "I'm afraid that if we let your friend go, you'll leave without helping us."

Damned right, I will. "I wouldn't do that."

Randy snorted. "You ain't a very good liar, boy."

"I'm afraid I can't release her," Jodie said. "She's the only leverage we have. Just help us find Dorothy. That's all we're asking."

"Please, Mr. Harlan," Janice implored, glaring at Jodie, "help us get Dorothy back. Surely you can see that she *belongs* here with her family."

I wanted to say that holding Callie hostage wasn't the way to win me over. I wanted to tell them that I no longer cared about saving Dorothy. I wanted to stand up and tell them that their problems were just that—*their* problems.

Then I remembered Callie, slumped over in the chair, and the bloodstains on her face.

Randy and Janice Korman seemed like the people I knew in Arcanum—rock-solid farmers, salt-of-the-earth folks, the kind who gave you the shirt off their backs if they knew you were in trouble.

But Randy possessed power, and I felt a little buzz coming from Janice, too. Jodie certainly possessed enough magical ability to give me pause.

The simple truth was that I didn't have the strength to fight them, and if what Randy said was true, I couldn't free Callie without the coven's agreement. I didn't know how many people were in Jodie's coven, but if Randy and Janice were indicative of their power level, I couldn't *force* them to release her.

The anger rose again, burning in the back of my throat, but there was nothing I could do about it.

They had me and they *knew* it.

I bottled the anger up and shoved it down deep inside. "If you can tell me where Dorothy is, I'll make sure she gets home safe and sound."

Kevin Lee Swaim

Chapter Eight

I swung Jodie's Prius into the park across from Meriwether's house and parked next to a dirty green picnic table. Randy had given me back my trench coat but had only laughed when I'd asked for my Kimber. Apparently the coven's trust in me to rescue Dorothy didn't extend to my firearm.

I *did* have my silver Bowie knife, though, as Jodie had agreed that I needed something for protection.

It was early in the afternoon, and a gentle wind rustled through the trees. The sun filtering through the park's tree branches cast a crazy patchwork of shadows across the grass, and the smell of damp leaves was thick in the air.

I left the Prius and headed east at an easy stroll. There was little traffic noise, and all I could hear was the sound of my own breathing and the scrape-scrape of tree limbs rubbing against each other as I hurried across State Street.

Jodie had informed me that Meriwether's property was protected by a potent magical spell. I reached into my coat pocket and fingered the leather bag Janice Korman had given me. She claimed it would allow safe passage onto Meriwether's property. She also claimed it would mask my presence.

The rolling lawn seemed a lot bigger now that I was on foot. The house sat a long way back from the road. If Meriwether's property was warded and the leather bag didn't work, I was a sitting duck.

Meriwether was a witch and I was about to trespass on his property.

I might as well paint a big fat target on my back. If only they didn't have Callie…

I stepped onto the brown grass and felt a tickling up my

spine. The coven's suspicions about Meriwether's house were true. It *was* warded. I took another step forward. It was like pushing against a wall of Jell-O. Another step forward and the pressure intensified until it finally gave way and I lurched forward.

Thank God the talisman worked.

I made a beeline for the side of Meriwether's property, where a stand of thick evergreens stretched to the east before turning south. The evergreens wouldn't provide much cover in the daylight, but it was better than nothing. I continued east until I reached the point that was roughly north of the house. Fifty yards of grass separated the evergreens from the house.

Randy and Janice Korman believed that Dorothy was being held in Meriwether's basement. Jodie thought Dorothy was being held in a bedroom on the third floor of the mansion.

I agreed with Randy and Janice. If Meriwether was holding Dorothy, the safest place to keep her would be in the basement, where the thick earth would muffle her screams for help.

Assuming Meriwether actually has Dorothy.

The basement windows were wide but short, the way basement windows in old houses used to be. Carefully sculpted shrubs dotted the sides of the house and I hoped they would shield me from view as I attempted to gain entry.

My stomach was doing flip-flops and a part of me recognized I was stalling for time.

It wasn't fear, exactly. I was a vampire hunter, or, at least, I wanted to be. Breaking into a witch's house to rescue a woman I didn't know wasn't the kind of job I pictured Jack doing.

Then again, I wasn't Jack.

And Callie was hurt.

Worrying about it isn't getting the job done.

I strode quickly across the lawn, heading for the house, and found that the line of bushes *did* shield me from view.

I peered into the nearest basement window. It led to a cluttered storage room filled with heavy wooden shelves lined with cardboard boxes.

The bottom of the window moved when pressed, but it didn't open. The window was hinged at the top and I pushed again, monkeying with it until the window gave way and swung inward. There was just enough room to squeeze through and drop to the concrete floor six feet below.

The room was big. Light streamed through the dirty windows and provided a surprisingly good view. The walls were brick. Ancient wooden floor joists ran above my head.

The house was old, but it was built to withstand the ages. I resisted the urge to whistle softly and crept around the room until I found a door that led south.

I twisted the brass knob, half expecting the door to creak and moan when I pushed against it, but it opened silently, exposing another room. Unlike the storage room, this room was semifinished, with white plaster walls and wooden stairs that led to the first floor.

Nicky Meriwether sat on the floor, playing with a set of Teenage Mutant Ninja Turtle dolls. The room was full of Teenage Mutant Ninja Turtle merchandise, including a plastic van the size of a small toaster oven and a row of three-foot-tall mannequins of the four turtles. At least half a dozen Ninja Turtle posters were taped to the walls, and the wooden shelf around the top of the room was covered in tiny turtle figurines. Nicky sat on the floor in the middle of the room, batting around a tall figurine I didn't recognize.

Before I could make my retreat, Nicky looked up, saw me, and smiled. "You came to play Ninja Turtles!"

My mind raced. I couldn't leave, but I wasn't about to hurt the man-child. "That's right. I came to play Ninja Turtles."

Nicky pointed to the room behind me. "Why were you in *there*?"

"I knocked on the front door," I lied, "but nobody heard me. I had to climb in through the window."

I prayed silently that Nicky would look past the blatant lie.

He nodded slowly. "Okay. Who do you wanna be?"

"Who do I want to be?" I asked.

"Yeah," Nicky said. "You wanna be Leonardo? I like Michelangelo. Michelangelo uses numb-chucks. You know about numb-chucks?"

I smiled. "I think they're called nunchucks. How about I play Rafael?"

"Rafael's cool," Nicky allowed, "but not as cool as Michelangelo."

He stood and handed me one of the turtles. "Okay, we're fighting Shredder. You gotta fight Shredder with Rafael."

I breathed a sigh of relief. "Okay," I said. "Rafael it is. So, how do we fight Shredder?"

"Like this," Nicky said, smacking the taller masked figurine with his turtle.

"Okay. Hey, Nicky? Is your dad home?"

"I don't *think* so," Nicky said. "He's always gone. He doesn't wanna play Ninja Turtles with me very much. Like, *never.*"

"That's okay," I said. "I'm here to play with you now." I picked up Rafael and hop walked him across the floor until I could swing his foot at the Shredder figurine.

"Take that, Shredder!" Nicky shrieked. "Here comes Michelangelo." He smacked the nunchucks into Shredder's side, knocking it over.

His laugh was full of wonder and joy, and for a moment I forgot that Callie was locked in the center of the pentagram, held with magic by the force of the coven's will.

Then, Nicky spoke. "Where's that girl?"

"What girl?"

"You know. That girl you were with."

The feeling of joy evaporated, as quickly as mist burning away from the morning sun. "She couldn't make it. She wanted to play Ninja Turtles with you, but she had to do something else."

"I wish she was here," Nicky said. "It's fun to have lots of people when you play Ninja Turtles."

"Isn't there anyone here who can play with you?"

Nicky frowned in confusion. "Huh?"

"Isn't there anyone else here?"

"Who *could* be here?"

"I don't know," I said. "A man or a woman?"

"No," Nicky said, shaking his head. "There's nobody here. We're all alone."

"There's *never* anybody here?"

Nicky pondered that, his face scrunched up in deep concentration. Finally, he said softly, "Well, sometimes there *are* people. I think they are Daddy's friends."

"Do you know any of them?"

Nicky shook his head. "They're *old* people."

"Old people?" I asked. "How old?"

"You know," he said, shaking his Michelangelo doll. "*Old* people."

I smiled in spite of myself. "Was there anyone here recently? An older woman?"

"Maybe," Nicky allowed. "I don't remember days too good. Maybe it was … yesterday?"

Yesterday?

"What did this woman look like?"

"I don't 'member," Nicky said slowly. "Old."

"Was she a friend of your dad's?"

"I *think* so. They yelled a lot."

"About what?"

"I couldn't hear too good, but when Daddy talks real loud like that, he's pretty mad."

"This woman was in the house? Where?"

Nicky eyed me suspiciously. "You ask lots of questions. You said you were gonna play Ninja Turtles."

"I know," I said. "I promised I would play with you, but I think I know that woman. I've been looking for her. Is she still here?"

"I said I don't 'member." Nicky turned his attention back to the Michelangelo figurine, bouncing it across the floor and kicking Shredder. "I don't wanna talk about her. I wanna play."

"I'm sorry. I didn't mean to upset you."

He turned his attention back to me, and a smile lit up his face. "That's okay. I'm glad you wanna play with me. I *guess* I can show you where she was."

"That would be great, Nicky. I'd really like to see her."

"Sure." He put his figurine on the floor and took Rafael from my hands, placing it next to Michelangelo. "C'mon. It's upstairs."

I followed Nicky up the stairs, through a doorway, around the corner, and up a set of stairs to the second floor. He led me down a long hallway lined with tiny alcoves set into the walls every five feet. Soft overhead lights shone on pieces of artwork. It reminded me of a hallway I'd seen once before, in Silas's house in Indianapolis. Just the thought made my blood boil.

We came to a door. Nicky smiled and pointed at it. "She was in there."

"Thanks, Nicky. This really helps me out."

Nicky smiled shyly. "You played Ninja Turtles with me. That means we're best friends."

"Best friends," I agreed, reaching out to spin the doorknob. "Ninja Turtles make the best of friends."

Nicky giggled as the door opened.

"Ninja Turtles *do* make the best of friends," a voice said from inside. My heart sank at the site of Carlton Meriwether sitting at a massive desk covered in rich black leather. "Hello, Mr. Harlan."

* * *

"Mr. Meriwether," I said.

Behind me, Nicky's breathing increased. "Daddy?"

Meriwether smiled and said softly, "Nicholas, I think you should return to your playroom. Mr. Harlan and I have business to discuss."

I turned to Nicky and nodded, forcing myself to smile. "It's okay, Nicky. I'll play Ninja Turtles with you some other time."

The man-child looked like he wanted to speak, but his gaze shifted back to his father and he nodded, his face crestfallen. "I guess so. Bye."

"Please," Meriwether said to me, "come in. Shut the door."

I reached for the door and saw Nicky, already halfway down the hallway, turn and offer a small wave. I waved back, then shut the door and turned my attention to the man whose home I had invaded. "I guess you know why I'm here."

"Have a seat," Meriwether said, motioning to the elegant chair in front of his desk.

Floor-to-ceiling bookcases lined the walls of Meriwether's office. Old-fashioned rolling ladders hung from brass pipes on each wall. A bay window provided a warm glow that gave the room a fresh, lived-in feel. I sank into the offered chair, my trench coat squeaking against the leather. "Is this where you threaten me?"

"I don't threaten, Mr. Harlan. Why would I?" Meriwether's brow furrowed. "I see the Sister isn't with you."

"How did you know she was religious?"

"Because I'm not a fool," Meriwether said. "I didn't need to use my gift. The Sister has a certain ... glow. She shines with an inner light. But you haven't answered the question."

"I didn't realize you had asked one."

Meriwether smiled sadly. "Jodie Rexford. I should have known. What has she done with your friend?"

"For a man with a small talent, you sure seem to know what's going on."

"Once again, I'm not a fool. Jodie is holding the Sister. She sent you to break into my house. She still believes I'm responsible for

Dorothy's disappearance."

I had to hand it to Meriwether. He *did* understand the situation. "You knew I was here," I said, withdrawing the talisman from my trench coat. "Even though I had this thing."

Meriwether pointed to a computer monitor on his desk. "I have video cameras. No magic necessary. Jodie must have you over a barrel to get you to come here like this."

I swallowed heavily. He was right.

She does have me over a barrel. Damn it.

"Nicky said he heard you yelling at an older woman. You're going to tell me that wasn't Dorothy Hamm?"

Meriwether laughed. "I assure you, I have not abducted Dorothy."

"I didn't ask if you abducted her," I said. "I asked whether she was *here*."

Meriwether leaned back in his chair and regarded me thoughtfully. "I will allow that I *might* have spoken with Dorothy in the last week. But I promise you, I had *nothing* to do with her disappearance."

There was something else there, something Meriwether wasn't saying. I could sense it. I thought back to everything he had said in our first encounter, and everything the Rexfords had said about him.

Something doesn't add up.

"Nicky said he heard you arguing with her. Is that true?"

"Sometimes friends disagree," Meriwether said, his eyes narrowing. "Arguing with an old friend isn't a crime."

"I thought you said you hadn't really spoken with Dorothy since your college fling."

Meriwether sighed. "I wasn't exactly honest about that."

"You lied about—"

"It's *nobody's* business," Meriwether said with a sudden heat to his voice. "That's the problem with people today. They think they have a right to know everyone's business. Some things are private for a reason. Dorothy and I *may* have kept in contact. So what? We weren't having an affair. It was just a few words here and there over the years. Why does Jodie think she has a right to know about that?"

He drew himself up in his chair and pulled at his sweater. "I don't know where Dorothy is. I don't know what happened to her. I'm not responsible for her. I never have been. She made that abundantly clear years ago."

I waited for Meriwether to calm down, then spoke carefully. "You said *you* broke things off with her."

Meriwether sagged back into his chair. "I'm not perfect, Mr. Harlan. When I tell a story, I might put a slant on things. Sometimes I … omit certain facts to make myself sound better. Who doesn't? Who wants to admit they got dumped by their first sweetheart? Yes, Dorothy broke things off with *me*. Are you satisfied? Now go back to Jodie and tell her that I don't have her sister."

Meriwether's voice was tinged with a long-buried hurt. He still clearly cared for Dorothy Hamm. "If *you* don't have her," I asked, "where else could she be?"

"I don't know," Meriwether said with a growl, slamming his hand against his desk. "I don't *know!*"

* * *

An electric shock ran up the back of my neck, and a vibration started in my rear molars. It buzzed along my jaw and I reflexively rubbed the skin below my cheeks. Meriwether stared at me, his eyes blazing with anger, and I finally understood why Jodie Rexford was so concerned. "Jesus…"

Meriwether's face softened, and the buzzing dropped a notch. "I'm sorry, Mr. Harlan. I didn't mean for things to … get out of control. I can assure you that I would return Dorothy to them if I could, but she's not here."

"That's a little more than a *minor* talent," I said.

Meriwether bowed his head. "I may have downplayed my abilities, but I am nowhere as powerful as Jodie's coven. You've met them?"

"Uh-huh," I said. The pressure in the room abated, and I managed to gulp. "I've met some of them. How many are there?"

"Thirteen, of course," Meriwether said. "The number is *always* thirteen. Otherwise, it's not a proper coven. They sacrifice much of their power if they don't have a proper coven."

"I met an old man," I said, still rubbing at my jaw. "A tall son of a bitch. He's strong."

"Randy Korman," Meriwether said, tilting his head to one side. "Yes. Randy and his wife, Janice. Randy is Jodie's uncle, you know."

"I heard. He's convinced that you're evil and that you took

Dorothy." Meriwether said nothing, so I continued, "He wanted me to kill you."

Meriwether bolted from his chair, sending it scraping against the hardwood floor until it smashed into the wall behind him. "He what?"

"Relax," I said. "I talked them out of it."

"I'm sorry, Mr. Harlan. I—I can't believe this is happening. It's a nightmare. I don't know what to do."

"I know what you mean," I said. "I just want to get my friend back."

We sat, taking each other's measure. I sympathized with Meriwether and felt ashamed that I could only think about getting Callie back and making sure she was safe.

Meriwether finally broke the silence. "Randy is an unpleasant man. He may seem like a country bumpkin, but he's one of the most arrogant men I've ever met. Combined with his natural ability, it makes him…"

"Makes him what?"

"Unpredictable. Before Randy's sister died, she passed control of the coven to Jodie. It easily could have gone the other way."

My eyes narrowed. "He said he let Jodie lead the coven."

Meriwether sighed. "It's none of my business. I've steered clear of him over the years."

"You know something."

"I know that Randy has always thought highly of his talent. I know that the other practitioners weren't prepared to blindly follow him. Jodie was a young girl, but she was a much better leader."

"Do you think Randy might have something to do with Dorothy's disappearance?"

He shook his head. "I don't know, Mr. Harlan. That's what scares me. He's so unpredictable…"

He didn't need to remind me of that. "He captured my friend, Callie. He basically forced Jodie to use her as leverage."

Meriwether frowned. "It all makes sense now. Save your friend. Randy could hurt your friend. Or worse. Escape while you can."

"What about you?" I asked. "How will you protect yourself? Randy doesn't seem like the kind of man who will let things go."

"I … don't know," Meriwether admitted. "But that's my problem, not yours."

I stood and offered him my hand. For all that Jodie had said about him, I found Meriwether a likable and caring man. "Thank you for understanding. I hope you figure out how to make Jodie see reason."

He took my hand in his and shook it firmly. "Good luck, Mr. Harlan."

Chapter Nine

The Toyota Prius was right where I'd left it. I got in, closed the door, then stopped and ran through my options.

I could go back to Jodie and her coven and tell them that Carlton wasn't a threat, but it didn't seem likely I would convince them.

They seemed so certain that Meriwether was a bad man and that he was holding Dorothy Hamm…

Telling them that I hadn't found Dorothy but had killed Carlton was another option.

What if they demand proof?

I sighed. My head hurt, my stomach was rumbling, and I wanted to go back to Iowa. Instead, I did the only thing I could think of.

I started the Prius and headed south on US-105 to Saint Michael Church.

* * *

Jameson asked a bunch of probing questions while I narrated the events of the past six hours. He would stop me occasionally to clarify a point, while Mosley kept nervously brushing his fingertips against his pants, looking horrified.

When I got to the part about Callie being held in the pentagram, Jameson shook his head and muttered, "Fools. The forces they're playing with…"

"Can you help me?" I asked. "Can we free her from that circle?"

Jameson tilted his head as if thinking, then said, "Perhaps. Continue with your story."

I dove right back in, finally reaching the part where I'd met Carlton Meriwether and he'd asserted that Randy might be planning a palace coup.

"That just doesn't sound like the people I know," Mosley said at last. "I can't believe any of them would do this."

I stared at him. "You mean kidnap me? Or threaten Callie? Which part doesn't sound like them? I mean, you know them, right? You live here, right? You didn't even know they were witches, for Christ's sake. How—"

"Sam," Jameson said sharply. "It's not Ethan's fault. It's easy to hide in plain sight. I'm concerned that there are more in Jodie's coven. Thirteen, you said?"

"Thirteen is the number Meriwether gave," I said. "That's a lot of witches for a hick burg like this, isn't it?"

"Yes," Jameson agreed. "It *is.*"

"You say you met with Meriwether?" Mosley asked.

"Yeah," I said. "About that. I don't think he's involved in any of this. Jodie is fixated on him—"

"She wants to find her sister," Jameson said.

"I get that," I said, "but I don't know if it's just that, or if Randy has her wound up. He's ... intense."

Jameson turned to Mosley. "Ethan? Have you met this man?"

Mosley nodded. "Once. I helped with a spaghetti dinner at the First Christian Church. His wife is such a pleasant woman—"

"Yeah, Janice seems like a peach," I said, "but her husband *isn't.* I can't tell how much of Jodie's convictions are actually hers or his. He's the one who took Callie, and he did it without Jodie's permission, I might add."

"Randy Korman is clearly a powerful man," Jameson said. "Did you sense that he's trying to assume control of the coven?"

I thought back to the encounter at the Korman farm. "He's powerful. Like, scary powerful."

"I don't believe a coven can be ruled by fear and intimidation," Jameson said. "Everyone must work together."

"Without the coven's support," Jameson said, "the coven falls apart."

I sat up straight. "That cop, Gary, seemed awfully torn between the two."

Jameson chewed at his lip. "If Randy wanted control, he needs the coven to agree to it."

"What if Jodie doesn't *want* to relinquish control?" Mosley asked.

"Perhaps it would require something happening to Mrs. Rexford," Jameson said.

"Yeah," I said, leaning back in my chair. "Like making her disappear. Am I the only one thinking that making Dorothy disappear might be the first step in that? She disappears, and Jodie loses some of her power base. And then something happens to her. The coven may suspect, but they don't know. Maybe Dorothy is just fine and Randy is just holding her."

There was a long silence, and then Jameson said, "You could be right. Or, perhaps Mr. Korman has done something more … permanent."

"To his own niece?" I said. "That's a pretty morbid thought for a priest."

Jameson's cheeks turned red. "It had to be said."

"So, he kills Dorothy, and then … what … kills Jodie? What about Gene?"

Mosley cleared his throat. "Gene Rexford isn't … he's not a strong man."

I cleared my throat. "Those are possibilities, and with all I've seen, I wouldn't put it past *Randy* to do something heinous. But, we're forgetting about the vampire's presence."

"Yes," Jameson said slowly, "there *is* that."

"Yeah," I said. "I haven't seen hide nor hair of a vampire. Jodie is convinced that Meriwether took Dorothy, but what if the vampire took her? What if it fed on her, killed her, and hid the body?"

Jameson's face went ashen. "What if it gave her the gift? She's been missing long enough. She might have turned."

Mosley looked ill. "We could have two of them?"

"We could," I said. "Maybe not, though. We just *don't know* what the hell is going on."

Both men winced and Jameson shook his head. "Sam—"

"Father," I said, slamming my fist against Father Mosley's desk hard enough to make the stapler on the corner of his desk jump. "I'm tired and sore and more than a little pissed off. This isn't what I signed up for. We didn't come here to get caught up in some metaphysical squabble. Now Callie is hurt and Randy has her trussed up like an animal."

"I've been thinking about that," Jameson said slowly. "There might be a way to rescue her."

"How?" I asked. "Jodie said the entire coven has to work together to release her."

"All things have rules," Jameson said. "Magic. Vampires. They *all* have an internal consistency. Just as there are ways to slay a vampire, there are ways to undo magic. No matter how complicated or powerful the spell."

"What do I have to do?" I asked. "Tell me and I'll do it."

Jameson frowned and rubbed at his eyes. "It's not as easy as that. I think ... I think I can unravel the spell if I can gain access to the room where Callie is held."

"You know how to do magic?" Mosley asked. His voice was accusatory but contained other strong emotions.

Fear, maybe, or dread.

"Not magic, exactly," Jameson said, avoiding eye contact with the younger priest.

"Then how?" I asked. "How can you free her from the circle?"

"It's complicated," Jameson said. "I told you that magic can lead the user down a dangerous path. When I was a young man, I studied about magic. In case I encountered it during an exorcism," he added hastily. "It turned out I was quite magically gifted, but I never practiced magic. Not ... exactly."

My stomach sank and I said quietly, "Why don't you tell us what you *did* practice—exactly?"

Jameson hesitated before clearing his throat. His jaw worked but no sound came out.

"Patrick?" Mosley said, leaning forward in his chair. "What did you do?"

"Nothing," Jameson said, turning away and facing the crucifix that hung over the door to the pulpit. "The problem with magic is that it makes things so ... easy. I learned a few simple things, like the manipulation of energy. I could light candles, move small things with my mind. I could peer into others." He paused, running a hand through his sandy hair. "I was a young man, and I thought I could control it until an exorcism went wrong. It was a woman. Almost thirty years ago. She was possessed by Haagenti."

"Never heard of him," I said.

"Haagenti isn't a *him*," Jameson said angrily, spinning to face me. "Haagenti is an *it*, a being of great cunning. The woman's name was Katherine, and I prayed for her night and day, until I commanded the demon to leave. It was then that it spoke to me in its terrible voice…"

"What did it say?" Mosley asked.

"It said it could help me with magic," Jameson said. "Haagenti knew all about me. It knew I possessed a talent, and it offered to teach me the art."

I couldn't imagine Jameson agreeing to any deal with a demon. "You didn't accept," I said.

"Of *course* I didn't," Jameson growled. "I would never give in to that kind of temptation. I would never betray my faith!"

"Something scared you," Mosley said, shaking his head. "I can see it plain as day. What happened, Patrick? What else did it say?"

Jameson smiled bitterly. "Demons have no sense of urgency. They are infinitely patient. They reckon time differently. Haagenti said many things, about how I could choose to use just enough magic to help with exorcisms, how I would always be able to pull back from the abyss. That's when I realized."

"Realized what?" I asked.

"Demons know what buttons to push," Jameson said. "They know what to offer. Haagenti knew my weakness, that I would try to justify using magic to help people all the while opening myself to possession."

Mosley sucked in his breath. "A demon's greatest feat is to turn a priest's love away from God."

"Yes," Jameson said, so softly I could barely hear him. "They have all the time in the world to eat away at our faith. They promise many things, and sometimes teach many things, but no matter what they say or do, their purpose is to lead us away from God. Haagenti knew that if I continued with magic, sooner or later, I would question God. Perhaps even *curse* God."

The priest made his way to the couch against the wall and sat down heavily. He looked up at us, and his hazel eyes were still haunted. "I cast Haagenti from Katherine. She cried out and fell to the floor, praising the Lord, and I joined her. After that, I never practiced magic again."

The room was silent. Mosley looked confused, so I decided to ask the question we were both clearly thinking. "How does this help?"

"Because I never *really* stopped," Jameson said. "Haagenti was right. I looked for any excuse. I finally found one. I quit doing exorcisms and started battling vampires, but I took every opportunity to learn what I could about magic. I only worked on stopping spells. On destruction, not creation. The few times I was exposed to magic, I practiced unraveling it. My minor talent, it turns out, wasn't so minor. With enough time, I can unmake almost any spell. My mind, you see, excels at turning the order of magic into chaos."

* * *

"I need your phone," I said.

Mosley frowned and leaned forward in his office chair. "What?"

"Your cell phone. You have a cell phone, don't you?"

Mosley started to speak, but Jameson stood up from the couch and handed me his phone without comment.

I dialed the number and it went immediately to voice mail. I growled and hit redial. This time, the phone rang once before it was picked up.

"No," Billy said. "I'm not getting involved." The phone clicked off and I punched the redial. This time, Billy picked up immediately. "Damn it, quit calling!"

"I don't have time for this, Billy. What did you find out?"

"Something is wrong," Billie said. "I can't…"

I sighed. "What happened?"

"I spirit-walked. It was nuts. Something has them stirred up."

"Stirred up? What does *that* mean?"

"Spirits aren't like people, Sam. They're more like remnants of people. All emotion and no reason."

"Did you find out about Dorothy Hamm?"

"No," Billy said anxiously. "The spirits didn't know anything about her."

"Then why are you so freaked out?"

"Because they were afraid."

"So?"

There was a long pause. "You don't understand," Billy finally said. "Spirits get sad, and angry, and lonely, but fear is the one thing they *don't* feel. They're beyond it."

I didn't understand Billy's point. "What does that mean?"

"It means that *something* is going on," Billy shouted into the phone. "Something bad enough to scare the spirits. Whatever you're doing, Sam, *stop doing it*. Run for the hills. Dig a hole and jump in. Hide out."

I sighed wearily. "I can't do that. I have a job to do."

"You sounding more like Jack every time we speak."

"Thanks?"

"That wasn't a compliment, dumbass."

"I appreciate it, man. I know it's … not easy."

"It's still thin," Billy allowed, "but not like it was during Halloween. I survived."

"Still," I said, "you took a risk for me. It means a lot."

Billy snorted. "You just won't listen to reason. Try not to get yourself killed."

The phone call ended and I tossed the phone to Jameson. "That didn't help."

Jameson raised an eyebrow.

"I'd hoped to find out if Dorothy was still alive."

"Is she?" Mosley asked.

I shrugged. "The magic eight ball says try again later."

Both priests stared at me as if I had lost my mind. "Let's go," I said. I stood and headed for the door. Mosley and Jameson followed me out of the church and crammed into the tiny Prius.

"How will we do this?" Mosley asked as I drove north.

"We don't have a lot of options," I said. "We'll park down the road and sneak up on them."

"Sneak up?" Mosley sputtered. "That's your plan?"

I turned to glare at him, driving with my peripheral vision. "Do you have a better one? Some way to make us invisible? A magic cloak, maybe?"

Jameson put his hand on my shoulder. "There's no need for this. Isn't that right, Ethan?"

Mosley nodded. "We can speak with them. They're reasonable people. They'll see how wrong they are."

I felt my mouth drop. "You think they're reasonable? Because they didn't *seem* reasonable. They *seemed* batshit crazy."

Mosley began, "I don't think—"

"People do desperate things in desperate situations," Jameson said. "You saw what Jack became. You should understand better than anyone."

Jameson had a point. I would've done anything to save my

daughter.

I would've crossed any line. Committed any sin.

It didn't make me any less angry. Just because Jodie's sister was missing didn't give her the right to drag me into their mess. It certainly didn't give them the right to hold Callie.

I turned on the side road and headed west. The asphalt was cracked and sloped sharply to the ditches on either side of the road. I retraced my route until we neared the Kormans' farm. There was a stand of trees east of the house and I pulled the Prius into the grass, using the skeletal trees for shelter.

The Kormans' farm lay one hundred yards past the tree line. "I wish I had my gun," I muttered.

"That shouldn't be necessary," Jameson said. "Should it?"

"You wouldn't think so," I said. "But I didn't expect an old farmer to run us off the road and put Callie in the middle of a magic circle." I gave the priests a hard look. "This is a damned dangerous little town."

Jamison looked like he wanted to argue, but he ran his hand through his hair and shook his head. "Just ... try not to hurt anyone. Violence is never the answer."

"Depends on what the question is," I muttered under my breath. I opened the door of the Prius and my boots sank into the dead grass. "Are you two coming?"

The priests frowned, but Jameson put his hand on Mosley's shoulder. They got out and Jameson quietly shut the door. I slipped my hand under my coat. The silver Bowie knife was still strapped to my belt.

I didn't know much about witches, but a slashed throat would cramp anybody's style.

If it comes to that.

"You're sure about walking to the shed?" Mosley whispered, eying the farmhouse nervously.

I couldn't resist a smile. "Would you feel better if I said yes?"

Mosley frowned and put his hands together. "Dear Lord, help us rescue Sister Callie. Protect us from these witches and any harm they intend."

I raised an eyebrow.

Mosley shook his head and rolled his eyes. "There's a prayer I never thought I would say."

"Look," I said softly, "I don't know what's gonna happen.

But either we try sneaking up and saving Callie or I'm going into that farmhouse and stabbing my way out. As a man of peace, I figured you'd prefer I try the sneaky way."

"Of course," Jameson said, shushing Mosley.

"Good. It's time to beat our feet." I motioned for the two priests to follow my lead and took off across the field heading west.

Walking across a frozen field takes an enormous amount of energy. There aren't more than a few inches of level surface within reach of your footsteps because the dirt is an endless series of oddly angled ridges. And, if that isn't bad enough, the remains of heavy-rooted cornstalks jut up, threatening to trip you.

To make matters worse, the sun was a little past its zenith and had warmed the earth just enough to melt the top inch of soil, making every footstep a squelching, sucking affair that drained my strength and made me question what kind of an idiot would go walking through the cornfields in the middle of the damned winter.

"We're totally exposed," Mosley whispered.

I glanced around at the priests, then pointed to the Kormans' house. "There aren't any windows facing east," I said, just loud enough for them to hear. "Not on the first floor, at any rate. We won't be seen as long as no one steps outside."

Jameson nodded approvingly. "That's smart, Sam. You're really thinking."

"It's *almost* like I know what I'm doing," I said, then hesitated. "Either it'll work or they'll kill us. Right?"

"Kill us?" Mosley said. His footsteps faltered in and he looked at me with concern.

"That's a joke," I said, continuing across the cornfield.

I hope.

* * *

We made it to the machine shed without incident. Either there weren't any magical wards on the Kormans' property, or they were set to prevent magical attacks, not three poor souls attempting a break-in.

The door to the shed was on the northwest side, and I turned to inspect the farmhouse. Windows faced south, with a clear view of the machine shed door. This was the part of the plan that worried me the most. If anyone happened to be looking to the south, we were totally screwed.

I stopped and waited for the priests to catch up. When they were pressed up next to me, I whispered, "We have to be quick about this."

They nodded, but they were clearly worried. I was, too, but I could almost hear Jack telling me that worrying didn't get the job done.

I took a deep breath, gave a silent prayer for luck, and twisted the knob, pushing against the door.

The door didn't budge.

Mosley and Jameson were standing so close I could feel their body heat. "It's locked," Mosley whispered. "What now?"

A firm shove opened the door with a scrape. "Not locked," I said. "Just stuck."

We entered the building and I shut the door behind us. A soft light streamed from transparent panels overhead, but not enough to fully illuminate the hallway.

I held up my hand and whispered, "Hold on."

The priests stopped in their tracks.

My hearing was better than it had ever been, and I turned my head, listening for movement.

It was quiet, but there was a rustling coming from inside the building, like the sound of fabric flapping in the breeze.

What the hell?

The rustling stopped suddenly, plunging the building into a deathly silence, then the noise resumed.

It wasn't a sound I could readily place, like a coat or a jacket snapping in the wind, but it definitely hinted at movement. I rotated my head, unable to pinpoint its source.

A low moan came from ahead. It was a sound that I *did* recognize—a woman's moan. The hairs on the back of my neck stood up and a cold ball felt like it was about to drop from my stomach and into my bowels.

I rushed forward. The door that led to the room where Callie was held wasn't stuck. It was locked. I growled in anger, then twisted the knob until it sheared off with a metallic ping.

Callie was right where I had left her, still tied to the chair in the middle of the room. Her head lolled to the side and she moaned again, a wet sound that rattled inside her throat. Jameson and Mosley stepped past me before halting in their tracks, held in place by the same invisible magical force that had trapped me.

"Step back," I whispered.

They were like flies trapped in molasses, but seeing Callie bound in the magic circle killed any humor I might have found in the situation. They finally managed to step back far enough to free themselves, and their bodies returned to normal motion.

"Yeah," I whispered. *"That's* what I was talking about."

Jameson turned to me and blinked. "Now I understand. There is something here, some magic that keeps us from approaching."

"Can you remove it?" Mosley asked.

"Let me see," Jameson said, crouching down to inspect the etchings in the outer rim of the circle.

While Jameson was doing his thing, I heard the rustling noise again. "Do you hear that?" I whispered to Mosley.

Mosley squinted at me and shook his head. "No."

There was another round of noise, a swish-swishing that was louder than before. "You don't hear that?"

Mosley closed his eyes for a moment, then said, "Hear what?"

I pulled my silver Bowie knife. "There's someone else here."

"Where are you going?" Mosley whispered.

"Follow me," I answered, "but stay behind, just in case."

The young priest's eyes widened. "In case of what?"

I shrugged. "In case they know we're here."

* * *

I eased down the hallway, heading back to the room where I'd been kept. Mosley followed a safe distance behind, panting heavily.

The door to the room with the pit stood open, but that wasn't the source of the noise. It was coming from another door on the west side of the hallway. I hadn't noticed the door before, but I hadn't been at my best, either.

I put my hand on the doorknob and felt the vibrations through the brass. The noise was definitely coming from behind the door. I turned the knob and found a room just like the one where I'd been kept. This room also contained a pit in the middle of the room, just like the one I'd woken in hours before.

"What's in there?" Mosley whispered.

"I don't know," I said, edging closer to the pit. "Maybe it's

Dorothy."

"Should you be … getting that close to the edge?" he asked.

"Probably not," I whispered, then took another step forward. I was almost to the edge when I felt an oily black presence grow stronger with each step. It was a familiar sensation that filled me with dread.

It was the feeling of evil. Of hunger. It was a stain against everything that was right. The darkness wrapped around my soul, and my own darkness rose to greet it.

I clutched my Bowie knife with shaking hands and peered over the edge, but I already knew what I would find.

A young woman at the bottom was moving almost too fast to see, the rustling coming from her clothes as she bounced against the concrete walls. She wore jeans and a black t-shirt with shredded sleeves, and her long brown hair flowed in the wind like a streamer as she spun around the room like a whirling dervish, her hands never quite touching the etchings in the walls.

She came to a halt and her hair finally caught up to her body, then she snapped her head back and glared at me with eyes of solid black.

"Jesus Christ," I whispered.

The woman was a vampire. Jodie Rexford and her coven had captured a vampire and bound it in a concrete pit, and the thing was staring up at me, its lips pulled back in silent rage and its ivory fangs fully extended.

I heard a gasp behind me and turned to see Mosley, frozen in fear. The young priest's face had drained of color, and I knew that he'd finally felt the vampire's presence. His mouth opened and closed soundlessly, and his eyes were full of panic.

There was a noise from the pit and I turned to see the vampire jump and sail up in the air as if shot by a cannon, only to smash against some unseen force and go hurtling back to the concrete floor. It stopped and became unnaturally still. The vampire had heavy black eyeliner and was dressed like a goth, but nothing could hide the utter hatred on its face.

"It's trapped," I whispered. I tried to sound calm, never taking my eyes from the vampire in the pit. "It must be held in place the same way Callie is."

Maybe I was exhausted, or hungry, or bruised from the wreck. Maybe I was in shock from finding a vampire. Or maybe my sluggish brain didn't fully comprehend the situation.

There was a stirring of something against the back of my neck, like the tickle of a feather, then it became more intense, like a lover's caress, and then the spell holding Callie gave way.

When it did, so did the spell warding the pit.

The vampire's eyes locked onto mine as the spell collapsed, and then it jumped with inhuman strength, flying over my head and over Mosley, heading for the door.

I wasn't about to let that monster loose into the world, not even if it meant announcing my presence to the witches.

Chapter Ten

I lunged forward, shoving Mosley out of the way and sending him sprawling to the ground. Amazingly, I caught the vampire's ankle with my left hand.

As surprised as I was, I wasn't half as surprised as the vampire. It turned to glare at me as it slammed to the concrete. A bone-rattling thump coursed up my arm and into my spine, making my teeth rattle. The vampire was barefoot, and it twisted, kicking at my wrist and forcing me to release my hold on it.

I was bringing the knife down when the vampire twisted out from under me. I hit the floor hard enough to knock the air from my lungs, then scrambled up, breathing hard and trying to regain my hold. I almost caught its ankle again, but I slipped and caught only the bottom cuff of its jeans. I yanked hard and sent the vampire spinning to the floor.

It was like trying to cage a lightning bolt. The vampire squirmed and rolled away every time I bought the knife down. It kept kicking me, its bare feet smashing into my stomach and ribs like a baseball bat, but I wasn't about to give up. It scrambled down the hall and I struggled after it.

I couldn't kill it, but it couldn't quite manage to break free, either.

It's a weak youngling. It could be the daylight weakening it, or maybe it hasn't fed recently.

The door to the room where Callie was held had opened, and Jameson was helping Callie through the doorway. Her eyes were open but unfocused, and she took a tentative step forward. The vampire turned and lashed out at her, and its claws raked across Callie's legs and narrowly missed slicing through Jameson's groin.

Callie jerked back and screamed, then Jameson was praying

and the crucifix around his neck was glowing like the sun, and I heard yelling from farther down the hallway.

The vampire recoiled and finally broke free of my grasp, heading for the north door. Officer Gary stood in the doorway, his mouth open in surprise, and Randy Korman stood behind him.

The vampire was on the police officer before I could catch up, and I heard a sickening squelch as the vampire shoved its claws through Gary's bowels, ripping his intestines out like long pink worms. Gary's face registered shock, then agony, as he was disemboweled.

Randy Korman backpedaled furiously, mouthing words in a language I didn't understand. A howling wind blasted down the hallway, but the vampire shrugged it off and lunged at Gary's neck, ripping out the officer's throat.

Blood sprayed in time to the man's heartbeat, long hot spurts that arced through the air and splattered against the plywood walls. Randy's eyes widened as Officer Gary collapsed to the ground. The vampire, energized from the fresh blood, lunged for Korman, its bloody claws outstretched.

It hadn't counted on me.

A white-hot rage washed over me as I finally neared the doorway and caught the vampire's t-shirt with my hand. I rammed the silver Bowie knife through the vampire's back and through its heart until the resistance gave as the tip erupted between its breasts.

The vampire whipped around, black eyes full of hate boring into mine, but it was too late. Flames burst from its chest, and it thrashed about on the concrete, the fire spreading across its body.

It grabbed for me, but I sidestepped its claws. The fire spread and it took only seconds before the vampire was reduced to a stinking pile of greasy ash.

The vampire's life-force, or whatever the hell animated it, rushed into me like an electric shock, sliding inside my skin and filling me with hunger.

I gasped, choking for air. For a brief moment I thought I would die from asphyxiation, then the dark energy settled down, joining the rest of the vampire energies rattling around my soul, the darkness that threatened to one day turn *me* into a vampire.

Like Jack.

The thought of turning, like Jack had in Tangier, scared the hell out of me.

I didn't have time to worry. I looked up to see Randy Korman, his lips drawn back in a snarl, waving his hands and then a wave of magic hammered me to the ground.

* * *

The voice was low and rough and insistent. *Wake up.*

I tried to speak, but the words didn't come. Finally, I managed something equally insistent. *Don't want to.*

The voice spoke with more urgency. *Wake up, boy. This ain't getting the job done.*

I don't care about the job. I want to rest.

You want to be me, boy, you got to get your ass up and do the job.

My heart hammered in my chest and I jerked awake. The light was bright and hurt my head. I blinked, then realized I was squeezing something soft and fleshy.

Father Jameson stood over me, his eyes bulging out of his head. His face was turning purple and he was making terrible choking noises and beating at my hands in a futile attempt to break free.

I realized I was choking the life out of the priest. Randy Korman was frantically pulling at my hands, trying to remove them from Jameson's throat. Korman's lips were moving and there was a buzzing against the back of my neck.

I released my hold on Jameson, who fell to the floor and clutched at his throat, and then turned my attention to Randy. "You go any further with that spell, old man, and I'll beat your fucking brains out before you finish."

Randy's grizzled face went red, but there must have been something in my voice because he took a halting step back and the buzz against my neck stopped.

I sat in the oak chair where Callie had been bound. Jameson lay at my feet. Korman stood behind him. A man and three women, all dressed in casual clothes and none of whom I recognized, stood against the wall watching me with fear and suspicion.

Another woman sobbed hysterically over Officer Gary's dead body, her black ponytail bobbing up and down as she cried, and I recognized her as the woman who had been with Gary at the Subway restaurant.

Janice Korman and Jodie Rexford were speaking in hushed tones to Callie, who sat on a stool near the door. They had stripped

Callie's jeans off and were working on her legs, which were covered in rivulets of blood all the way down to her ankles. Father Mosley held Callie's hand, looking like he might vomit at any moment.

Callie was writhing in pain, almost falling from the stool. Her face was pale and sweat rolled down her cheeks.

I felt the buzzing again and knew they were performing magic. My anger rose, a blazing white-hot thing that made my blood sing in my ears. "Get away from her," I growled loudly, "or they'll find pieces of you spread across the nearest five counties."

Janice Korman turned to me, her face white as a sheet, and dropped the bloody towel she'd been pressing against Callie's leg.

Jodie Rexford started to speak, but Gene Rexford appeared in the doorway, putting his hand on Jodie's shoulder. Her mouth opened and closed, but Gene squeezed and shook his head.

"Sam," Jameson said, choking out the words, staring up at me from the concrete floor. "They're … trying … to help."

"Sam," Callie said, her voice full of pain. "It's okay." She made eye contact with me and nodded her head.

I tried to relax, but the sudden surge of adrenaline made the muscles in my arms twitch. "How long was I out?"

"Just over an hour," Jameson said. He stood and rubbed at his throat. "We've had a … chat and agreed to work together."

The woman crying over Officer Gary's body was making snuffling noises. My eyes drifted to her and I said, "We have, have we?" I paused and licked my lips. "These people were holding a vampire. A *vampire*." When I said *vampire*, the men and women standing near the wall winced and their eyes darted to Jodie and Gene Rexford.

Jodie brushed her husband's hand from her shoulder and stepped forward. Randy glared at her as she passed, but shook his head and shuffled out of her way.

"It isn't what it looks like," Jodie said.

I grunted. "It looks like you played with fire and got burned." I pointed to Gary's body. "*That's* what happens when you mess with vampires. You're a witch. You should know."

A hint of red appeared on Jodie's cheeks. "It wasn't supposed to be like this. We're not bad people, Mr. Harlan."

I couldn't take my eyes off the dead man's body. "Lady, you got a real funny way of seeing things." Randy Korman took a step toward me, his face going hard, but I was through playing games.

"What in the hell were you going to do with a vampire? What plan could you possibly have had for that … *thing* … that doesn't make you bad people?"

"We *had* to arm ourselves," Jodie said. "We had to do *something*."

"And you thought a vampire would help? Jesus, lady, that's the opposite of a good idea. They're inhuman killing machines—"

The woman leaning over Gary's body stood up. Her face was a mess of running mascara, and she shouted in a nasal voice, "Show some respect!"

One of the women rushed to her and cradled the grieving woman in her arms. "Molly, please. He doesn't understand…"

I felt a momentary stab of guilt. Officer Gary was dead, and the crying woman was clearly his wife or girlfriend. I was betting on wife. I quickly counted up the people in the room. There were nine locals, counting the dead police officer.

Most of Jodie's coven.

The crying woman glared at me, wiping at the black streaks under her eyes, then turned back to the dead body. I didn't blame her. The loss of her husband must have come as a shock.

I was beginning to suspect that Jodie Rexford had undersold the vampire's danger. "You attacked us," I said to Jodie Rexford. "You held Callie hostage. You blackmailed me into doing your bidding, and now you act surprised when the most dangerous creature in the world breaks free and kills one of your own? You got off *lucky*."

Jodie shrank back from the tone of my voice. "It's not like that…"

"Sam," Callie said softly. "Can I speak with you?" She turned to Janice Korman. "Alone, please?"

Janice bit her lip. "Let's leave them alone."

Jodie looked like she wanted to argue, but she shook her head and said, "Everyone out. Clear the room."

The men and women grumbled as they left. Randy looked like he wanted to take a swing at me, but Jodie urged him out the door. Jameson led Mosley to the door and gave me an appraising glance before leaving and shutting the door behind him.

Callie and I were left alone in the room with Bobby Gary's dead body. The smell of blood was thick in the air, but it was overwhelmed by the bitter stench of urine. Underneath that was the odor of bowel and feces, the terrible odor of death that I had come to know so well.

I stood on rubbery legs and made my way to Callie. "How badly are you hurt?"

She dabbed at the wounds on her legs with a wadded-up ball of gauze. "It cut through the muscles. I don't know what the coven did, but it helped." She sucked air through her teeth. "It hurts, but they kept me from bleeding to death. I think I'll have the use of my legs."

I looked down at her thighs. The vampire had sliced through her skin and muscles like butter. The skin was shades of purple and yellow, and the edges of the cuts were held together with butterfly tape. Black clots had already formed around the edges of the wounds and they were starting to pucker and turn waxy.

"You realize," I said, "that the only reason you're hurt is because of them? They ran us off the road, Callie. *They risked our lives.*"

She nodded. "They told me."

"Did they tell you they wanted me to kill Meriwether?"

"They're terrified, Sam. Can't you see it?"

"It's not our problem," I said. "I killed the vampire. Our job is done."

She shook her head. "I know you see it. You must."

"How is any of it our problem? *They* caused this," I said, pointing to the blood covering the milky-white skin of her legs.

"I know," Callie said. "But we're here. We're in the middle of it." She groaned softly as she repositioned her legs, wiping at the blood seeping from the clotting wounds. "We have to do something. We *have* to help them."

"Help them how?" I asked. "What they need to do is sit down with Meriwether and work things out before they get themselves killed."

"You *can* help them," Callie urged. "You can make them listen to reason."

I laughed bitterly. "They don't *want* to listen to reason. We said we couldn't take on every cause. We agreed we would fight vampires."

"Can you really turn your back on them?" she asked, raising an eyebrow. "Can you walk away, knowing they might destroy themselves?"

I turned away and found myself looking at Gary's body. His

sightless eyes stared at the rafters above, eyes that were now glassy and looked almost artificial.

I hadn't cared for Gary in life and I sure as hell didn't care for him in death, but I was experiencing several emotions, not the least of which was anger. Callie's words kept eating at me, though, until I finally said, "Damn it. *Damn it!* You *know* I can't."

"You're a good man," Callie said, the ghost of a smile playing across her face.

* * *

Janice Korman had taped fresh gauze across Callie's legs and given her a pair of brown slacks, forty years out of date, to wear. Callie sat at the kitchen table, next to Janice Korman, and across from Jodie and Gene Rexford. Randy stood behind his wife, glaring at everyone.

Jodie's coven filled the rest of the kitchen, barely offering enough standing room for Father Jameson and Father Mosley, who were stuck in the corner. The air was stifling hot from all the bodies and a trickle of sweat ran down my back. The coven members were deathly quiet, waiting for me to speak. I glanced at Callie, who nodded her encouragement.

"You *need* to make peace with Meriwether," I said. "I'll help if I can, but if you continue like this, you're going to wind up dead."

There were several gasps around the room, but I didn't take my eyes off Jodie. She glared at me, but her expression finally faltered and she spat out, "Carlton has my sister."

I shook my head. "Do you *think* he has your sister, or do you *know* he has your sister? I've been to his house. She wasn't there."

"Don't give us orders," Randy said. "You're an outsider here." He pointed to the two priests. "All of you. This ain't your *place*."

"Bullshit," I said. Several of the coven started murmuring, but I silenced them with a glare. "You made it my place when you caught that vampire. You're witches. I get it. Do you know what I am?" Before Randy could answer, I pointed to Jodie. "You saw what I do."

Jodie remained silent, but the members of her coven turned to her. A bald-headed man in his late thirties wearing blue jeans and a heavy flannel shirt spoke up. "What's he talking about? You said he could get Dorothy back, but you never said how."

Gene Rexford turned to the man. "You didn't need to know,

Brady."

"This isn't a dictatorship," the man said, his face reddening. "We're not servants. I'm getting tired of being told what to do." He put his arm around the thin woman next to him, a pretty young blonde close to him in age. "We're supposed to be part of something bigger, but the only thing we've done lately is listen to you bitch and moan about Dorothy."

"Shut your trap," Randy said, turning to the man. "With a talent as weak as yours, you should be thankful we allow you to be a part of this coven."

The pretty blonde next to Brady spoke up. "That's unfair, Randy. That's really unfair. We may not have your level of talent, but I don't remember you complaining when you asked us to join."

Brady nodded vigorously. "Rachel's right. You begged us, remember?" He turned to Jodie. "You said we were equals—that the coven was greater as a whole. You said all that, but then you run it with an iron fist. You tell us what to do and where to go. That *has* to change." He pointed at me. "What is he talking about?"

"I kill vampires," I said loudly. The murmuring stopped and the room fell deathly quiet. "Callie and I came for the vampire. I don't care about your coven, or your power struggle."

There was an immediate reaction in the room, a sense of pressure building. The coven's fear was causing them to instinctively draw on their power.

Callie frowned and I knew that she sensed it, too.

"We just want Dorothy back," Jodie said wearily. She searched the faces of her coven. "Can't you understand that? Carlton has her. I know it!"

Brady, the bald-headed man, frowned. "I know you think that—"

"I don't *think* it," Jodie said, her voice rising. "I *know* it!"

"Why?" I asked.

Jodie turned to me, her face suddenly blank. "What?"

"*Why* are you so convinced that Meriwether took Dorothy? He's a witch. I got it. He had a fling with her. Yeah. That's all true, but why are you so convinced *he* took her? Is it those stupid Tarot cards?"

Everyone in the room turned to stare at Jodie. Her lips moved, but no sound came out.

"Don't," Randy said. "You don't have to explain."

Janice placed her hand on her husband's shoulder. "They should know."

"What?" Brady demanded.

"Nothing," Randy said. He was still angry but his voice had lost its edge. "It's family business."

Jodie sighed. "It's too late for that, Randy. No more excuses. Carlton may be Nicky's father, but Dorothy is Nicky's mother."

A hand grenade going off would have caused less of a reaction.

"What?" Brady said. His wife clutched his arm, pulling at him, but he brushed her hand aside. "How?"

Everyone began speaking at once. The noise was so loud I could barely hear myself think, but Father Jameson barked out over the din, "Quiet. Let her speak."

The room fell silent. Jodie sat in the middle of the group, looking lost. "Carlton told you that he dated Dorothy. He didn't tell you that she got pregnant. Carlton's father threatened to disown him, so he abandoned her. He met his wife and got married right after that. A few months later, Annette got pregnant and died during childbirth."

"How did he wind up with Nicky?" I asked.

"A child born out of wedlock was shameful," Randy said. "No one knew Dorothy had got herself pregnant. She wore loose clothing and quit going out." He shrugged. "That was what women did back then."

"She gave birth in secret," Callie said. "You used magic, didn't you?"

Jodie exhaled heavily. "It was simple magic. Just enough to keep people from asking questions. We took Dorothy to a Springfield hospital. She almost died delivering the baby, and we … well, we knew as soon as he was born that something was wrong. Dorothy wanted to keep him, but Randy talked her out of it."

Everyone turned to Randy. There was a tremor in the old man's hands and he tucked them into the pockets of his overalls. "The baby wasn't right. I could see it. The boy was never gonna be normal."

I blinked. Randy sounded so sure of himself, and his attitude had probably been common in the late sixties or early seventies. But I had noticed his hands shaking and wondered how sure he was now. "That still doesn't explain how Nicky wound up with Meriwether."

"Dorothy found a couple to adopt the boy," Randy said, his gruffness giving way to a more plaintive tone. "They knew about him and would take him and love him as their own. Carlton found out, but he didn't care 'bout Nicky until that wife of his died during childbirth. He thought he was gonna have another son. A better son. When it all went south, he found Nicky and convinced that couple to give him up."

"No one knew about this?" I asked.

"Nicky was only six months old," Jodie said. "Carlton kept him hidden until he was almost two. By then, the age difference wasn't apparent. As far as anyone was concerned, Nicky *was* Annette's baby. He told everyone the child had survived her death."

"Dorothy knew," Janice said. "She was heartbroken. The idea that Carlton would raise their son? Well, it crushed her. She *hated* Carlton for it."

"He wanted to be with Dorothy," I said in sudden understanding. "The two of them, raising their son together."

Jodie's eyes widened. "How did you—"

"It's all starting to make sense," I said.

"Dorothy wouldn't have anything to do with Meriwether?" Callie asked.

"No," Janice said. "She *hated* him. She wanted Nicky back, but she wouldn't give Carlton the time of day."

"*That's* why you think he's taken Dorothy," I said. "You think he wants them to finally be together."

"Carlton is a very dangerous man," Jodie said. "He is used to getting his way. It infuriated him that Dorothy wouldn't have anything to do with him."

"Why now?" Callie asked. "After all these years, why take her now?"

"Ain't none of us young pups," Randy said, shaking his head. "Maybe he got to thinking it was time for action. Or he finally got so full of himself he decided to *take* what he wanted."

I studied the old farmer. The man was resolute. Every time he spoke Meriwether's name, he looked like he wanted to spit on the floor. "All these years and you still dislike him," I said. "It can't just be about Dorothy."

"I used my sight to look at that baby," Randy said. "It wasn't just touched in the head. There was an evil in it."

"I'm supposed to believe a baby," I said, "a newborn baby,

contained evil? That's the most absurd thing I've ever heard."

The old farmer squinted at me. "You know about vampires, boy, but I know magic. It may sound crazy to you, but I saw *inside* that baby. Call it what you want, but the evil in that baby came from somewhere, and it *weren't* from Dorothy." He turned to his wife. "Tell them. Tell them I'm not crazy."

Everyone in the room watched Janice, waiting for her to speak. She blinked furiously, then spoke in a hushed tone. "He saw it, Mr. Harlan. Randy is a lot of things, but he's not a liar. He sees things. Strange and terrible things. It's his gift."

* * *

The coven slowly filtered out of the kitchen and into the living room, giving us a chance to speak privately. Several of the coven members cast hostile glances at Jodie on their way out, especially Officer Gary's widow, Molly.

When they were finally gone, it was just Gene and Jodie Rexford, Janice and Randy Korman, and Callie crowding around me at the kitchen table.

"What are you going to do?" Jodie asked.

I hesitated. "I can speak with Meriwether again. Try to make peace."

"No," Randy snapped. "You don't make peace with the Devil."

"If I may?" Father Jameson interrupted. "Speaking with Meriwether will give Sam an opportunity to question him in person. He might find your sister's whereabouts. And, if Sam is correct and Meriwether *doesn't* have your sister, you'll have eliminated a possible threat."

"Weren't you listening?" Randy said. He placed his big palms on the table and glared at me. "His boy is *evil*. I saw it."

It dawned on me that the old farmer's gruff exterior was actually fear. Nicky terrified the old man. I shook my head. "I don't know *what* you saw, but I talked to the kid. He's no more evil than I am."

Jodie raised her head. "You've asked him twice about Dorothy. Ask again. The power of three."

"The power of three?" I asked.

"Three is a magical number," Callie confirmed. "It has power among those who practice witchcraft. Meriwether can lie, but not when asked three times."

Jodie looked startled. "How on earth did you know that?"

Callie looked to Father Jameson, who gave a nod of permission. "The Church knows many things about witchcraft," she said.

Janice Korman jerked back from the table. "You've been spying on us?"

"Not you," Jameson said. "But in general terms, yes, the Church stays abreast of such subjects."

There was a look in Jameson's eyes and I wondered if anyone else caught it. "If I ask him again, he has to tell the truth? Even if he lied before?"

"Yes," Jodie said. She took a deep breath and slowly exhaled. "If he says he doesn't have my sister, I'll believe it."

I pointed to Randy. "Even though he's convinced that Nicky is an evil beast who got it from his father?" Randy started to speak, but I silenced him with a raised finger. "Don't. Whatever you want to say, just don't. I've only been here two days and I can already see that you've been egging this on."

Callie's hand found mine and she squeezed tightly, but I continued, "You've made Meriwether into the biggest threat you could imagine. You captured a vampire. Don't think I've forgotten about that. What were you going to do, unleash it on him?"

Jodie couldn't look me in the eye and even Randy looked abashed.

"You were going to sic it on him," I said. "What a bunch of morons. You thought you could control it? You saw what it did. It's like a nuclear bomb. It goes off and everything near it dies."

I saw some emotion flash across Jodie's face, something I couldn't quite place. She turned to Randy and stared at him until he finally looked away. "Tell him," she said.

"We think Carlton has a vampire," Randy said.

A ball of ice settled in my stomach. "What?" I waited for them to continue, but they were busy looking everywhere but at me.

It was Janice who finally spoke up. "We were visited by a vampire. He had business with our coven. He wasn't a bad man—"

"He's *not* a man," I said. "You people are unbelievable. Vampires only care about blood and terror and making other vampires."

"Not this one," Jodie said. "He isn't like that. Then he ... disappeared. Carlton has him. It's the only explanation."

"Wait," Callie said. "We were at Meriwether's house. We would have felt the vampire's presence."

I started to agree, then remembered how Jodie's coven had captured a vampire without me sensing it. "How did you hold the vampire?" I asked. "How did you bind it to the pit? I didn't feel it until I was right on top of it."

Randy pointed at Callie. "An old spell, like the one we used on her."

"Meriwether *could* have a vampire," Jameson said, rubbing at his chin. "Sam, you have to investigate."

"Sure," I said. "Or let me offer another explanation. The vampire abducted Dorothy, and is going to drain her and dump her body in a ditch, if it hasn't already."

Gene Rexford had been sitting quietly next his wife, showing a mix of concern and guilt, but he finally spoke up. "Please, Mr. Harlan. I know we haven't given you much reason to trust us, but we need your help. If Carlton has Dorothy, we need to know."

"What if he doesn't?" I asked.

Gene shrugged. "Then we need to know that, too."

I turned to Callie, but I knew it was too late. She had the same look I'd seen in Marshalltown. Jameson was nodding his head. Father Mosley was looking at me expectantly, even though he was still looked like he might faint. "Bobby Gary died here today because of you," I said, pointing to Jodie. "That's on you. But if there is a vampire and I leave without investigating it, then that's on me."

Everyone breathed a sigh of relief, but I didn't feel relieved. I felt manipulated. I leaned close to Callie and whispered, "We need to talk."

"Of course," she whispered back.

Randy stood and stuck out his hand. "I'm sorry, Mr. Harlan. I truly am. These hard times have turned us to desperate measures."

I glowered at him until his hand dropped to his side. "Don't thank me. If Meriwether has a vampire, it's my job to kill it."

* * *

The sun had just set, but there was still a faint glow to the west that lit up the clouds a deep shade of purple. The temperature had slid back below freezing, and Callie was pulling at her jacket for warmth as I led her outside.

Callie limped heavily but managed to walk without my assistance. When we reached the end of the gravel driveway and were well out of earshot, she turned to me and said, "I'm going with you."

"You're in a lot of pain," I said.

"I don't care." She circled me, staggering as she did. "See? I can walk."

I sighed. "Yes, you're walking. That's a good sign—"

She snorted. "You'll be lost without me."

I smiled. Callie was beautiful, even in the dark. Then she winced in pain and I felt a surge of anger that made me want to hit things. "You're hurt," I said, clenching my teeth. "I'm not taking any chances. If Meriwether has a vampire, I'm not going to risk your life."

"But you don't think he has a vampire."

I was amazed by how well she could read me. "It just doesn't make sense. Everything I've seen says Meriwether's not like that. Let's get real. Jodie's coven had the only vampire we've seen."

Callie took my hand in hers, an eerily familiar gesture that brought up a mix of emotions I preferred to ignore. "They're afraid. Fear makes people do crazy things."

"More Church wisdom?"

"No," she said, smiling. "Just common sense."

I pulled my hand away. "I suppose you think that's why I don't want you to go. You're right. I *am* afraid of you getting hurt. You shouldn't be putting yourself in more danger."

She grunted and turned away. "Fine, but you're not going alone. Take Father Jameson or Father Mosley. Their faith will protect you."

"Worrying about me, Mom?"

She spun on wobbly legs and slapped my arm. "Don't be silly. You don't stand a chance without God's protection."

"Ouch," I said, placing my hand over my heart. "That hurts."

She shook her head, all humor gone, and put her hands on my shoulders. "Take one of them with you, Sam. If Meriwether does have a vampire, it's better to be safe than sorry."

I started to make a smart-ass remark, but the worry in her eyes made me reconsider. "It *is* a good idea."

"See," she said, slapping my arm again, "you're not as dense as you seem."

Chapter Eleven

We waited in the Kormans' kitchen for Randy to retrieve Jodie's Prius while Janice and the rest of the coven finished working on Callie's legs. It didn't take long for Mosley and Jameson to come to a decision.

"Ethan will go," Jameson said, pointing to the young priest.

"Really?" I asked.

Mosley was five foot six, at most, and didn't look like he could punch his way out of a wet paper bag. In a fight with a human, he'd lose every time.

With a vampire? It would be a slaughter.

Jameson, on the other hand, was closer to my six-foot frame, but thicker through the arms and legs. He looked like he had spent time doing hard labor. In a fight, Jameson was the one who might actually provide some assistance.

Father Mosley didn't bother hiding his surprise. "I don't have the experience—"

"Wouldn't you be a better choice?" I asked Jameson skeptically.

"Nonsense," he said. "Ethan's faith is strong. Besides, I'm needed here. Mrs. Gary is distraught. I'll comfort her as best I can—"

"I can provide comfort," Mosley said, glancing down at his feet. "I—I think I might be better suited to providing comfort..."

"Nah," I said. "You come with me. I think the Father wants to poke around."

Mosley looked taken aback. "Is that true?"

"I'll comfort the widow Gary," Jameson said, then dropped his voice to a whisper to add, "*and* poke around. Maybe I can discover what is really going on."

"You don't trust them," I said.

Jameson nodded toward the living room. "Magic is never as it seems, and witchcraft is *never* without consequences. I'm not sure they've been completely honest."

"Okay," I said. "I'll take Ethan. Snoop around, but make sure they don't do anything weird to Callie."

Jameson nodded, and there was concern in his eyes. "Watch yourself, Samuel. These people may have abused the truth, but they *are* afraid of Meriwether."

I clapped the priest on his shoulder. "Be careful, Father. They were willing to cage a vampire."

"God go with you," Jameson said.

There was a heavy clomp-clomping up the porch steps and then Randy opened the door, stepped inside, and handed me an old cloth sack. "I reckon you'll be wanting this back."

I looked inside the sack and withdrew my Kimber, still in the Galco shoulder holster. "There's my baby." I checked to make sure it was still loaded with silver ammunition and that it was cocked and locked, then strapped it under my left arm.

I was glad to have it back. I still had the silver Bowie knife, but I felt a lot safer with the Kimber.

Randy's eyes never left me as I checked the gun, and he finally said, "You think that peashooter is gonna protect you?"

"Silver bullets tend to grow holes in vampires, and if that doesn't work, I can always count on the Lord." I pointed to Mosley. "Right, Father?"

Mosley swallowed hard. "Of—of course."

"See? We'll be fine," I said. "Where's my truck?"

"A coven member owns the town's garage," Randy said. "He's working on it. Trying to make it right. He said he's replaced the radiator and some other parts and done a realignment. The body needs work—"

"We're lucky *our* bodies don't need work after crashing into that ditch," I said, with a little more heat than I'd intended.

"Sorry about that," Randy said, "I truly am." He frowned and leaned in close and handed me a set of keys. "Take my van and remember what I said about the boy. You don't got to believe me, son, but you keep an eye peeled. Understand?"

"Yeah, we're on it," I said. "C'mon, Father. Let's go knock on the Devil's door."

* * *

I pulled Randy's Dodge van between the brick columns that guarded Meriwether's house. It was shortly after six, and the nearest streetlight did little to beat back the night. The trees in the park across the street looked like crooked black skeletons. As I pulled up to the house, I noticed just how menacing the place appeared at night.

Get a grip.

I stopped the van in front of the house, turned off the engine, and tapped Mosley on the arm. "You feel anything?"

Mosley was craning his neck, trying to look everywhere at once. "What?"

"Do you feel a vampire?"

"No. I mean—wait, let me…" He grabbed for the heavy silver crucifix around his neck and rubbed at it with his thumb. "I don't *know.*"

I sighed. Mosley was a good man, and very sincere, but I didn't *need* sincere. I *needed* a badass servant of the Lord. "Calm down, Father. Just take a moment and breathe."

Mosley gulped for air and managed to bring his breathing down to that of an old steam train. "Thank you."

"I don't feel it, either," I offered, "so I think we're good."

"That *doesn't* make me feel better," Mosley said.

"It's not supposed to," I said. "Look, don't freak out, but don't stop listening to that voice in the back of your head that tells you you're in danger. If you feel *anything*, take it seriously. I didn't sense the vampire at the Korman farm until I was right on top of it. I don't think the coven is right about Meriwether, but it would suck to be wrong."

I just hope if I'm wrong, it doesn't get anyone killed like it did in Marshalltown.

Mosley squinted at me. "I *pray* that you're not wrong."

"You and me both, Father." I opened the van door. "Just follow my lead."

Mosley followed me up the steps to Meriwether's front door, pulling his brown wool coat tight to protect himself from the chill. I pushed the doorbell and waited. There was the sound of footsteps from within, and then the door opened and Meriwether greeted us. "What cockamamie story does Jodie have you chasing now?"

"Can we come in?" I asked.

Meriwether turned to the priest and smiled, exposing a pearly white set of teeth that probably netted him a boatload of insurance policy sales. "Who is this?"

Mosley stuck out his hand. "Ethan Mosley. I'm the priest at St. Michael's Church in Bement."

There was an uncomfortable silence as Meriwether stared at Mosley's outstretched hand. Mosley finally let his hand drop and Meriwether said, "Nothing personal, Father Mosley, but I'm feeling less charitable as the day wears on." He turned to me and frowned. "What? I'm not allowed to be upset? How many accusations will that woman hurl at me?"

"You're right," I said. "She's a chore, I'll agree, but she provided some new information."

There was another awkward silence before Meriwether opened the door and beckoned us in. "Fine."

We followed him down the hallway and into his gigantic living room. Meriwether pointed to the sofa. "Have a seat." He removed a crystal carafe from a small mahogany table next to the fireplace and poured a glass. "Would you gentleman like a drink?"

"No, thanks," I said.

Meriwether raised the tumbler of dark liquid to his lips. "Suit yourself." He drained the whiskey in a long swallow and smacked his lips together. "Smooth. Sure you wouldn't like one?"

"We'd like—we'd like to talk," Mosley stammered. "I'm sorry for the inconvenience, Mr. Meriwether, but if we can just—"

"Fine, fine," Meriwether said, taking a seat on the couch across from ours. "What crime has Jodie accused me of *this* time?"

"It's personal," I said. "She claims that Dorothy is Nicky's mother."

Meriwether's expression never changed. "It's true, of course. I won't even bother trying to deny it."

His acknowledgment wasn't surprising. Every time I had questioned Meriwether, he'd been more than reasonable, offering solid explanations for his behavior.

"You knocked up Dorothy all those years ago and dumped her when you found out," I said.

He leaned back against the couch, watching me thoughtfully. "I'm sure that's how she remembers it, but let me offer a different explanation."

I glanced at Mosley. "We're listening."

He sighed heavily and removed his glasses, rubbing at a spot above the bridge of his nose. "Family has a magical power all its own."

"I don't follow."

"My father has been in the ground for thirty years," Meriwether said. "Thirty years, and he still somehow has the ability to influence my decisions." He chuckled bitterly. "Let's say Jodie's version doesn't quite place the events in the correct order."

"You didn't dump her after she got pregnant?"

"As I told you earlier, she broke things off with me." He sighed again. "I made the mistake of bringing her home to meet my father. He was a … complicated man. And, if we're being truthful, he was also a cruel bastard. We dined together and my father insulted and belittled Dorothy throughout the meal. After that, she wanted nothing to do with my family. I didn't blame her. Dorothy couldn't understand how I put up with him."

"You were a young man," Mosley said, leaning forward. "He was your father."

"Of course," Meriwether said. "I knew he was uncouth, but he was the only father I had. Dorothy didn't appreciate that. Then she came to me one night and told me she was late. She'd missed her period. I was the father, of course. She hadn't been with anyone else. I thought … that I might have another chance with her. We could get married and raise our child."

I caught myself leaning forward, as well, all concerns about the vampire gone. "Your father didn't agree."

Meriwether nodded, his expression turning ugly. "I made the mistake of telling him as soon as I'd found out. He was an ambitious man. He thought we could regain our status among the wealthy Chicago families. I didn't care. My life here was more than enough for me. We were the wealthiest family in Monticello, the big fish in the little pond, so to speak. Why give that up?" He shook his head. "No, I was happy here. Then he…"

"He what?" I asked.

"He made comments about Dorothy. How he could … have his way with her." He licked his lips and there was a tremble in his hand as he put his glasses back on. "He could make her do things she would *never* do."

"He threatened to rape Dorothy?" Mosley asked, clearly horrified at the thought.

"Worse," Meriwether said. "He would charm her. Subvert her will. Make her think it was her idea. Then, when it wore off, she would realize what he'd made her do. The mind reacts by going into shock. It can lead to dramatic changes in personality. It can make someone suicidal."

"You're right," I said.

Meriwether raised an eyebrow. "About what?"

"Your father *was* a cruel bastard."

"You have no idea," he said. "I didn't seek Dorothy out again. I told my father she left me, then I went back to school. I met Annette shortly after that. She was warm and loving and beautiful, but mostly she was from a wealthy family. My father strongly approved. We were soon married and Annette became pregnant."

I knew what was coming next. "It didn't work out."

Meriwether shrugged. "Life is cruel, Mr. Harlan. She became quite sick. As I told you earlier, I tried to use my gift to heal her, but healing is something I have no talent for. I watched her fade away, until one night she collapsed. I rushed her to the hospital, but it was too late. She died. So did our unborn son." He took a deep breath and exhaled slowly. "I was devastated. I slept late. I drank heavily. I quit bathing. I … was a mess."

"Then Dorothy gave birth," Mosley said. "You found out that she was giving up the child. *Your* child."

"My father found out, actually, and he also learned about Nicholas's handicap. He blamed me. He said it was a mistake in my genes and that I'd given Dorothy a retarded baby. Retarded," he said, his voice breaking. "That was the word they used back then." The muscles in his jaw tightened. "They didn't even have a proper name for it. My father said the same defect had cursed my second child. He said it killed both the baby and Annette."

By the time Meriwether finished, his eyes had narrowed and his cheeks reddened, and the temperature in the room had dropped by ten degrees. Meriwether blinked and there was a popping as one of the overhead lights blew out, plunging the area nearest the hallway into darkness.

"Holy Father," Mosley whispered.

Meriwether's eyes glanced in the direction of the hallway. "Sorry," he said.

"No," I said. "I understand. Cruel bastard, right?"

"Yes," Meriwether said. "Quite a cruel bastard. But I did

something then. I was so angry. I met the people adopting Nicholas and I charmed them, convincing them to give my boy to me."

"I bet your old man wasn't happy about that," I said.

Meriwether glanced at Mosley. "That's where the story takes a dark turn, I'm afraid. I did something I shouldn't have. My father was furious. He didn't want Nicholas in the house. He thought it better to let the boy die than ruin the family name."

"What did you do?" I asked.

"I used my talent against my father," Meriwether said. "I pressed him. Charmed him. He resisted, but I pushed harder than I ever had before. I wanted Nicholas to come home with me and I wasn't going to take no for an answer."

"You subverted his will," I said.

Meriwether chewed at his lip. "I'd never done anything like that before. His own talent in that area resisted, and when I finally overcame him, it did something."

"You took away his free will," Mosley said. "One of humanity's most sacred possessions."

Meriwether stood and glared at the priest, his hands clenched into fists. "It's a terrible thing, but I'd do it again. No matter how much it hurt him, or how much it hurt me, I'd do it again to have my boy with me. I'm not an especially religious man, Father, but surely He will forgive me. When my father died, I was sure of only one thing. He wasn't judged favorably."

Mosley looked abashed. I didn't blame Meriwether one bit. "We're not concerned about that. We're concerned about Jodie's claim you wanted to be with Dorothy."

"You think I've harbored feelings for her all these years? Please. I've raised Nicholas as best I can. I've loved him and protected him while Dorothy kept her distance. Jodie Rexford is clearly insane."

"What about Randy Korman?" I asked.

Meriwether raised an eyebrow. "What?"

"Randy said he used his gift to look into Nicholas. He thinks the boy is evil."

"That's what this is all about?" Meriwether asked. "All this time they've been accusing me because of that? Magic is unpredictable. I've learned that the hard way. You think it would be different for him? Randy's family never liked my father, and I suffered because of that. What a farce."

I had heard enough. "Jodie's coven took it seriously enough to trap a vampire."

Meriwether collapsed against the couch, stunned. "You—you can't be serious."

"They kept it in a pit on the Kormans' farm," I said. "They claim it was in self-defense because *you* had a vampire."

Meriwether's face went pale, his eyes big and shiny. "Do they still have it?"

"It's gone. I put a silver knife through its heart."

"They've gone insane," Meriwether said, waving his hands in the air. "They've *all* gone insane. I'm not safe here. Nicholas isn't safe here."

"I killed the vampire," I said. "You're safe. Speaking of your son, where is he?"

"He's staying with friends," Meriwether said, nodding dismissively.

"Mr. Meriwether?" Mosley spoke up. "You never said whether you had a vampire."

Meriwether's face was blank. "What? Don't be ridiculous. How on earth would I capture a vampire? Where would I keep it? And to what purpose?"

"Relax," I said. "We promised the coven we'd look around. If we didn't find anything, they said they'd let the issue go."

"Let it go? You mean they will finally come to their senses and quit blaming me for their problems?"

I nodded. "That's what they agreed to."

Meriwether smiled sadly and shook his head. "Congratulations, Mr. Harlan. You have done the impossible. You brought them back to reality. Unless you prefer traipsing around my house looking for vampires?"

"That won't be necessary," I said. The fear and anxiety I'd been feeling evaporated and I relaxed for the first time since we'd arrived. "I'll tell them we found nothing and that they need to make their peace with you."

Meriwether stood and offered me a hand up from the couch. "Thank you, Mr. Harlan. I owe you for this. You might have saved my life. You might have saved my *son's* life."

"Don't mention it," I said. "I'm going to go back and give Jodie the news."

"You're an interesting man, Mr. Harlan. I wish we'd met

under different circumstances."

I smiled and shook Meriwether's hand, then led Mosley to the front door. As I climbed into the van, I had the nagging sense in the back of my head that I'd forgotten something important.

* * *

"He wasn't what I expected," Mosley said.

I turned to him, momentarily taking my eyes from the road. "What did you expect?"

"Someone more … dangerous."

I turned my attention back to the road. We were heading up a large hill near the south side of Monticello, passing a monument on the west side of the road with a sign I didn't bother to read. "If there's one thing I learned, Father, is that *anyone* can be dangerous under the right circumstances."

"I know that," Mosley said, "but based on how scared they were—"

"Yeah. How could the coven have been so wrong?"

"I've lived here for almost two years, Mr. Harlan. These are good people. They tend to be suspicious of outsiders, but they genuinely care for one another."

We drove in silence for several minutes, "Their secrets caused most of these problems," I said. "If they had just *talked* to each other, maybe it wouldn't have come to this."

"It's been difficult," Mosley said, staring out the window. "Dorothy's disappearance certainly didn't help."

Dorothy?

That's what I had forgotten.

So weird that I blanked on that.

I slowed and turned east to the Kormans' farm, puzzling over the missing woman.

The van's headlights sliced through the night and illuminated Jodie, who was waiting for us in the driveway. The temperature had dropped into the upper twenties, and her breath trailed behind her in little clouds as she paced back and forth in front of the garage, wrapped tightly in her black windbreaker.

We barely had time to get out of the van before she demanded, "What did he say? Does he still claim to be innocent? Did you find the vampire? Now do you believe us?"

"Let's go inside where it's warm," I said.

"You didn't find anything," she said, her voice full of disappointment. "You think we made it up."

"I don't think you made *all* of it up. I think you've been under a lot of stress and maybe put things together that didn't necessarily go together."

Crestfallen, she turned to Mosley. "What about you, Father? You saw Carlton. What do you think?"

"I think he's not—not the way you made him out to be," Mosley stammered.

"But I was *so* sure," Jodie said more to herself than to us, tugging at her windbreaker. "He's been asked three times. He *can't* lie."

"It's easy to get things wrong when it comes to family," I said. "I know a bit about that."

Maybe it was my tone, or maybe she was tired of hating Meriwether for so long, but Jodie nodded and said, "I guess that's true. I'm sorry to have included you in this, Mr. Harlan. You've been more than patient."

"It's okay," I said. "I suggest you speak to Meriwether as soon as possible. As for your sister's disappearance…"

"Yes?" Jodie asked.

Funny, I can't remember what I was going to say.

Jodie gave me an odd look, then shrugged her shoulders and opened the kitchen door when I didn't speak. "Please, come in."

We followed her into the kitchen. Callie sat on a chair with her legs propped on another. Brady Warren's wife, Rachel, was stroking Callie's legs and humming softly. I stopped next to them. Callie looked up and smiled faintly. "You made it."

"No vampire," I said quietly. "Your legs are better?"

"It's amazing. The wounds have closed." She patted the black sweatpants she now wore. "Rachel says that as long as I take it easy, the pain will be gone in a few weeks."

The woman, Rachel, stopped humming and smiled shyly before brushing her hands through her short blond hair. "She needs to rest for the muscles to knit correctly. We owe her this much."

Callie leaned forward on the chair and whispered, "I'll heal as fast as you do."

A shiver ran up my spine as Jameson's words came back to me.

All magic comes at a cost.

"Where's Jameson?" I asked.

"He went to check on Dawn McKie. Everyone seems to have forgotten about her. Her mother is still missing, remember?"

I blinked. "How could I forget?"

Except, I *had* forgotten. Something buzzed against the back of my neck, a fleeting sense of unease, then it was gone. "Good for him."

Mosley took the seat next to Rachel. "How is Mrs. Gary?"

Rachel frowned. "Molly is … she's taking it hard. She's still crying. I don't know *how* Jodie's going to explain this…"

"Anything like this happen before?" I asked.

"Never," Rachel said. "Not *ever*. Magic is a force of nature. It's to heal and to help those in need." She paused, and when she spoke again, it was wistful. "When Jodie asked us to join the coven, it was all so different. So peaceful. It was … sexy. We danced naked around the fire—" She blushed and gave Mosley an apologetic smile. "Sorry, Father. I didn't—"

"I understand," Mosley said, a hint of rose to his cheeks. "I'm not blind to the temptations of the flesh."

"Does Molly have any kids?" I asked.

"No," Rachel said. "They tried for two years, but nothing worked. They had treatments at Carle Hospital, but the doctors finally said she couldn't have kids."

"At least she won't have that to deal with," I said.

Rachel's mouth dropped. "I hadn't thought of that. Oh my. Could you imagine?"

"Yes," I said, perhaps a little too harshly, and left it at that.

There was an uncomfortable silence. Finally, Rachel said, "I just meant I couldn't imagine someone telling *my* kids. Especially without telling them about … you know. The *other* world."

The words just slipped out of me before I could stop myself. "You mean about magic and monsters and things that tear people's heads off?"

Callie shook her head reproachfully. "Sam…"

"Sorry," I said, embarrassed by my lack of control. "I didn't mean to—"

"I know about the world," Rachel said. "The *real* world. I just never expected it to hurt us."

Damn. There goes the anger again.

"If you didn't expect anyone to get hurt," I said as gently as I could, "then you weren't paying attention."

"Sam!" Callie said, louder than before.

"Yeah, yeah, I know." I started to apologize to Rachel, who looked hurt by my comments, but then I felt it.

The oily, unclean feeling crept up my neck, buzzing against the back of my teeth, and the lizard part of my brain started screaming that danger wasn't just coming, it was right damned there.

It was a vampire's presence.

* * *

"Vampire!" I screamed. My hand moved so fast that the Kimber appeared as if by magic.

Callie's eyes went wide and she grabbed the crucifix around her neck, her mouth moving as she prayed for the Lord's protection.

Rachel jerked back like she'd been stung. "What?"

Father Mosley stared at me in horror. "My God. My God!"

I pointed to the living room. "Take them, Father. Keep them safe."

Randy appeared in the doorway, a puzzled look on his face. "What's going on in here? Why are you yelling?"

"A vampire," I said, spinning to the front door. There was a small window in the top of the door and I flipped on the outside light and stood on my toes to peer outside. "Don't you sense it?"

The driveway held a few cars and the Kormans' van, but there wasn't a soul in sight and certainly no signs of a vampire. I turned back to Randy, who was looking at me like I'd gone crazy, but he closed his eyes and muttered a few words. "There's magic near."

Magic?

"Get everyone to the living room," I ordered.

Randy nodded, visibly shaken. Rachel helped Callie from the chair and they followed Randy deeper into the house. Mosley stood and asked, "What should I do?"

"You'll follow me. Got it?"

"Got it," Mosley said, then grabbed his stomach. "I don't feel well."

"It's the vampire. You feel it now. Plus, you're scared. It makes it worse."

Mosley's face went pale. "You've felt like this before?"

I twisted the doorknob with my left hand, keeping the Kimber aimed and ready with my right. "It's not what you *feel*," I said, "it's how you *act* on it. Fear just means you're smart."

"What are we going to do out there?"

"We're going to kill a vampire," I said.

The evening air was frigid and held the sharp smell of cold earth and decay. The feeling of wrongness grated against my nerves. "It's close," I said. Based upon how creepy-crawly my skin felt, it wasn't a youngling. "Watch yourself."

Mosley nodded, his head whipping back and forth, staring into the night. I twisted my head and tried to find a position where I could mute the dull roar from the blowing wind, listening for footsteps.

It was too late.

A surge of energy battered into me and knocked me to the gravel driveway.

"Sam?" Mosley shouted.

It was magic that hit me, not a vampire.

"Get back in the house!" I tried to say, but a wave of arctic cold descended on me. My face went numb and my breath froze to my lips. "There's a witch," I croaked.

Mosley was staring at me with concern. "Sam? What's happening?"

I was on my hands and knees. The sharp edges of the gravel slashed at my palms and knees. "Witch," I mumbled. "There's a *witch!*"

Mosley's crucifix blazed to life, a pure white light imbued with God's power. It lit Mosley's face, making his eyes dark and hollow, then the vampire was on him, slashing through Mosley's brown wool coat and sending blood splattering across the gravel.

It all happened incredibly fast. The vampire was an overweight man with deep sunken eyes and chubby jowls. He turned to me and there was a moment of recognition in his eyes.

I gasped. The milksop of a man in the red tracksuit was Milford Barlow, a vampire from Indianapolis that I had last seen holding his dying wife's hand.

"Milford?" I croaked.

Mosley had fallen to the gravel and was scrabbling to get away. Barlow frowned and grabbed the young priest, lifting him as easily as I would a rag doll, and tore the young priest's head from his body.

There was a fountain of blood as the priest's heart spasmed its last beats, then Barlow casually tossed Mosley's head to one side and his body to the other.

"No," I moaned. "Oh, no."

The vampire spun on his heel and his lips moved wordlessly, then his jaw slammed shut and his lower lip quivered. His gaze lingered on me, then he was moving faster than my eye could follow, through the door and into the farmhouse's kitchen.

I struggled to stand. The cold intensified around me, plunging from merely frigid to subzero. Crackling came from my face and it felt like someone was gouging my eyes with needles. My vision went blurry and I rubbed at them, desperately trying to wipe away the thick frosting of ice suddenly covering my face.

I had to do something or I was going to freeze to death.

The Kimber was still in my hand, and I used the last of my energy to flip myself over on the loose gravel. I landed awkwardly and there was a cracking sound from my ribs, like sticks breaking, and I gasped.

There was a tall man standing in the tall grass next to the field, waving his hands and chanting.

The man was thin, with a sharp widow's peak, and wore a long black trench coat similar to my own. He saw me and his eyes widened in surprise, then my Kimber barked and the man looked shocked as the bullet tore through his chest and dropped him to the cold earth.

The cold dissipated and I took a deep breath, trying to ignore the stabbing pain in my side. I crawled across the gravel to Mosley's body. The blood had stopped its furious pumping and oozed from the neck. It appeared black in the darkness, and long flaps of flesh and muscle and ligaments trailed from the stump.

Mosley's head lay sideways on the gravel four feet away, his sightless eyes wide in shock and his mouth open in a terrible scream.

The eyes were what did it for me. It was always the eyes. Mosley's brown eyes were once so full of life, but now they looked so empty, reduced to jelly-filled orbs that no longer served any purpose.

I retched, but only green bile came up. I spat on the gravel, trying to clear my throat.

This isn't getting the job done.

I stood on rubbery legs and spun, searching for more

intruders. The light above the kitchen door spilled its pool of light onto the driveway, but the darkness beyond was empty. The buzzing against the back of my skull was gone, but the vampire was still nearby, a fact readily apparent by the screams coming from inside the Kormans' house.

Callie!

I stumbled forward, yanked open the kitchen door, and entered the house. The kitchen was empty except for Randy, who sat on the floor, leaning against the living room doorjamb and facing away from me. "Randy?" I called out softly. "Randy!"

The old farmer didn't move. The screams coming from the living room were louder and more anguished.

"Randy?" I said, crossing the kitchen and putting my hand on the man's shoulder.

Randy slumped back, his head striking the white rug in front of the stove with a dull thump, and I saw why the old farmer wasn't responding.

Barlow had torn Randy's throat from his body, leaving a gaping chasm where the esophagus and larynx should be, and the smell of the old farmer's urine was bitter in the air.

There was no need in checking the old man for a pulse. There wouldn't be one. One of the screaming voices from within the living room choked out a garbled sob and then fell quiet.

Damn it.

I stepped over Randy's body and entered the living room. It was like a slaughterhouse. Bloody streaks stained the walls, garish splashes of scarlet that stood out vividly against the white paisley wallpaper.

Barlow held Jodie Rexford by her throat, and Gene Rexford lay at Barlow's feet. Gene was covered in blood and moaning in pain.

Janice Korman sat on the brown carpet nearest the door, her right hand delicately holding in her intestines which were threatening to spill out between her fingers. She looked confused when she glanced up, and I realized she was in shock.

Rachel Warren was hunched over her husband with her arms spread out protectively, trying to shield him from danger. It was a useless gesture, as her husband was most likely dead. If he weren't, he'd be the first person to live with their heart ripped from their chest. Rachel wailed like a banshee, a high-pitched keening that contained more agony and despair than I'd thought possible.

Callie huddled on the floor, her arm wrapped protectively around Molly Gary, and Callie's crucifix glowed like a mini-supernova.

"Where is she?" Barlow demanded in his reedy voice. "*Tell* me. *Where is she?*"

Chapter Twelve

I trained the Kimber on the doughy little man. "For Christ's sake, Milford. Stop it!"

Barlow spun around before I could pull the trigger, putting Jodie in the line of fire. "I must find Dawn McKie. I won't stop until I do."

"Milford!" I screamed. "It's me!"

The vampire growled. "I know, Sam. I *know*. I must find this Dawn woman. Where is she?"

What could Barlow possibly want with Dawn McKie? The last time I'd seen him, he had been with his wife, Eva. "Tell me what's going on, Milford. I can help."

The vampire uttered a string of curses, then said loudly, "I *must* find Dawn McKie. Do not delay my quest."

Quest?

Barlow wasn't acting like himself. Unlike most vampires, Barlow had mastered his hunger relatively quickly, living a quiet life in Indianapolis and only feeding on his wife, who willingly provided her blood. "This isn't like you."

"I must find Dawn McKie," Barlow repeated, his eyes darting around the room.

"Okay," I said slowly. There was a bay window along the west wall of the living room, and I squinted. I didn't see anyone in the darkness, controlling Barlow from afar, but it was the only explanation. "She's not here," I said, trying to buy some time. "I don't know where she is."

Barlow shook Jodie hard enough to make the woman gurgle in pain. "Do not oppose me and no one else will die. Bring Dawn McKie to me or I shall lay waste to the rest of these humans." A flash of anguish crossed Barlow's face and then it was gone.

"I *really* don't know where she is," I said. "I'm not lying—"

"Silence," Barlow hissed, his chubby cheeks quivering. "You *will* find her. I *must* have her."

The glow from Callie's crucifix grew brighter, bathing the room in a light so bright that it was almost a living thing.

Barlow still held Jodie, but his arm drooped, allowing Jodie's heels to touch the ground. A light steam arose from Barlow's arms and oozing blisters erupted on his skin where the light touched.

"It's going to take some time," I said. "Give me a few hours."

"You'll bring her to me within the hour," Barlow said, his face contorted in a strange mix of emotions. "Bring me the girl and you shall live."

There was the sound of movement behind me and another light joined Callie's. "Leave this place, you foul thing," Father Jameson shouted, emerging from the kitchen.

I turned and saw Jameson, his crucifix held high, his free hand dragging Dawn McKie behind him. Dawn's face was as white as a sheet and her eyes wide with disbelief.

Barlow screamed in frustration.

I spun back to face him, but Barlow latched onto Callie and jumped through the bay window, smashing through the glass and into the darkness beyond. Callie's crucifix cast a furious white light across the brown grass, all the way to the edge of the empty field to the west.

"Damn it!" I shouted, then jumped clumsily through the window.

It was too late. Barlow slowed and Callie's crucifix fell dark. I tried to follow his movement, but he was too fast, moving faster than I could run.

I considered emptying the Kimber into Barlow's back, but while I might hit the little man, there was a good chance the bullets would pass through the vampire's skin like papier-mâché and strike Callie.

"Damn it. Damn it!"

Barlow disappeared into the night, taking Callie with him.

* * *

"I'm going after her," I said to Jameson.

Jameson stood in the living room with a stern expression on his face, his crucifix still dangling between the lapels of his tan jacket.

"You can't leave," Jameson said.

I felt my anger rising. "The hell I can't."

"You don't know where that monster took her," Jameson pointed out.

I sighed. The dead and dying filled the living room, but I wasn't in the mood to comfort them. "I need my stuff."

"Look around you," Jameson pleaded. "These people *need* your help."

"*These* people," I said, "have caused nothing but trouble and kept me from doing my job."

Jodie Rexford was kneeling over Janice Korman. As I spoke, she stood and glared at me, her hands sticky with blood. "Look what Carlton did to us. *He* sent that vampire."

"I don't know if that's true," I said. "I don't know what's been going on around here, and I don't care anymore. You've stood in my way. You've told me half-truths. You've conspired to send me after your enemy. You're a deceitful little witch." I snorted, unable to stop myself. "*Literally.*"

I stepped over Randy's dead body as I made my way to the kitchen. Randy's empty eyes stared up at the ceiling, but I could swear there was an accusation in them.

Not my problem.

Jameson caught up to me as I opened the kitchen's storm door. "Sam, please. You don't even know where you're going."

"Anything is better than standing here doing nothing."

"Damn it, Sam!"

Perhaps it was the desperate tone in his voice, or perhaps it was the curse, but I turned to the priest. "Look, Patrick." I grabbed Jameson's arm and dragged him outside to the driveway. "Look at your friend," I said, pointing to Mosley's body. "He's dead because of them. He didn't deserve this. You know what? I don't even blame the vampire. I blame *them.*"

Jameson's eyes settled on Mosley, and there was a depth of grief in them that I couldn't begin to understand. "I know, son. I *know.* You want to lash out. Sometimes you have to put other people first."

"That's what I'm doing," I said. "I'm putting *Callie* first."

"Do you think she wants that?" Jameson asked softly. "Do you *really* think she wants you to neglect these people?"

I started to speak, but Jameson continued, "Callie would want you to help them. Deep in your heart, you know it's the Christian thing to do."

"You think Callie wants to be held by a vampire?" I countered. "You think she wants it feeding on her? Or giving her the gift?"

The thought of Barlow using Callie as a meat treat made my stomach churn, but the more I thought about it, the more confused I became.

Jameson noticed my hesitation. "What is it, Sam?"

My anger slipped away. It felt like I could finally think straight. "I know that vampire. *Knew* that vampire. It doesn't make sense."

Jameson scowled. "What doesn't?"

I pointed to Mosley's body again. "Milford's an eighty-year-old vampire. He's in control of his hunger. He wouldn't kill like this."

"Things change," Jameson said, turning away from Mosley's body. He blinked away tears, then said, "Vampires are unpredictable."

"Milford *is* predictable," I insisted. "He's not like the others. Why kill Ethan?"

"Perhaps this is his true nature."

"After all these years?" I shook my head. "No, it doesn't make any sense. When he was holding Jodie, it's like … he wasn't in control of himself. He kept asking for Dawn. What would he want with her?"

"You believe Meriwether set the vampire upon them?"

I crossed the driveway and walked through the grass until I reached the man I'd shot. I rolled him over and inspected him. It was hard to tell in the dark, but he looked to be in his late forties or early fifties. His clothes were slick with blood, and his bowels had released, soiling his black slacks. The man was handsome, in a way, almost delicate enough to be considered pretty, but death had taken that from him, slackening his face and making him look like a dime-store mannequin.

"Who is he?" Jameson asked, bending over to look at the body.

"No idea." I fumbled in the dead man's slacks until I found his wallet and held up his driver's license. "Collin Stevens," I said, squinting to read by the light from the kitchen window. "Lives in Champaign. Forty-seven. Six foot, one hundred and eighty pounds. He isn't an organ donor."

"Why would that make a difference?" Jameson asked.

"It could mean he's a selfish asshole," I said, "but yeah, it probably doesn't mean anything. Except for the part where he tried to freeze me to death with magic and was working with the undead, so I'm sticking with asshole."

Jameson shook his head. The priest headed back to the driveway and knelt over Mosley's body. I trailed behind but stopped when I heard him speaking softly in a language I couldn't understand. He finished, stood, and noticed me watching. "A special prayer for those killed while battling vampires."

"Of course," I said. "Why *wouldn't* the Church have something like that?"

Jameson shook his head. There were tears in the priest's eyes, and when he spoke, his voice was full of emotion. "Ethan was a good man. A brave man. We should all be so lucky."

"Lucky?"

"To die in the service of the Lord," Jameson said. "Few answer the Lord's call."

"Does that mean *I* answered the Lord's call?"

Jameson wiped at his tears with the sleeve of his jacket. "It may not seem like it, but you've been blessed."

"I'm *anything* but blessed," I said bitterly.

"You've been tested in ways that would have destroyed most men. You've not only survived, you've found your purpose."

I stared at the man in disbelief. "Remember what you said about Jack? About what he was becoming? You said there's always a price."

Jameson shrugged. "I might have been wrong about that. The Lord's plans don't often make sense. We are mortals, after all. We cannot always make sense of His will."

"*His* will is more like a curse," I said, my throat suddenly raw. "I'd give up His blessing if it meant getting my wife and daughter back."

"You don't mean that," Jameson said.

"The hell I don't," I muttered, spinning back to the house. A thought occurred to me. "Why did you bring Dawn with you?"

"What?"

"You showed up with Dawn, just in the nick of time to help fend off Barlow. Why bring her into this?"

Jameson paused, perplexed by the question. "I guess I

thought it was time she knew the truth about her mother and her aunt. I … just had a feeling."

"A feeling?" I asked. "Is that more of God's will?"

Jameson jerked back as if struck. "That's … funny. I was speaking to her about her mother, trying to prepare her for the worst. Then, I was urging her into the car. When we got here, I saw Ethan was dead. I—I felt the vampire's presence and knew that I must do something."

"Huh." I didn't know what else to say. Perhaps it was God's will. Maybe it was just a lucky coincidence.

I didn't know which unsettled me more.

* * *

We made it back to the living room and found Janice Korman breathing fast and rhythmically, followed by long pauses, with an occasional rattling in the back of her throat. Rachel Warren and Molly Gary waved their hands over Janice's head and chest, chanting loudly.

Rachel glanced up when I entered the room, and her face was pale. She stared at me for a moment but went back to chanting when I didn't speak. Her voice was softer than before, less urgent, and Molly said, "Don't stop, Rachel."

Jodie Rexford was kneeling next to her husband, Gene. Gene wasn't moving. "I need help," she pleaded. "Help me!"

I threaded my way through the room and stopped next to Janice Korman. "I don't think she's going to make it," I said to the two witches. "Maybe you should help Gene."

Molly's hands slowed. She looked up and choked back a sob. "But she'll *die.*"

Jameson had joined us. He leaned over to check on Janice, then put his fingers against her throat. "I know something of what you're attempting," he said, shaking his head. "Her pulse is weak and thready. I'm afraid your magic won't be enough."

Molly's hands slowed. "But—but…"

"She's beyond your help," Jameson said gently.

Rachel looked like she was about to speak but then started crying. "It's not fair." She stroked Janice's hair. "It's just *not* fair."

Molly stood and grabbed Rachel's hand, pulling her up and frog-marching her across the living room. They began their chanting and motioning over Gene's body while Jameson sat down on the blood-soaked carpet and took Janice's hand.

"She's not long for this world," Jameson said quietly.

"What are you going to do?" I asked.

Jameson shook his head. "I can only make her comfortable."

I didn't have a response for that. I didn't know the woman very well, but she seemed like a decent sort. She'd been more than polite to me, even with all that was happening. I watched her blue eyes, like the sky on a summer day, staring off into space as her life drained away.

Jameson spoke softly, administering last rites to the woman. The smell of death was thick in the room. In the center of it, across from the broken window that now admitted a freezing-cold wind, Dawn McKie sat on the Kormans' ugly couch.

Dawn's eyes would occasionally focus, first on Brady Warren's dead body, and then on Jameson as he tended to Janice, then her face would go blank. The girl was in shock, tuning out the dead and dying.

I wish I could tune this out.

"What about her?" I asked Jameson. "Is she safe here?"

Jameson looked up, then over at Dawn. "None of us are safe, but as long as you're here…"

"That's a low blow, Father, even for you."

Jameson cradled Janice's head in his lap, stroking her hair as her breathing slowed. There was a long pause, longer than before, then she drew in a deep breath. There was a pause that went on for so long I thought she had stopped breathing, then she exhaled in one long gasp.

This time, Janice's breathing didn't resume.

Her face looked relaxed, like she was taking a nap, but there was nothing left in her. Whatever made her the nice woman I'd met earlier was gone.

Maybe she was somewhere else. Maybe she was in the next life, or Heaven, or wherever the soul goes after death, but all that was left in *this* world was the fleshy shell she'd left behind.

Jameson shook his head. "Such a tragedy," he said so quietly I could barely hear.

A wailing started, a sound so full of agony that my skin crawled. Jodie pounded on her husband's chest, shrieking loud enough to make Rachel and Molly pause their ministrations. They watched helplessly as Jodie sobbed, her mascara running in dark streaks down her face.

"Jodie," Rachel started to say. "He's—he's…"

"Please come back," Jodie begged her husband. "Please. *Please!*"

Gene Rexford clearly wasn't coming back.

Chapter Thirteen

I snapped my fingers in front of Dawn's face. "Snap out of it."
Dawn's listless eyes found mine. "This isn't real. It *can't* be real."

"Sam," Jameson began.

"Dawn," I snapped. "It's happening. Magic exists. Vampires exist. You're caught in the middle of it."

Dawn blinked, her face empty of emotion. "This isn't happening."

I could have been talking about the weather for all the reaction she gave, and I resisted the urge to give her a light slap across her face. "Your mother has been taken, probably by the same vampire that took my friend. Your mother is a witch. Your aunt is a witch. Your great-uncle Randy was a witch."

"Uncle Randy?" She slowly turned her head until her eyes found Randy Korman's dead body. "No. Magic isn't real. You—you aren't real. I'm dreaming. This *has* to be a dream."

"Sam!" Jameson barked.

"I don't have time for this shit," I said, then grabbed Dawn's face in my hands. I stared into her eyes, so close I could almost kiss her, and used the force of my will to push against her mind. "*Snap out of it.*"

Dawn jerked back like she'd been struck. "What? What's going on?" Her eyes darted around the room and horror filled her eyes as the realization sank in. "No. No, no, no!"

"The vampire wants you for something," I said. "Why?"

"Vampires aren't—"

"Real?" I asked, my voice ringing out louder than I'd intended. "Hell, yes, they're real. They feed and they kill. They're like sharks. Why does this vampire want your mother? Why does this vampire want *you*?"

"I—I don't know," Dawn said.

I felt the footsteps approaching and then Jodie Rexford was standing next to us. "Dawn, honey, I know this is a shock, but you're a strong girl. You'll be okay. I just need to speak with Mr. Harlan."

Jodie grabbed me by the sleeve of my trench coat and yanked me up. "We need to talk," she said. "Follow me."

I nodded and followed her to the kitchen. She stumbled over Randy's dead body, but caught herself. As soon as we were out of Dawn's earshot, she said, "Carlton is behind this. I'm sure of it."

I had to give Jodie credit. She'd lost coven members and family members, but she'd put that aside and focused on what she perceived as the threat. "You think Meriwether is responsible? Fine. I'm tired of arguing. I'll pay him a visit."

She laughed. It contained a hint of hysteria. "You've already talked to him three times today. You've discovered nothing. Nothing! I saw you, Sam Harlan. I saw into you with my sight. How can a man like you be so easily fooled?"

A surge of ice ran through my veins. "I'm going to let that pass, since you just lost your husband."

There was a tug on the sleeve of my trench coat. "I need to speak with you," Jameson said.

I shrugged. "Take care of your niece," I said to Jodie.

"What do I tell her?" Jodie asked. She turned away from me and leaned heavily on the gleaming white counter. "How do I explain this?"

I sighed. "You've known about magic," I said gently, aware of how the loss of her husband had shaken her, "but she's new to this. Explain it to her. Tell her what happened. She needs you."

Jodie ran her hands along her legs and I could almost see her putting herself back together. "Right. You're right."

"You might want to help Rachel, too," I said. "I think the shock will wear off soon. She lost her husband, too."

"Of course," she said and headed deeper into the house.

Jameson watched me with approval. "Good, Sam. That's good."

"What?"

"Getting her to focus on others," he said. "It gives her purpose."

"It keeps her from falling to pieces," I said. *"Temporarily."* I leaned against the counter, feeling tired and hungry.

"You think confronting Meriwether is a good idea?" Jameson asked.

I wanted to take a seat at the kitchen table and put my head down. "You were right. I don't have any idea where to start, but if Jodie's right, I'll find Callie. If she's wrong, it won't make a difference."

"If she's right," Jameson said, "then Meriwether has control of that vampire."

"Yeah, I've been thinking about that. I need to make a phone call."

"To?"

"A friend."

Jameson handed me his cell phone and went to help Jodie tend to the living.

And the dead.

* * *

The voice on the other end of the phone was gruff. "This isn't a good time, Sam."

I sat down heavily at the kitchen table. "Hello to you, Henry. Working tonight?"

There was a pause on the line before Henry Hastings said, "Yes, as a matter of fact."

"The Ancients?"

There was a snort on the other end of the line. "No. Some fool kid high on meth missed a turn north of town and ran his truck off the road. He was thrown from the vehicle. It's … amazing how fragile humans are. Never ceases to amaze me how often they take the opportunity to prove that."

Henry Hastings wasn't just the Vampire Sheriff, tasked with keeping vampires hidden from the rest of the world, he was also the sheriff of Hot Springs County, Wyoming. "Sorry to hear that. I have a question for you."

"Got yourself into a piece of trouble, eh?"

I watched as Jodie led Dawn and Jameson through the kitchen, the screen door slamming shut as they exited the house. "What makes you say that?"

"You haven't called since Marshalltown, so I reckon you got yourself a vampire."

I don't know why I was surprised. Henry had a thousand years of experience to draw from. "Yeah, I got a vampire. Central Illinois."

"Heh. That place is as flat as a flapjack. What's your problem?"

"I have a question. It's not about a vampire," I said. "Not exactly."

Henry's voice was curious. "Then what is it?"

"Can a vampire be controlled?"

There was a long pause before Henry replied. "Whatever do you mean?"

"I mean ... can someone use magic to control a vampire?" This time, the silence lingered so long that I was starting to think I'd lost the call. "Henry?"

"You have to understand," Henry said, "that if such a thing *were* possible, I could be in a heap of trouble for even thinking of answering."

It made sense. Henry worked for the Ancients, the oldest vampires on earth. They were at the top of the food chain and determined to keep it that way. Henry disposed of the young vampires that threatened to make the world aware of vampires, but he also killed the older ones before they threatened the Ancients.

The magic that could control a vampire might be as much of a threat to them as the world rediscovering the vampire menace, if not more so.

Little was known about the Ancients, but if the strength and power of a vampire increased with age, then the Ancients were close to gods. The idea of a witch controlling one of the Ancients was enough to make my sphincter pucker with fear.

"You know I wouldn't ask if it wasn't important," I said.

"I'm sure you wouldn't, but even *knowing* this information could spell trouble for you."

"If—"

"It could spell trouble for me, too," Henry said.

"But—"

"I didn't say I wouldn't tell you," Henry continued. "You got to understand that magic and ... what makes vampires what we are ... they ain't in the same wheelhouse."

"That's a no?"

Henry cleared his throat. "We may not be in the same

wheelhouse, but we're not that far off, I guess."

"Okay. So, that's a yes, then?"

"If someone has the know-how, and that's a helluva big if, then yes, it can be done. Whatever you got yourself into, boy, it's *serious* business."

"Yeah, I kinda figured that out."

Henry's sigh, even over the phone, conveyed a sense of bone-weary exhaustion. "I can't help you out, Sam. I got my own problems. Sit tight for a couple of days and I'll get there when I can."

I wanted to say yes. I wanted to tell him that I wouldn't lift a finger until the Vampire Sheriff was here and then we'd kick ass and take names together. I wanted him to ride in with all his power and all his experience and bail me out of my mess, save Callie, and make everything right again.

But it was night, and it was damned cold out. The screen door opened and Father Jameson helped Dawn and Jodie carry Father Mosley's body into the house. Well, Dawn was carrying Mosley's head, holding it to her chest like a basketball, looking like she might cry at any moment.

"It can't wait," I said to Henry. "I'm going to have to do this alone."

There was another pause. "What about the Sister?"

"She's been taken," I said, "by Milford Barlow."

"You're joshing me."

"I know," I said, "it kinda shocked me, too. What's weird is that her crucifix was glowing. It hurt him. His skin was blistering, but he managed to carry her into the night before I could stop him."

"That kind of control is beyond most mortals," Henry said, his voice deeper and more guttural than usual, the way he got when he forgot his aw-shucks folksy charm. "To subvert a vampire's will that way requires the kind of magic that bespeaks things older than the mortal world. Do you understand, boy?"

"Not really, no. Does it matter? Anything can be killed. You told me that yourself."

"Anything *can* be killed," Henry agreed, "but it takes a hard man to do what needs to be done. You need to be that hard man, Sam. Don't hesitate. You're Jack's kin, but you haven't really embraced that. You need to let it out."

"Let what out?" I asked.

"The killer," Henry said. "I can't help you this time. You got to do it yourself. Good luck, son. Don't die on me."

The phone went dead as the call ended, but I continued as if Henry was still on the line. "I hope I don't let you down."

* * *

"Tell me truthfully," I said, "that part about asking Meriwether three times and him having to tell the truth. Were you serious about that?"

Jodie Rexford was sitting across from me at the Kormans' kitchen table. Father Jameson was sitting to my right, listening intently, and Dawn McKie was sitting to my left.

"I didn't lie," Jodie said.

I glanced at Jameson, who nodded his head. "If that thing about asking three times is true, then how did Meriwether get around it?"

"I don't *know*," Jodie said. "Somehow he bent the rules."

Jameson's words rattled around in my head. Part of me felt that I didn't owe her anything, but there was a vampire involved, a vampire I knew personally. Callie's life was now in danger. If there was a chance I could save her, I had to take it. "I need my stuff back."

Jodie nodded. "I'll make a phone call."

Within minutes, I heard a familiar thrum. I followed Jodie outside as the man climbed out of my truck. "This is Robert Schrock," Jodie said.

Schrock was in his late thirties, with big muscular hands, long scraggly brown hair, and a goatee. "She needs a little bodywork," he said, "but I got her running good."

I walked around the Chevy, giving it a quick inspection. The driver's side front quarter panel had been patched with Bondo where Randy Korman's plow had ripped through the sheet-metal. The front grill was cracked and there was a new ripple in the hood, but nothing a little time and effort couldn't fix.

"She'll get you where you need to go," Schrock said. His smile evaporated as he saw the look on Jodie's face. "What's going on?"

"We've got ... bad news," Jodie said.

I watched as she led him to the house. I didn't particularly want to watch as Schrock heard about the dead members of his coven. Watching the truth filter through Dawn McKie's eyes had been more than enough for me.

The toolbox was in the back of the truck, right where I'd left it, and I rummaged around inside until I found what I was looking for, then headed back to the kitchen. Robert stared at Randy Korman's dead body still sprawled across the living room doorjamb.

Jodie hugged Robert tightly, but Robert looked like he might faint.

Jameson glanced up from the kitchen table, saw what I was holding, and said, "Oh, no."

"Oh, yes," I said, shoving the Ingram M-10 across the table along with a handful of magazines loaded with silver. "You're staying here. I trust you, Patrick. Your faith is strong. But, just in case, I want you to blow the hell out of anything that comes your way."

Jameson eyed the gun with distaste, then slammed a magazine in and cycled the bolt with practiced ease. He caught me staring at him and raised an eyebrow. "You think this is the first time I've handled a weapon?"

"I guess not," I said. "Where's Dawn?"

Jodie had stopped tending to Robert and was watching our exchange. "She's in the living room," she said. "Molly and Rachel are working on a defensive spell. We should be able to put up something to ward off trouble when the rest of the coven gets here."

"Was this place warded before?" I asked.

Jodie bit her lip. "We weren't sure of the threat. We had many wards, but most of them weren't specific to a vampire. Robert, call Carly and tell her we need her. I'll call Jaime and Karrie."

"Will that be enough?" Jameson asked. "You've lost so many of your coven…"

"Uh, about that," Robert said. "I'm not sure I want Carly involved with this-"

Jodie spun around at glared at him, her hands resting on her hips. "This isn't the time to second-guess me. We stand together or we all die. *All* of us. It doesn't matter if she's not here. Carlton will track her down and slaughter her. Who will take care of your kids then? Who's going to—"

"Mrs. Rexford," Jameson said. He had stood while Jodie spoke, and put his hands on her shoulders. She turned her glare on him, but it quickly faded and she staggered back against the counter.

"Sorry, I'm sorry," Jodie said. Tears rolled down her cheeks and she wiped at them with the sleeve of her sweater. "Robert, please. We need your help. We need Carly's help. It's not about my sister anymore. We're all in danger now."

Robert swallowed hard. "I don't know…"

"I believe Mrs. Rexford is correct in this, my son," Jameson said. He waved the M-10 around and spoke slowly, his voice full of emotion. "If you pull together, you might survive this, but if you choose to run and hide? You will all surely perish."

* * *

The rest of the coven arrived thirty minutes later. Carly Schrock, a trim blonde with pretty blue eyes and thick glasses, joined her husband. With Robert's help, Jodie had moved Randy's body from the doorway. Carly took one look at the bloodstain on the floor and promptly vomited into the kitchen sink.

Karrie Showalter, a willowy college student with long black hair and carefully applied black lipstick, arrived next. She wore dark blue sweatpants and a black shirt, and carried herself with a world-wise sophistication, but like Carly Schrock, she vomited as soon as she saw the blood trail in the living room doorway.

Carly held Karrie's hand as Karrie heaved until her stomach was empty, then Jameson led them to the living room to join the rest of the coven.

Jaime Alcorn arrived last. He was a stout man, almost six foot tall, with thinning brown hair and a large bald spot on the back of his head tanned a dark copper that matched his arms. He wasn't exactly the most impressive man to look at, but he didn't fall apart when he saw the pile of dead bodies stacked in the living room like so much firewood.

Jodie gave him a brief hug and then turned to the rest. "The coven has convened. We will protect this home and all within it. By the power of the Goddess."

There were nods all around and Jodie motioned me to the kitchen.

"Hurry," she said quietly. "We'll do what we can, but I don't know if we can ward off a vampire that powerful."

My mouth dropped. "I thought—"

"I'm their leader," Jodie whispered. "They expect me to lead. I wasn't wrong about the danger we're in. If I left it to them, we'd die hiding in our basements."

Jameson held up the weapon I'd given him. "Go, Sam. I'll

keep them safe."

I eyed Jodie critically. "You sure?"

She started to nod, then shrugged. "If I stop to think about … about Gene … I'll fall to pieces. I've buried my feelings. I … hope I can make it through the night."

My opinion of the woman went up a notch. She'd lost her husband, and things weren't looking good for her sister, but she kept on going. "I'll do what needs to be done."

"Do that, Mr. Harlan. Do it for our sakes."

I can't argue with that.

Chapter Fourteen

It felt good to be back in my truck, eating up the miles. The wind had picked up and snowflakes swirled in the truck's headlights. There wasn't enough to cover the ground, but the flakes caught the light like a flurry of shiny diamonds blowing in the wind.

It was almost ten when I crested the hill just north of Monticello and there were few cars on the road. A few minutes more and I was through town and heading north on State Street.

The elegant homes appeared different at night. A few Christmas lights glowed from porch fronts and windows, but most of the decorations had been taken down, leaving the vast lawns empty and the houses looking like soulless dark shells.

There was no sense in hiding my presence. I took a right turn into the driveway, slowing just enough that the tires wouldn't chirp on the asphalt, then slammed on the brakes.

The driveway was filled with cars and trucks, at least seven different vehicles by my quick count, and although it looked like Meriwether was entertaining guests, only a single light illuminated his front window.

There wasn't time for hesitation. I opened the truck door and ran to the front of Meriwether's house, not bothering to close the truck door behind me. My Kimber was in my right hand and I took the steps two at a time, then stopped long enough to grab the door handle. The door wasn't locked.

I shoved it open and entered the house, my boots clacking against the hardwood floor. I was halfway down the hallway when I felt the slimy evil of the vampire clawing up the back of my neck.

Then I was in the living room where Carlton Meriwether stood. He was tending to a roaring fire in the fireplace, a drink in one hand and a poker in the other. He turned and I had just enough time to register the smile on his face—then there was movement behind me and a fist came rocketing out of nowhere, smashing against my temple and knocking me unconscious.

* * *

I floated on a warm cloud. It was like my body was covered in syrup. My thoughts were slow and lazy. Golden light filtered through my eyelids.

I could almost convince myself I was in Heaven.

My stomach began to hurt like I'd been kicked in the gut. The bile came up the back of my throat and I choked it out as my eyes finally opened. I couldn't see anything except for the gray concrete as I heaved and heaved. My body felt like it had been beaten by a linebacker after a three-night bender.

When I finally stopped retching long enough to take stock of my surroundings, I found myself in Meriwether's basement, surrounded by strangers.

Men and women stood in a semicircle, wearing shit-eating grins. A naked woman who bore a striking resemblance to Jodie Rexford was stretched out on the hard concrete floor with closed eyes, tied to metal hoops embedded in the concrete. Fluorescent lights flickered and buzzed overhead, giving the woman's ample flesh and sickly pallor.

Meriwether stood in front of me, his brown loafers just inches from the bile I'd vomited over the concrete, watching me with a self-satisfied smirk.

There was the slimy presence of a vampire nearby, and I saw Milford Barlow standing to my right, as still as a statue, his doughy skin marking him as something other than human.

Then I saw Callie and my heart thumped in my chest.

They had tied her up with hemp ropes and hung her from a wooden beam overhead. She had a gag in her mouth and whimpered when my eyes found hers.

She had been stripped to her bra and panties, and runes had been carved into her skin, just deep enough to have already scabbed over. They covered her back and her sides, even curving around her thighs and stretching down to her calves.

The writing could have been Celtic, or Aramaic, or Egyptian, for all I knew. It didn't look like they were designed to hurt so much as to humiliate her.

Anger overcame me, and a pool of red swam around the edge of my vision. I had never felt anger like it before, the kind where each breath felt like my last. I was prepared to kill anyone or anything that got between Callie and me. It didn't matter. Nothing mattered except the urge to kill and to save my friend.

I was moving without even realizing it, rushing to Callie's aid, and then it felt like steel clamps had latched onto my hands. I turned to see Barlow holding me with ease. I growled and started to pull away. Barlow held on tight, but I wasn't about to stop.

Barlow's eyes widened as I took a step forward, in spite of his grasp, and then another. Even Meriwether, who was looking bored, suddenly became interested.

"Stop, Mr. Harlan," Meriwether said. "Stop or I'll have the woman hurt. She may look … ill-used … but I assure you she hasn't suffered any *permanent* damage."

Callie.

The world spun. I didn't *want* to stop. I wanted to smash Meriwether's face in, to claw his eyes out, and to rip his throat out with my teeth. "If you bastards touch her—"

"Oh, *please*," Meriwether said. "Do tell. Would you shit yourself as the vampire snapped your neck? Or would you rather scream in agony as we used magic to flay your skin from your body? That hasn't been done in two hundred and forty-eight years, but I'm sure I could arrange it."

My anger lessened as I realized that Meriwether had my gun tucked in the front of his black slacks and my silver knife strapped to his waist. I was defenseless. "What do you want?" I finally asked.

"What do I want?" Meriwether mused. He cocked his head back and laughed. "The list of things I want is so long and varied I'm afraid I don't have the time to name them all."

"Why are you doing this?"

"Finally," Meriwether said. "Finally, you ask the most important question of all. Why does anyone do anything? Money, sex, and power, obviously."

Maybe it was my pounding head, but I didn't understand. "What?"

"Just kidding," Meriwether said. "I'm like you, Mr. Harlan. I peeked into your soul. I know you better than you know yourself. You're a very suspicious man. Do you know how I charmed you so thoroughly?"

"No," I growled, "but you damned well won't do it again."

"You think you're clever? You don't *trust* anybody. That lets me warp the truth around you, twisting my words. I spun them in your mind, like the finest silk, turning those suspicions against Randy Korman and Jodie Rexford. By the time I was done, you shook my hand and wished me the best."

My right eye twitched. "That's *not* how it happened."

"That's *exactly* how it happened," Meriwether said, clearly relishing the moment. "Don't blame yourself. You couldn't have known. Oh, wait. Jodie *did* tell you. You *did* know."

It wasn't his words that stung, it was the look in Callie's eyes.

He's right. He charmed us. He charmed me.

"What will it take to free Callie?" I asked.

His smile grew wider. "Ah, perhaps you really are clever."

"You obviously want something from me," I said, "or you would have killed me by now."

"It's amazing that such a reasonable conclusion could come from such a dull-witted man, but it's not what I want *from* you, it's what I want you to *do*."

The men and women had watched our exchange, but now they were leaning forward in anticipation, and I could almost feel the energy building in the room. "What?"

Meriwether smiled, exposing his gleaming white teeth. "You're going to bear witness."

There was the sound of a door opening. Plain wooden stairs led up from the basement, and Nicky descended them, watching us intently, still wearing his Teenage Mutant Ninja Turtles shirt. He smiled shyly as he took the last step to the basement floor. "Hey, Sam."

* * *

Nicky came to a halt in front of me. He had a simple grin on his face. "Are you gonna play Ninja Turtles with me?"

The cold pit in my stomach started to rise, aiming for my heart, and I addressed Meriwether. "Don't do it. Please."

"What do you mean?" Meriwether asked.

"Whatever you have planned. You can't—"

"Ah, but I must," he said. He approached Nicky, placing his

arm around his son's shoulders. "I love my son. I *never* lied about that. Never."

The men and women shuffled backward, and I could finally see the pentagram inscribed in the concrete floor. The naked woman at the center was strangely still. A woman I recognized as Lisa Doll stepped forward and said, "You have to come with me, honey."

Nicky frowned. "I thought I was gonna play with Sam."

The woman gave Nicky a thousand-watt smile. "He's just here to watch."

"Lisa," Meriwether said sharply.

"I'll play with you," Lisa said. "Just like we used to in kindergarten."

"I don't know," Nicky said doubtfully. "You were *mean* to me. You said things about me when you thought I couldn't hear."

"That was a long time ago," Lisa said. She turned and I saw her husband, Del, was among Meriwether's coven.

"She won't be mean to you," Del said. "She'll play real nice. I promise and that's a guarantee you can live by."

"*Please* don't do this," I said to Meriwether.

He shook his head. "I take no pleasure in this, but I must heal Nicholas."

Heal?

"You think whatever you're about to do will … what … make Nicky right?"

"I *know* it will," Meriwether said. He turned to Nicky, who was sitting on the floor with Lisa. Lisa kept snapping her fingers, drawing Nicky's attention from the woman, the woman I'd been desperately searching for.

The naked woman tied to the floor was Dorothy Hamm—Jodie's missing sister, Dawn's mother and, as it turned out, Nicky's mother.

Meriwether nodded and an older couple, a matronly older woman with a crooked grin and a man with a shiny bald head and stylish glasses, came forward and squatted on the floor next to Dorothy. The woman stroked Dorothy's hair and whispered something while the man closed his eyes and mumbled to himself, causing the hairs on the back of my arms and neck to prickle.

I'd been trying to avoid looking at the naked body of Dorothy Hamm. She started tossing and turning against the cold concrete, her eyes still closed, her lips moving like she was talking to herself.

It was the nudity that bothered me. She didn't seem the kind of woman who would appreciate being nude in front of a crowd, and yet there she was, her heavy breasts sagging to each side and the dark mound of wiry black hair between her legs on full display to Meriwether's coven.

The coven members watched with hungry looks on their faces, an almost sexual sense of anticipation, but if I'd learned anything of late, it was that they weren't hungry for sex.

And, when an old man wearing a heavy sweater and clubby brown shoes brought the matronly woman a long, curved knife with an ebony hilt, I knew I'd been right.

They hadn't bound Dorothy Hamm nude on the floor for sex.

Nicky turned to stare at the old man, then noticed the curved knife. "Are—are we gonna play with that?"

Lisa laughed, and it was too loud and too high-pitched to carry mirth. "Honey, *you're* going to play a game with it."

Nicky tilted his head. "I am?"

"Yes," Lisa said. "This is the best game of all."

Nicky frowned. "How do you play?"

The matronly woman held the blade up to Nicky and it caught the light, gleaming like silver.

For all I knew, it probably *was* silver.

"I don't know," Nicky said slowly, his eyes never leaving the exposed blade. "Daddy only lets me play with Ninja Turtles. I like numb-chucks."

"Nicholas," Meriwether said loudly, in full-on parent command voice. "You may play this game. I give you my permission."

Nicky licked his lips. "What do I do?"

Lisa said, "It's easy-peasy, honey." She motioned for Nicky to take the knife.

"What if I don't wanna?" Nicky asked.

"This is the make-Nicky-better game," Lisa said. "Don't you want to get better?"

Nicky frowned harder and his eyes finally left the blade and found his father. "Is there sum'thin wrong with me?"

"Yes," Meriwether said. He entered the pentagram and took the knife from the older woman, who nodded and smiled gratefully as if he'd given her a gift.

Meriwether's coven backed up, leaving Nicky alone with his father and mother. Meriwether placed the knife in Nicky's hand and guided Nicky's hand until the blade was pressed against Dorothy's neck.

"I—don't wanna do this," Nicky said, his voice cracking.

"It's the easiest thing in the world," Meriwether said. "You're going to pull the knife across her throat. That's all. It will make you better."

"It will?"

Meriwether smiled. "It will."

There was a series of grunts from Callie. She was staring at me, her eyes wide, pleading with me to do something.

There's a moment before something bad happens, something truly bad, where time slows and you think of all the ways you could stop it if only things were different.

Things weren't different.

"No," I said. "No!"

I watched helplessly as Nicky drew the knife across his mother's throat.

I'd been desperate to find her, and now I had to watch as blood spurted from Dorothy's neck. The knife had cut deep enough to sever an artery, and Meriwether guided Nicky's hand as the knife continued to slice deeper and deeper until Dorothy's throat was laid bare to the world in a crimson mess.

I struggled against Barlow's icy-cold grip. The blood pooled around Dorothy like a scarlet halo, then it flowed to the lines of the pentagram etched into the concrete, filling them.

"No!" I screamed.

Dorothy's eyes opened and her mouth went wide in a silent scream. Her body jerked and pulled at the metal hoops inserted into the floor. A terrible gurgling came from her ruined esophagus.

She had a moment of clarity as the spell to pacify her gave way and her heart beat its last. She died before my eyes, there on the concrete floor.

A metallic gong sounded inside my head as Meriwether's spell concluded and I managed one last, halfhearted "No!"

Kevin Lee Swaim

Chapter Fifteen

Nicky stood and looked around at the assembled coven with a beatific look on his face. "Wow," he drawled.

Meriwether wrapped his arms around his son, hugging him tightly. "Do you feel better?"

"Better?" Nicky asked. "I dunno. I feel ... *different.*"

Meriwether pushed his son back and stared at him with unblinking eyes. Nicky glanced around the room, shuffling his feet, but Meriwether held his arms. "The process didn't work," Meriwether finally said.

"It should have been enough," he continued, his voice losing its confidence. "You said it would be enough."

"What?" I asked.

"Nothing is certain," Meriwether said, his voice deepening. "There was always a chance. That's why we kept Harlan."

"What are you talking about?" I asked.

Meriwether ignored me. Lisa approached Nicky and took his hand. "Let's go upstairs, honey."

Nicky smiled tentatively. "Okay."

As they walked past me, Nicky slowed and said, "Sorry we couldn't play."

I gritted my teeth. "Maybe next time."

Nicky smiled, but it wasn't quite as innocent as it had been moments before. "You betcha."

Nicky clomped up the stairs as Lisa urged him on. The door at the top of the stairs slammed shut and the room fell still. The coven members were staring at Dorothy's body, and the room was filling with the smell of death.

There was a twitch in Barlow's hand as he stared at the blood on the concrete, and for a brief moment the vampire relaxed his grip, but then it clamped back down on me before I could capitalize on the momentary distraction.

The vampire's strength was so much greater than mine that it wasn't even close. I realized that Barlow could crush me—literally crush me—and there was nothing I could do about it. The only reason I'd been able to offer any resistance had been because Barlow was trying not to hurt me.

"What do you really want," I finally asked.

There was a murmuring around the room, and Meriwether smiled, exposing his gleaming white teeth. "I *want* Dawn McKie."

"I'm supposed to give you Dawn?" I asked. "You've *got* to be kidding."

"I'm really not," Meriwether said, his black eyes focused on me with a ferocious intensity. "On this, I promise. I *want* that girl and I want you to *get* me that girl."

"I can't give you a girl. I'm not some…" I trailed off, unable to come up with the words to describe the kind of man I'd be. "I won't do it."

"You will," Meriwether said confidently. "You'll help me or I will hurt your friend. Even a nitwit such as you must have figured out that I'm willing to do whatever it takes to get what I want."

Even though my head was still pounding, and even though I felt like I might vomit again, I glared at him and said, "The stick man."

"Hah. Yes, the stick man."

"You thought you could kill us."

"I *thought*," Meriwether said slowly, "that you were a nuisance, but now you are going to make yourself useful."

"And you want me to … what … to give you Dawn McKie?"

Callie shook her head, but a giant of a man kicked her with one of his pointy-toed cowboy boots hard enough to make her grunt.

My arms jerked, but Barlow held fast. "Damn it!" I shouted. "Stop that!"

"Chester," Meriwether said without turning around, "if our guest gets out of line again, kick that useless whore as hard as you can."

The big man smiled, flashing his brown-stained teeth, and chuckled.

I wanted to kill that man with the cowboy boots and the button-up western shirt. I wanted to kill him more than I'd ever wanted anything in my life, but I said through gritted teeth, "How do you expect me to give you the girl?"

"Tell Jodi you found nothing," Meriwether said. He withdrew a white medallion the size of a silver dollar from his pocket and held it up. The medallion was delicate, etched with runes, and looked to be made from bone. "Break this. It will remove the wards I'm sure they've put up since you left."

My mouth felt like it had sand in it. "What if I don't?"

Meriwether shook his head. "Then I kill you and tear the wards down myself. You just don't understand. I work smart, not hard, Mr. Harlan. My coven has the power, but why waste the energy when I have you?" He raised his hand and pointed at Callie. "Just to be clear, if you don't do as you're told, I'll rape Sister Calahane. *Repeatedly.* In between the torture. Then, after a year or so, when I've had my fill, I'll sell her to a few of my Egyptian friends. They *do* love redheads…"

"I'm going to kill you," I growled. "I don't know how, but I'm going to kill you."

The men and women began to laugh and Meriwether raised his hands. "Oh, Sam. You should have been a comedian. You've been so busy since you murdered your wife and daughter that you haven't realized how little you know."

My wife and daughter?

There was something more to Meriwether than magic. There had to be. He knew too much. "How did you lie to me?" I asked. "I questioned you three times. That's the magical number, isn't it?"

Meriwether's smile faltered. "So many questions." He fingered the bone medallion as the coven's laughter died out. "You asked why I'm doing this? I'm doing it for family. That's the currency you understand, isn't it? Family?"

My eyes were drawn to the body of Dorothy Hamm. "I see what *you* think of family."

Meriwether frowned. When he spoke, his voice was higher and not quite as confident. "I gave her the chance to do the right thing. She refused to offer herself."

"You thought she'd kill herself?" I asked.

"And why not?" Meriwether asked. He pointed to Dorothy's dead body. "*She's* to blame for this. Now I have to take stronger measures."

Callie watched our exchange with widened eyes. She grunted

and moaned, but there was nothing I could do. I felt the shame from not saving Dorothy's life burning in my gut. "What kind of stronger measures?"

Meriwether rocked back on his heels. His face went blank and his voice deepened. "Go back to Jodie's coven and do as I ordered."

I shook my head. "I can't—"

"You *will* do it because you have no choice." He put the medallion in my coat pocket and patted it. "You're out of *options*, Mr. Harlan, and out of *time*. You tried. You did your best. There's no shame in that."

"You want me to hand over Dawn so you can sacrifice her like you did her mother." I resisted the urge to spit at him. "Killing Dorothy wasn't enough?"

Meriwether shook his head and said simply, "No. It wasn't. Blood magic is difficult, even for someone with my knowledge."

"Dawn's just a ... a thing to use to get what you want."

"Of course," Meriwether said. He raised an eyebrow in bafflement. "What else would she be?"

"How do you know it will work?" I asked. "You couldn't do it this time."

He blinked. "There's a way around every obstacle."

"How can you make Nicky do that? How could you make your own son—"

"These sacrifices will do for Nicky what I never could," he said loudly. "It is a *small* price to pay."

"Why don't you tell that to Dorothy?" I asked. "Oh, wait, you just slaughtered her like a sacrificial lamb."

Meriwether's eyes widened and I barely had time to register his fist as it connected with my jaw. There was an explosion of pain, and I would have collapsed if Barlow hadn't held me upright.

"No more arguments," Meriwether said. "You will do as you're told or I'll kill your friend." He must have seen the look on my face, because he continued, "You have twenty minutes. If you haven't removed the coven's defenses, I won't bother raping your little friend. I'll have the vampire rip her heart from her chest."

Callie moaned, shaking her head, trying to signal me. I knew she would rather die than have me follow Meriwether's orders.

I wanted to tell him to go to Hell, but in that moment which seemed to last forever, I realized that Callie was the thing I loved most in the world.

She was all I had left.

My eyes burned and I felt tears roll down my face. "Fine," I whispered.

There was a murmuring among Meriwether's coven. He smiled and leaned close to my face. "What did you say?"

Callie went wild, shaking and yanking against the rope, stomping her bare feet against the concrete. She shook her head, whipping it back and forth, pleading with her eyes.

I bit my tongue hard enough to draw blood and said, "I'll do it."

Meriwether laughed, a deep belly laugh like the world was his joke and he'd just heard the punchline. "Oh, Mr. Harlan, I like you *very* much. Do as you've been told, and I promise I won't lay a finger on you. When this is all over, you can comfort yourself knowing that you restored my son's life. You are giving him the opportunity to achieve his true potential."

There was a deep sense of shame burning in my belly. "I doubt it," I said, watching Callie glare at me.

* * *

Barlow led me to my truck. "They removed your supplies while you were unconscious," he said. "Don't even think of resisting."

"Why are you doing this?" I asked. "He's controlling you, isn't he?"

Barlow opened the truck door and shoved me inside. "I'm sorry."

"Yeah," I said, "there's a lot of that going around."

Barlow shook his head. "I can't—"

"What's really going on?"

"I'm…" He paused and stared at me with hooded eyes. The muscles in his jaws worked. "I'm … unable … to say more."

"I don't understand."

"I *know*," the vampire hissed. "Go now. Do as you've been told." He turned and headed back into Meriwether's house.

I was left alone in the cold. There *had* to be a way to rescue Callie and save Jodie's coven, but my brain felt like it was full of cotton. I didn't have any weapons and I was still woozy from being knocked out.

What am I supposed to do? There's no way I can take Barlow. Not without weapons.

I'd staked my first vampire, completely by accident, with a broken chair leg. If I could sharpen the end of a piece of wood and fashion it into a stake, I could kill Barlow.

Except I don't have any wood and the clock is ticking. It will take me at least fifteen minutes just to get back to the farm.

"Damn it," I said to myself, smacking the steering wheel.

There was nothing else left to do. I was out of ideas and out of time.

I gunned the Chevy, roaring through Monticello, and was halfway to Bement when I remembered that Callie kept a spare cell phone in the glove compartment.

Assuming they didn't take that, too.

Fate was with me. I rummaged through the glove compartment with my right hand while steering with my left, until my fingers touched the heavy plastic of the burner phone under a stack of old-fashioned maps that had belonged to Jack. I yanked it out and called the only person I thought could help.

There was a ringing on the other end and then Henry asked, "You have good news?"

"I'm ... in trouble," I said. "A witch is forcing me to hand over a girl or he'll kill Callie."

There was a low whistle on the other end. "You got problems, boy."

I was nearing the side road that led to the Korman farm. "The witch sacrificed a woman to heal his son. He's the one who's controlling Milford."

"A blood sacrifice," Henry said, "*and* controlling a vampire? Get the hell out of there, Sam. Blast your way through them, get the Sister, and get the hell out. Don't look back."

I turned on the side road and headed west. "What? What is it?"

He sounds scared.

That, more than anything, scared *me*. Henry was the most powerful vampire I'd ever met. If he was scared, then I was in *serious* trouble.

"You're dealing with something you got no experience with," Henry said. "I can be there in a day. Don't do anything until I get there."

The Korman farm was quickly approaching and I hit the

brakes, making the turn into the Kormans' gravel driveway. "I can't, Henry. They'll *kill* her."

"Listen to me, boy," he said, his voice low and guttural. "Your life is in danger. *Serious* danger. Worse than anything my kind can inflict."

The door to the Korman farm opened and Jameson stepped out, looking at me quizzically.

"I have to go," I said.

"Wait! You—"

"Sorry, Henry. I'll call you later."

"Don't—"

I clicked the button to end the call, wondering what new terror I faced.

It didn't really matter. It had been almost thirteen minutes since I'd left Meriwether's house and I figured it was a few minutes for Barlow to put me in the truck…

I was almost out of time.

Jameson opened the truck door. "Sam? Did you find anything at Meriwether's house?"

"I need to speak to Jodie," I said, jumping out of the truck and heading for the kitchen door. "Now!"

Jameson frowned but followed me into the farmhouse.

Jodie was sitting at the kitchen table with her niece. She saw the look on my face and grabbed Dawn's hand. "What happened?"

"You were right," I said. "Meriwether was behind *all* of it. He's controlling the vampire. He took your sister. He's got Callie and is threatening to kill her."

Jodie's mouth dropped. "How do you know?"

"Because," I said, "I found him. I *saw* Dorothy."

"You saw Mom?" Dawn asked. "Where is she?"

Jodie's face fell before I could stammer out a response and she said, "He killed her, didn't he?"

Dawn shook her head. "No. That can't be."

"He sacrificed her to cure Nicky."

"Nicky who?" Dawn asked.

"You didn't tell her?" I asked Jodie.

She bit her lip. "I … hadn't gotten to it yet."

"*Who* is Nicky?" Dawn asked.

"He's your half-brother," Jodie said. "He's Carlton's son."

"I don't *have* a half-brother," Dawn insisted.

"Sam," Jameson said, "what *aren't* you telling us?"

They all turned to stare at me. I removed the bone medallion from my pocket. "I have to use this in the next few minutes or he kills Callie."

"You *can't*," Jodie said. "He'll just kill her anyway."

Jameson took the medallion from my shaking hands, as carefully as one would hold a bomb. "What does he really want?"

My eyes found Dawn and I blurted out, "He wants her. Nicky's half-sister."

Jodie covered her mouth with her hand. "You can't do this."

I shook my head, fighting back tears. "I don't have a choice."

"You're going to trade Dawn's life for your friend's life?" Jodie asked. "How could you live with yourself?"

I wanted to tell her that I didn't know, but Jameson spoke first. "It's not your fault, son. You've done all you can."

"Father," Jodie said, her voice rising in panic, "you can't condone this. Carlton will kill Dawn and then kill us. He'll kill the Sister, too. He won't honor any agreement."

There was an ice-cold ball in the pit of my stomach, and I couldn't seem to get enough air in my lungs. "Father," I said, "I can't wait any longer. What should I do? It's like I'm trapped in Hell."

"When you're going through Hell," Jameson said as he snapped the medallion in half, showering the floor with bone dust, "keep going."

My mouth dropped. There was a whooshing sensation in the room, then my ears popped and a high-pitched whine filled the room, then the air went unnaturally still.

The blood drained from Jodie's face as the bone dust settled to the floor. She stared at the priest and asked, "*What* have you *done?*"

* * *

"We only have a moment," Jameson said, handing me the Ingram.

"What are you talking about?" I asked, still in shock.

"Do you really think this is all a coincidence?" Jameson asked.

Jodie stared at the priest in horror. "You've killed us."

"Perhaps," Jameson said. "Perhaps not."

My hands, the only part of me that was working correctly, methodically checked the Ingram. "I don't understand."

The priest grabbed me by the shoulders, a sad smile on his

face. "Free will, Sam. It's the one thing humans possess that defines us among all of creation. You will understand when the time is right, the Lord willing."

Jamison's crucifix began to glow a pure white that filled the room like the heart of the sun. There was a crash from the living room, and then screaming. I turned and raised the Ingram, another crash sounded behind me as Barlow burst through the kitchen door, splintering the wood and shattering the glass.

I heard the sounds of engines outside and car doors slamming. I spun, ready to pull the Ingram's trigger, but Barlow yanked it from my hands with inhuman speed.

There was an explosion of pain as his fist struck my nose. I dropped to the floor, stunned. It blinded me, filling my eyes with tears and making me see stars. The room filled with sound and movement, and Jodie's screams mixed with Dawn's as I heard Jameson shout, "Get back! In the name of the Lord—"

The room fell silent. I frantically wiped the tears from my eyes, propping myself up on my knees.

Barlow held Dawn and Jodie by their throats. Jameson stood, arms spread wide, his crucifix glowing fiercely. Barlow's skin smoked under the harsh light, blackening where the power of the Lord beat against the vampire's unprotected skin.

Barlow appeared unfazed.

He continued holding the women, seemingly unaware of the damage Jameson's faith inflicted.

The screams from the living room had turned into gurgling shrieks, and I could only imagine what was occurring. "Damn it, Barlow," I pleaded. "You can't do this."

"He will do as he is told," a familiar voice said from the doorway. Carlton Meriwether stepped over the remains of the door, glancing around the room with a smile on his face. "Thank you, Mr. Harlan. I had my doubts about you. I was terribly afraid I was going to have to kill your friend."

I stood there, helplessly watching as Meriwether strode around the room, inspecting the Kormans' kitchen as if he were doing a victory lap. He smiled as he passed Dawn McKie, then came to a stop in front of Father Jameson.

He carefully plucked the crucifix from the priest's neck before casually tossing it out the front door and sending it spinning into the night. "Hello, Patrick."

Jameson shifted uncomfortably. "I know who I'm talking to. I know who you *really* are."

Meriwether rocked back on his heels, his smile fading. "You do, do you?"

"Yes," Jameson said. "It all makes sense."

"Say it," Meriwether demanded. "Who am I?"

Jameson sighed heavily. "I've never forgotten you, Haagenti."

* * *

Haagenti?

Meriwether laughed. "Oh, how surprised I was when I saw you through the little vampire's eyes," he said, his voice deepening and becoming more melodious. "I almost lost sight of my goal. I've waited a *long* time for this, Patrick."

"Time has no meaning to a demon," Jameson said. "It's been but the blink of an eye for you."

"It's true that we don't register time the way humans do," Meriwether said. "But we *do* notice its passing."

"He's a demon?" I asked Jameson. "A real demon?"

Meriwether held up his hands. "Guilty as charged. Carlton was nice enough to offer me his body if I could give him what he wanted."

"That's what you do, isn't it?" Jameson asked. "You offer people what they want."

"You're not still upset, are you?" Meriwether asked.

Jameson shook his head. "How could I be upset? Demons never give what they offer."

"Ack," Meriwether said, putting his hand to his chest. "You wound me. I would have taught you magic beyond your wildest dreams. The means to work with the forces of creation."

"You were never going to deliver," Jameson said. "You cannot tell the truth. It's beyond you. It is in your very nature to deceive."

"When did I ever deceive you?" Meriwether asked.

"Wait," I said. "If you're a demon, then why bother with Nicky?"

"Ah," Meriwether said. "Even the Harlan understands. I honor my promises. The knowledge to cure the boy was a small price to pay for a willing host. And what power this body *contains*."

"That's because you have none of your own," Jameson said. "You're impotent."

Meriwether clucked his tongue. "Petty insults are beneath you, Patrick."

"You have no power here," Jameson said. "Only that which you steal."

Meriwether cocked his head to the side. "Call it what you wish, but I have knowledge, and knowledge *is* power. Take the vampire. Do you know how difficult it was to ensnare?"

Jameson nodded to Jodie, still dangling from Barlow's grasp. "The coven figured out how to do it *without* your help."

"The youngling?" Meriwether scoffed. "They caught a fly, but they hadn't figured out how to control it." He glared at Jodie, his face full of malice. "Amateurs. You give your kind a bad name."

Dawn sobbed, great wracking sounds that shook her chest, but Jodie was trying to maintain a brave face. "Don't do this," she choked out. "Please."

Meriwether frowned. "Would it surprise you to know that I derive no pleasure from killing?"

"You lie," Jameson said.

"That's the problem with being a demon," Meriwether said, shaking his head. "No one believes when you tell the truth. I realize you think me a monster—"

"Because you *are* a monster," I said.

Meriwether whipped around to glare at me. "Spoken like a little man with a little mind. What do you know of the world, Sam Harlan? You've seen so little of it. I don't enjoy death, but I'm not afraid of it."

"Of course not," Jameson countered, "because you don't die. Your spirit is everlasting, forever doomed to live in Hell, far removed from God's glory."

"God?" Meriwether said. "You think He cares about you? Where is He? He's abandoned you!" He practically spat the last words at me. "Where was God when your family was murdered? Did He help you? Did He offer you solace? Did He right the wrongs against you?"

"How do you know my family was murdered?" I asked.

"Knowledge *is* power," Meriwether said. "I broker in fact, and I know all the facts about you, human."

"He's lying," Jameson said to me. "That's what he does."

"I've given humanity so much," Meriwether said. "Your little mind can't begin to comprehend it. I gave humanity the knowledge of fire. How to cook with it, and how to keep the night at bay."

"Which made us afraid of the dark," Jameson said. "We used fire to make war on each other."

"What about gold? I taught you how to mine it and how to refine it. I taught you how to craft it and make such beautiful things—"

"You taught us greed," Jameson said, his voice rising. "You bred ignorance and envy."

"Gibbering little monkeys. You're *never* satisfied," Meriwether said. "I give you something, anything, and you demand more. Do you think knowledge comes without a price?"

"You will go," Jameson said. "You will go back to Hell, where you belong. This place is not for you. Leave this place! I command it!"

Meriwether threw his head back and laughed, then hitched his thumb at the priest and said to Barlow, "Can you believe this guy? Your faith isn't as strong as it used to be, Patrick. You don't have the juice to banish me. Besides, I'm not ready to leave. Not yet." When Barlow said nothing, Meriwether continued, "I'm so unappreciated. Of course you wouldn't think so, would you, little beast?"

Barlow's eyelid twitched, but it was the only indication that he was listening. He continued to hold the two women in his iron-like grasp.

The screams had died out from the other room and there came the sound of shuffling, like something scraping across the floor. A stick man appeared in the doorway to the living room, just like the one that had attacked us in the Best Western.

"Cleaned up the riffraff?" Meriwether asked.

The stick man's head was made of thick branches with a few dead leaves still attached, and its eyes were emotionless orbs. It inspected the room, then dipped its head in acknowledgment.

"Fantastic," Meriwether said, then yelled toward the door leading outside, "Chester, it's safe to come in now, you coward!"

The big man from Meriwether's house entered the kitchen. "I ain't a coward."

Meriwether grinned. "Sure you aren't."

"Besides," Chester whined, pointing at the stick man, "you got those things."

Meriwether smirked. "Calm down, big fella. I was only teasing. Get them and get moving. Miles to go and all that." The big man nodded and followed the stick man into the living room. "Carlton wants to savor this moment, but I have business to attend to. Patrick, you'll be coming with us."

"Where are you taking me?" Jameson asked.

"I'm going to make you watch as Nicholas slashes Dawn's throat. Your God will do nothing to stop it, I'm afraid. That's just the first step, my pet. I'll force you to watch *everything* and then you'll realize how powerless your little God is."

Chester returned with Molly Gary and Rachel Warren's bodies thrown over his broad shoulders. A stick man followed him, carrying the unconscious forms of Jaime Alcorn, Carly Schrock, and Karrie Showalter.

"What about them?" I asked. "You said you didn't enjoy killing."

"I don't," Meriwether said, "but I have plans for them. I discovered how to control vampires a long time ago, but what they are and how they work remain a mystery." He pointed at Barlow. "I'll feed them to the little beast. He will turn them. They call it 'giving the gift,' but I will be the one receiving the present. I will *finally* learn how vampires work and where they come from."

I had a sinking feeling in my gut. "What about us?"

Meriwether's head swiveled to Jodie, his neck turning just a little too far to be considered normal. "I have no use for Jodie. She could muck up the ceremony and make a mess of things." He turned and removed his glasses, staring at me with unblinking eyes. "As for you, Sam Harlan, a man such as yourself presents an interesting opportunity for study. But…"

I was afraid of the answer. "But what?"

"You simply *aren't* worth the effort."

"You said you wouldn't kill me."

He shook his head. "I said I wouldn't lay a finger on you, and I shan't."

I swallowed hard. "Let Jodie go, too. She won't be a problem."

Meriwether raised an eyebrow. "She won't?"

"She's offered you no threat," Jameson said.

"True," Meriwether said to Jameson. "But she greatly offended my host with her churlish attitude, and let us not forget her pathetic band of losers. No, Carlton would love to make you suffer, but frankly, she's not worth my time, either. She is just one more loose end to clean up. Like Harlan."

"If you want me to beg," Jameson said, swallowing hard, "I'll beg."

"Of course you would. That's what makes this so delicious. Little beast, bring the girl and the priest." Meriwether snapped his fingers as Chester and one of the stick men reentered the kitchen and pointed in my direction. "Kill Harlan and the Rexford bitch. Meet us when you're done."

"You said you wouldn't lay a finger," I said.

"I won't." Meriwether pointed to the stick man. "It will." He threw his head back and laughed. "I can't *believe* you fell for that. There's a sucker born every minute."

"Wait," I said. "What about Callie?"

Meriwether spun and faced me, his wide smile displaying his teeth. "Did I forget about the Sister? I said I would hurt her if you *didn't* break the medallion, but I never said I *wouldn't* hurt her if you *did*. No, I will break her, just as I'll break dear Patrick. When they've finally given up their faith? It will be … exquisite."

Chapter Sixteen

Meriwether left as the stick man grabbed me by the throat. I tried to resist, but the thing was just as strong as the one that had attacked us in the hotel. I tried to grab its chest, but it wrapped its left arm around me, pinning my arms to my sides as its right hand squeezed my throat with inhuman strength.

I panicked. The stick man was preventing me from breathing, but it was also pushing against the arteries in my neck, and I knew that if it continued much longer, I wouldn't have to worry about a lack of oxygen to my lungs.

I'd have no oxygen to my brain.

My vision was swimming when I pulled back just enough to loosen its grasp. My heart was hammering in my chest and my ears were ringing, but blood rushed to my head for a second and my vision cleared.

Chester held Jodie against the kitchen cabinet next to the sink. He grabbed Jodie by the arm, removed a kitchen knife from a wooden block next to the sink, and was busily trying to put it to Jodie's neck.

Jodie struggled, kicking and biting at Chester, but the big man simply overpowered her. His mouth was stretched back in a crazy leer and his face was practically glowing. He clearly enjoyed her struggle. The knife was long and thin, more of a boning knife, and he stabbed the point into Jodie's shoulder.

When she screamed, Chester looked euphoric.

It stirred an anger in me and I pushed against the stick man, but the golem was stronger and it clamped back down on my neck.

My vision swam again and I tried to kick the stick man. It was like kicking a tree stump, for all the good it accomplished. I was getting lightheaded and black spots appeared before my eyes. I saw

Chester stab at Jodie's face, leaving a bloody gash in her cheek.

She turned to look at me and whispered something, then Chester was slashing at her face and she was screaming and screaming.

I was desperate to break free. My head felt like it was going to explode and there was a roaring in my ears. I batted at the stick man, but my energy was fading. The last thing I saw before everything went black was the stick man's giant eyes, its rectangular pupils like two black slits staring into an unyielding abyss.

* * *

The darkness was absolute.

There was neither sound nor shape nor form. It was both peaceful and terrifying, and it went on for an eternity.

I heard a little girl's voice in the void. The words were unrecognizable, but it was the tone more than anything that stabbed at my heart. The girl was terrified. For me.

Something nagged at me, something that my mind couldn't quite work around. Father Jameson said that humans have free will.

What did that truly mean? And, more importantly, why did it matter? Clearly I was somewhere else.

Nothing really matters anymore, does it?

Except...

Free will. What a funny thing.

I'd never really considered it before. Jameson said that free will was something that separated us from demons.

The attack in the diner had changed my life. What decisions had I made since? Jack had pushed me to follow in his footsteps, but he'd been manipulating me, both by words and by mental pushes from the vampire essence he had absorbed over the years.

Jack had left me everything he owned, a small fortune in silver and gold, and urged me to settle down, finally free of Silas Harlan.

Instead, I'd followed in Jack's footsteps and almost died in Marshalltown as a result.

Was it really my decision? Was I still suffering from a lingering desire to please him? Was it Jack's influence?

Inside me burned the essence of Jimmy Munzinger, my first vampire kill. I'd staked him on the floor of my house in Arcanum. He wasn't my last. I'd killed Silas, too, after Jack had tortured him with silver, slashing away at him like a maddened butcher. I'd killed Jack, too, after he'd changed.

I'd killed my wife. My daughter.

I'd killed Ignacio Santiago, finally, in Marshalltown, after I'd lost almost the entire Mendoza family.

I'd killed the vampire Jodie's coven had captured.

It wasn't as many kills as Jack, but I carried each within me, an insatiable hunger that gnawed and burned and was still changing me.

That was before I died, strangled by an animated bundle of sticks.

What a shitty way to go.

Jodie had whispered something to me before the world went black.

What was it? What did she say?

It seemed important. I searched my memory until the word came to me.

Rise.

That simple command took hold in my mind as the vampire essence flooded through me.

The blackness pressed against me, offering to take away my remaining thoughts, but I could have sworn I heard an old man's voice telling me to get it done.

No. I have free will. I'm going to survive this. I'm going to save Callie and I'm going to kill Carlton Meriwether.

The more I thought about it, the stronger I felt, until I opened my eyes and saw the stick man still throttling me.

Only seconds had passed and the thing was still trying to kill me, but I felt a rush of strength and broke free of it.

I screamed incoherently, and Chester turned to glare at me as I broke the stick man's arms with a crack, and then the stick man was scrabbling to get away from me.

The thing hardly had time to move before I rushed it and grabbed for the heart at its center, tearing away branches in a frantic bid to reach the magic animating it.

The stick man's head jerked back and forth and it fell against the wooden floor. When it did, it exposed the heart and I took the opportunity to squash it so hard with my boot that blood and viscera exploded across the floor, soaking the leg of my blue jeans in crimson goo.

I don't know how I knew, but as surely as I knew that the sun rises in the east and sets in the west, I was certain Haagenti was watching me through those amber goat eyes.

I also knew, somehow, that the demon was enraged.

Then I moved on to Chester. The big man was slashing and stabbing at Jodie's stomach, but he staggered back as I grabbed him, knocking his head into the cabinet and splitting the cabinet door in half, sending dishes and bowls crashing to the floor around us.

Chester slashed the knife against my trench coat, but I jerked back and smashed my fist into the big man's mouth. There was a crunch as his green teeth shattered, and I felt the thrill of wounding my enemy. I almost didn't notice the stabbing pain in my knuckles, and it didn't matter anyway because I was punching the man's face over and over until blood sprayed from his broken and ruined nose.

I cocked my fist back as he screamed in a nasal voice, "Son of a bitch! I'm going to kill you!"

He tried to knee me in the crotch, but I shoved him back against the cabinet with everything I had left. He struck so hard that the doors of the nearby cabinets sprang open and spilled their china all over the counter and floor.

Chester stared at me in shock, and I took the opportunity to grab his head by the sides and spin his head like a basketball, breaking his neck with a satisfying snap.

The big man dropped to the floor, his mouth opening and closing like a fish, then he went still and the room filled with the smell of his bowels.

* * *

I slipped and slid through the broken dishes to Jodie. She was bleeding from a dozen slashes and punctures, some extensive, but none appeared life-threatening.

As long as I can stop the bleeding.

There was a pair of holes in her left cheek that leaked sheets of blood down her face, but she opened her eyes and nodded at me.

Then the hunger hit.

I hadn't eaten since earlier in the day and I'd almost forgotten about it. What came rushing up from my core wasn't something I could ever forget. Wave after wave roiled my stomach. The smell of blood filled the room and I dropped to my hands and knees, sniffing at Jodie's face like a dog.

What the hell am I doing?

It was like watching someone else. I kept telling myself to stop, but my tongue flicked out and lapped at the blood on Jodie's face.

Bliss I had never dreamed possible enveloped me and I licked faster. The blood was hot and salty and burned the back of my throat as I swallowed.

The vampire essence in me went wild. I'd have gotten less of a reaction throwing a bucket of chum into a shark tank. A fire built inside as the vampire part of me stretched its metaphysical legs and declared it good.

My strength returned in seconds, my body healing itself, and then I saw Jodie cringe, trying to pull away from me.

No!

I rolled and vomited fresh blood onto the floor, splashing against Chester's dead body. I choked out a scream that made Jodie wince.

"Sam," she croaked. "Sam!"

I turned to her and shouted, "I'm dead. I'm dead!"

Jodie managed the ghost of a smile. "You're *not* dead."

It was like a splash of cold water against my face. "I'm *not* dead?"

Jodie shook her head and coughed bloody bubbles from her mouth. "I woke the thing inside you. It was the only way to help."

"Oh, thank God." I rolled onto my back and stared at the white paneled ceiling. "*Thank God.*" My lungs pumped like bellows and I savored the cool air, gathering my fill, then said, "I thought the golem had killed me and I'd turned—"

"I didn't have the power to stop them," Jodie managed. "I thought maybe you could..." She nodded at Chester's body. "It worked."

The beast within me slithered back down into the darkest reaches of my soul, making itself at home again, and I was left cold and frightened. "I—I didn't know what was happening." I shivered in the cold air rolling in through the outside door.

"Sam," Jodie said. "I can't ... can't..."

I rolled over and looked at her. She was pale and her eyes were rolling back in her head. I had to do something. "I'll be right back."

She nodded, then leaned against the cabinets and closed her eyes.

I staggered to my feet, slipping on ceramic shards from the broken plates, and made my way to the door. I had to step over Chester's dead body, resisting the stab of anger that made me want to stomp the dead man's face to mush.

I found Callie's backup medical pack hidden behind the driver's seat, grabbed it, and stopped on the way back to the kitchen to retrieve the Ingram that Barlow had thrown to the ground. I slung it over my shoulder and hurried back to check on Jodie.

Her breathing was shallow and the pulse in her neck was racing. I leaned over her and said, "Stay with me."

I fumbled with the pack. My hands were clumsy and my fingers useless, so I dumped the contents on the kitchen counter. It took a moment, but I successfully pierced the tube of superglue. "This is going to burn," I said, "but it *will* stop the bleeding."

She opened her eyes. "What if you don't?"

"You've lost a lot of blood. You could go into shock."

She licked her lips. "I don't want to die."

"That's a good place to start." I raised her sweater to expose her surprisingly muscular stomach. Two deep slashes accounted for most of the bleeding, so I squirted glue in the edge of one of them and pinched it shut. Smoke rose as the glue set and Jodie grunted, slapping at my hand. I ignored her and worked my way across the wound, then paused long enough to ask, "How are you doing?"

"I would have been better off dead," she said.

"Hang in there." I started on the second gash. She moaned several times but held relatively still while I finished gluing it shut. "I need to work on the others."

"Ugh," she said, closing her eyes and gritting her teeth. "It *hurts.*"

"I *know.*" I pulled her sweater back down and moved the neckband to expose her shoulder. There was a deep puncture above her clavicle where the knife had cut through muscle, and I glued it shut and hoped for the best.

The wounds to her face presented a problem, as the glue *might* hold the wounds shut but would leave nasty scars. "You need to sit up."

She opened one eye. "I need to rest for a bit."

"You can rest later." I glued the skin together while she

kicked at the floor, sending broken china spinning in all directions. I cleaned the wounds as best I could with antiseptic wipes. When the alcohol had dried, I covered them with butterfly tape, just in case, and handed her three pills from the medical pack. "Swallow these."

She stared at the pills in my hand. "What are they?"

"Antibiotics and something for the pain." I grabbed a glass from the floor and filled it with water from the Kormans' refrigerator dispenser.

Jodie wolfed down the pills and drained the cup in one long gulp, coughing and sputtering at the end. "Those taste horrible."

"It should help with any infections," I said. A little color had returned to her face and she finally opened both eyes. "We have to go after Meriwether."

"You—you can't be serious," she said, her eyes widening. "You saw what he did. What he is."

"He's got Callie," I said. "And Jameson. He's also got your coven members. The living ones, at least."

She shook her head and winced in pain. "He's not human."

"I know," I said. "He's a demon. Haagenti."

"I can't—I can't deal with that."

"You must," I insisted. "We can't abandon our people."

She looked away. "I don't know how to deal with … with *that*."

I understood. I could barely comprehend the threat a vampire posed, let alone a demon, but Haagenti had Callie, and I would stop at nothing to get her back. "Jodie, I'm going to tell you something a wise old man once told me. *Anything* can be killed. I know you care about your people and I know you want to save them. I'll kill that demon and send it back to Hell, I promise you, and nothing on this earth will stop me."

She stared up at me with a funny look on her face, then said, "I'll help."

I smiled wolfishly. "Goddamned right you will."

* * *

Jodie staggered to her feet.

"Can you walk?" I asked.

She took a faltering step and I caught her before she collapsed. "No."

"Let me help," I said. I carried her to my truck and deposited her in the passenger seat, careful not to jostle her too much.

"I need you to do something," Jodie said. "Go to the shed behind the house. There's a room in the corner with a metal box about this big." She held up her hands to indicate something roughly the size of a breadbox. "It's covered in writing. You may have to hold it up to the light to see. Bring it to me."

"What is it?"

She closed her eyes, then said carefully, "It's the only help I have left to give."

I made my way to the shed behind the house. I clutched the Ingram, expecting to get jumped by some nasty thing that Meriwether had left, but the farm was quiet. The shed was dark and I flipped the switch next to the door. The overhead lights flared on, but I found them far from comforting.

I rushed down the hallway, past the room where Callie had been imprisoned and past the rooms where the vampire and I had been held captive, until I reached a door at the end of the hallway that led west.

I kicked the door open and found myself in a small shelf-lined room. Plastic boxes were piled to the ceiling, but I finally found the metal box on a shelf near the floor in the corner. It was heavy, close to ten pounds, and made of a dull material that appeared to be lead.

I didn't see any writing on it, then remembered what Jodie had said about it. I stood in the middle of the room and held the box up to eye level. The faintest hint of symbols glowed in the light. They weren't etched into the metal. It was more like they floated on top.

I hurried back to the truck and handed the box to Jodie. She took it and cradled it between her breasts.

"That thing will help us?" I asked, frowning.

"As much as your gun," she said, nodding at the Ingram that hung from my neck.

"It better be a magical box of kick-ass."

She squinted at me. "It's a magic wand."

I smiled, and when she didn't smile back, I said, "What is it really?"

"A magic wand," she repeated with a steely-eyed gaze.

"I thought you were joking."

"The coven prepared this months ago," she said, fighting to hold her head upright. "It was the last major piece of magic we created." She sniffled a little. "This is the last I have of them."

"We'll save them. I promise." I slammed the door and got in the driver's seat, started the truck, and backed out before gunning the engine and heading east.

Chapter Seventeen

Henry answered on the first ring. "Tell me you're gone. Tell me you left."

"It's a demon," I said. "The man who took Callie is a demon."

"Damn it," Henry growled. "I was afraid of that. You steer clear of this thing. I'm loading up now."

"There's no time," I said. Jodie was staring at me as I pushed the truck to its limit. "I've got to kill it."

"You *can't* kill it," Henry said. "Demons are immortal."

"What *can* I do?"

"It's got to be exorcised. Once the demon is gone, it can't come back. Not for a long spell, anyway. It takes them a hell of a lot of energy to break through. No pun intended."

"How am I supposed to exorcise a demon?" I asked.

"First you need to find a priest—"

"I've got that covered."

"Really? Well, once the priest has exorcised the demon, kill the host. You got a problem with that?"

"I don't think that will be a problem," I said. "That won't be a problem at *all*."

* * *

I came to a screeching halt in front of Meriwether's darkened house. "Looks empty," I said to Jodie.

She had fallen silent on our way to Monticello but opened her eyes long enough to inspect the house and make an oddly delicate gesture with her left hand. "It's empty."

I growled in frustration. "Where are they?"

"I think he's gone to…"

"Where?"

"Allerton Park," she said. "It's west of town."

I drove, following her instructions, as she explained how Robert Allerton had built a European-style estate and filled it with hedge mazes and statues before eventually donating it to the University of Illinois.

"Why there?" I asked doubtfully.

"The place has a certain … energy," she said. "If the demon needs more energy to heal Nicky, that's the best place to do it."

Something had been troubling me. "Why didn't he kill Dorothy there?"

"There's an energy there. A certain natural magic. It's built on a flood plain, and it's beautiful and remote. That's probably why Allerton found it so appealing. It's a thin spot between our world and…"

"And what?"

"And whatever comes next," Jodie said softly.

"That's bad?"

"It might give him more power, but a spot that thin comes with risks. Things happen there. Things are *seen* there."

We continued on in silence. The snow had picked up, changing from a spit to a flurry. "Like what?" I finally asked.

"The place is rumored to be full of snakes and deer. Bobcats have been reported, but there have also been other sightings. People claim to have seen an eight-foot-tall hairy beast—"

"You have got to be kidding. A Bigfoot?"

Jodie grunted. "That's not worries me."

"A Bigfoot doesn't worry you? What does?"

"I'm worried that Carlton, or the thing in him, has called up something worse."

"Something worse than Bigfoot?" I said, trying not to sound too skeptical.

Jodie grunted. "You've never been anywhere like this place. It's dangerous."

"More dangerous than a demon possessing the body of a witch?"

She sighed and pointed her finger. "There's the turnoff."

I hit the brakes just in time to make the right turn onto the narrow road that led to the park entrance. Towering pines lined the road and my headlights dimmed, forcing me to drive slower.

Creepy.

"Did it get darker?" I asked, glancing in the sideview mirror.

Jodie ignored me. "Stop the truck."

I stopped just as we came to a bridge. "What's going on?"

"I have to check something." She held up her hand and made an elaborate series of gestures. "Okay."

A tingle ran down my spine. "What the hell was that?"

"A small charm guards the river. I removed it."

"What kind of charm?"

"If we had passed through, we wouldn't have seen things as they *really* are."

I had no idea what she was talking about. "Good to know."

She settled back against her seat and closed her eyes again. "Drive."

I drove past several gravel patches where tourists could park and walk the trails before I finally came to an intersection, where Jodie instructed me to turn left.

"Does this place have any kind of security?" I asked.

"It belongs to the University of Illinois and Carlton sits on the board of directors. The security gets sent home with extra pay when the park is being used by the covens," Jodie said. "The place will be abandoned if he is here."

We passed a small parking lot to the left but she insisted I keep going. I followed the winding road as it split to avoid a tree and passed something that Jodie described as a sunken amphitheater until we reached a point deep in the woods.

Three black Dodge Durangos were parked against the side of the road, and Jodie said, "I told you. Pull over and turn off your lights."

I stopped and flipped off the headlights. "There's nothing *there.*"

"It's down that path," she said, pointing to a spot in the darkness.

I squinted, barely able to make out the gap between the trees that led deeper into the park.

"Can you make it?"

"I'll—I'll try."

I got out and pulled my trench coat tighter. The temperature had plunged into the low teens. The moon was a barely visible distant crescent over the treetops. Most of the trees were bare of leaves, except for a few stragglers that hadn't yet dropped, and the smell of wet and rotting leaves burned my sinuses.

The trail was difficult to navigate. Thick roots caught my boots with every footstep and I stumbled and jerked around, aiming the Ingram at the darkness around us. The going was slow but we were soon far from the truck.

"We're sitting ducks out here," I whispered.

"I know," Jodie whispered back. She pointed left at a fork in the path. "That way."

We followed the left path, and within a dozen yards, we noticed a glow in the distance. "Is that it?" I whispered.

She nodded. "There's a stone altar in the middle of the clearing for ceremonial purposes. We must be careful."

"Careful?" I whispered. I didn't mention how foolish it was for us to interrupt a demon in the middle of a magical forest.

She stopped, held up the box, and whispered something. I felt a now-familiar tingle up my spine as she opened the box and withdrew a small wooden branch that had been stripped of its bark.

"That's it?" I whispered. "*That's* your magic wand?"

Before she could reply, there was a rustling in the bushes. I smelled something like the musk of a lion I had smelled once at a zoo and heard a growl so low that it was more vibration than anything else.

An animal approached from the woods, but it wasn't like any animal I had seen before. It appeared to be some kind of Chinese dog, the kind printed on restaurant menus.

That was, if a Chinese dog could stand five-foot-high at the shoulders and glow a deep iridescent blue.

"What the hell is that thing?" I whispered.

"Don't move," Jodie warned, so softly I could barely hear. "Not an inch. It's a Fu Dog."

I steadied myself and the Fu Dog held its ground, watching us with eyes like giant rubies that pulsed with energy.

"If I shoot," I said quietly, "they'll know we're here."

"If we *don't* stop it," Jodie said softly, "it's going to rip our spines out and eat our livers. Fu Dogs *love* liver."

The Fu Dog's head rolled to the side and it opened its mouth impossibly wide. Razor-sharp teeth glinted in the moonlight. "This is magic, isn't it?"

"Have you ever seen anything like that in *nature*?" Jodie whispered bitterly. "Allerton bought dozens of Fu Dog statues, but one of them wasn't *just* a statue. Silver bullets won't stop it. Only magic will."

"What are you waiting for?" I asked. "Kill it."

"It's going to take every bit of power in this wand. I won't be of much use to you after that."

The Fu Dog growled again, and it sounded like the rumbling of a freight train. "Maybe we can run for it."

"I *can't* run," Jodie said. "And even if I could, it's faster than us."

"How do you know so much about Fu Dogs?"

"I'm the one who figured out how to activate it," she said. "I never thought anybody would be stupid enough to actually do it."

Electric sparks zapped between the Fu Dog's teeth like the old-fashioned bug zapper that used to hang from my porch back in Arcanum. A wave of bitter-smelling ozone rolled our way. The Fu Dog took a step forward, then another, then it was moving so fast it became a ghostly blur.

Jesus!

Jodie yanked me to the ground as the Fu Dog sailed over us. I struggled to help Jodie up as the Fu Dog landed hard and clawed the dirt and leaves before spinning like a cat and turning back to us, its mouth wide and teeth sparking like a thunderstorm in the spring.

The smell of ozone was overpowering and there was another smell, too, a fetid stench of rotten meat that turned my stomach. Its eyes flared until they were red lanterns that lit the Fu Dog's face in a devilish glow. It sprang forward and its paws kicked up leaves and dirt in a rooster tail behind it.

We're dead. We are so dead!

Jodie pushed me to the side and raised her magic wand, shouting words I didn't understand, and the woods exploded in sound and light as a cone of fire three feet wide at the tip of the wand and ten feet wide at the end struck the Fu Dog.

It was like an atomic bomb going off. I closed my eyes and held my hand in front of my face, but I could see through my eyelids like some kind of weird X-ray.

The sound was deafening. I'd once had the unfortunate luck to have an aerial bomb go off just above my head, an accident at a Fourth of July fireworks show when I was a kid. That aerial bomb didn't hold a candle to the fury that Jodie unleashed.

The Fu Dog didn't simply explode—it was erased from existence. The light died down and I blinked, trying to adjust my eyes to the dark, except it *wasn't* dark. The leaves and twigs in the path of the cone of fire had been vaporized, but the wake of Jodie's spell had ignited pockets of dead branches in the Fu Dog's vicinity. Even the muddy leaves nearby were smoldering.

Jodie groaned and collapsed against me. "They know we're here."

"You think?"

"What should we do?"

I never got a chance to answer because it was then that Barlow arrived, drawn to the explosion, and smashed me across the face with inhuman strength.

* * *

My head thunk-thunked against tree roots as Barlow dragged me to the clearing by my leg. Jodie was hanging from Barlow's shoulder. She twisted and shook in a futile attempt to escape his grasp. I kicked at him, but it was like kicking stone.

"*Stop* struggling," Barlow said. "You're only making it *worse*."

"Let us go," I said. "You can fight this."

Barlow didn't respond. He just kept walking briskly like he was out for an evening stroll.

Meriwether was waiting for us in the clearing with a leering grin on his face, my Kimber still tucked in his black slacks. He wore a black sweater as his only protection from the cold.

Barlow deposited us in front of him like a pair of prize trophies.

Meriwether's coven wore black hooded cloaks and was arranged in a semicircle in front of a roaring bonfire. In front of the fire sat a white stone altar as big as a door, carefully balanced upon two large boulders. Dawn McKie was stretched across the altar, tied by thick ropes. She was naked and shivering and clearly terrified. The remaining members of Jodie's coven knelt in the dirt, their heads bowed. Jameson and Callie were lashed to wooden poles driven into the ground at each end of the altar.

Nicky stood next to the altar, awkwardly holding the knife from Meriwether's basement. He was staring at Dawn's breasts in obvious fascination.

I wondered if Nicky knew the young woman he ogled was his sister. Given the hungry look on his face, I wasn't sure it mattered.

There was a creaking noise from the edge of the clearing and I caught sight of the remaining stick man swiveling its head to watch everything with its lidless eyes. Snowflakes fell from the sky, small and perfectly formed. Meriwether held up his hands so they could land gently on his palms. "Marvelous," he cried out. "It's simply *marvelous*. I love snow. It reminds me of home."

"That's because you live in the eternal cold, away from God's warmth," Jameson shouted.

"Clever," Meriwether said, rolling his eyes. "You continue to amuse me, Patrick."

There was a long silence as the fire crackled and popped. The flames licked skyward and sent a stream of embers riding on currents of hot air. Jodie's coven members were shaking, and most of them were sobbing quietly.

Meriwether regarded them coolly, then asked me, "What happened to Chester?"

I raised my chin and gave him my most intimidating stare. "That redneck hillbilly? I broke his fucking neck."

A murmur arose from Meriwether's people, but he just smiled and shook his head. "That's a shame. He wasn't the smartest man, but he *did* serve his purpose."

I nodded at the members of his coven. "That's all these people are to you, isn't it? Just interchangeable widgets to serve your purpose."

"Nice try," Meriwether said with a grin. "They know what I am. They know I honor my promises. They *worship* me."

"They don't understand what you ask of them," Jameson said. "They haven't realized—"

Meriwether flicked his hand, palm up, and Jameson gagged on his own tongue, banging his head backward against the wooden pole. "That's just about enough out of you, Patrick. What can you possibly say that will sway them? What can you offer? Your God? What has He done for anybody lately? Where are His blessings?"

Jameson choked out, "Look around you." He coughed and cleared his throat, then addressed Meriwether's coven. "You stand in the middle of His creation and you think He has abandoned you? He has given us the greatest gift of all. Free will."

"Free will?" Meriwether said as the fire continued to crackle. "How worthless. Where has free will gotten you, old man? Trussed up like a turkey? What about the Sister? She's married to God, isn't she? What a letdown that must be, eh?"

Callie, who had silently watched their exchange, spoke up. "You mock what you don't understand. Each of us has sin within us and the free will to ask for forgiveness. That's something you'll *never* understand."

Meriwether sighed. "Your pretty words have no meaning here. The only thing that matters is the strength of my will. I'll finish with Nicholas and then I'll feed the Rexford woman to the vampire. Sooner or later I'll discover the truth about vampires, even if I have to feed every one of them to the little beast."

He squinted at me. "And, if that doesn't work, I'll tear Harlan apart and see what makes him tick." His eyes narrowed and he focused his attention on me. "Oh, I know what you did, Harlan. My golem told me. You touched the beast within you. I can't *wait* to play with it."

I struggled against Barlow's iron grip. "I'll do it again, you bastard. I'll call it up and rip your damned head off."

"Oh, I'm sure you'll *try*," Meriwether said, "but I doubt you can manage it. You got lucky. Now you're just a helpless little man. What a shame, too. I know so much about your family."

A chill that had nothing to do with the bitter cold ran up my spine. "What?"

"As I said, knowledge *is* power," Meriwether said. "I've watched the vampire hunters for a *very* long time. That kind of knowledge is—"

"I know all about Jack," I said. "I'm the one who killed him."

Meriwether tilted his head back in delight. "Ah, I'd wondered about that. Thank you for that piece of information. That connects many dots. But I *wasn't* talking about Jack Harlan."

"Don't listen to him," Jameson said. "Never trust a demon."

"I *could* help you," Meriwether mused. "I could tell you things about your family that would finally explain so much. Heh. I could, but I won't." He turned to the altar, where Nicholas still held the knife. "It's time, Nicholas."

* * *

Nicky raised the knife and took a halting step closer to the altar. The tip of the knife jerked back and forth and Nicky turned back to Meriwether. "I don't think I wanna do this."

"It's just a game," Meriwether said reassuringly. "You *love* games, and after this game, you'll be right as rain."

"It doesn't *seem* like a game," Nicky said. "It seems like—like a *bad* thing."

"It's a *small* bad thing that leads to a *good* thing," Meriwether said, his voice rising in frustration. "This should cure you."

Nicky blinked, watching his father with eyes full of reproach. "You told me I wasn't sick. You told me I was just the way I was s'posed to be."

Meriwether's face went blank, losing any semblance of expression, and the voice that spoke was Haagenti's. "You suffered brain damage at birth, Nicholas. This blood sacrifice will heal that damage and make you whole and will release me of my debt."

"Why are you talking funny?" Nicky asked. "Why are we here? I don't like this place. It's *cold*."

Before Meriwether could respond, I shouted, "That's not your dad, Nicky. It's a demon, and it wants you to kill your sister."

Nicky's eyes widened. "I don't understand *any* of this. I just wanna go home. It's *scary* here."

"Don't listen to *him*," Meriwether said angrily. "Slit the bitch's throat. I have things to do and this is a waste of my time."

"Free will," I said, as the snowfall turned heavier and the thick flakes sizzled and spattered as they struck the roaring fire. "You've got free will, Nicky. *You* make your own choices. If you slit her throat, terrible things will happen!"

"Do it," Meriwether ordered in a hard voice that had lost all its humanity.

Nicky stood poised over Dawn and slowly lowered the blade to her throat, putting just enough pressure on the tip to cause a fine bead of crimson to trickle down Dawn's throat.

There was a collective intake of breath among the coven members. A humming thrummed through the earth, making my feet vibrate, and Barlow tensed, tightening his grasp on my shoulder.

"Daddy?" Nicky said. His hand was shaking and he sounded on the verge of tears. "I don't wanna do this."

He knows. He feels guilt! He didn't understand before, but now he knows it's not a game.

"Don't do it," I shouted. "It's your choice. Don't let him make it for you."

"What are you waiting for?" Meriwether asked. "Why don't you kill her?"

"Free will is a bitch," I said to Meriwether. "We all make our own choices. The Father is right. You don't understand free will because you don't have it."

As I watched Nicky struggle with the knife, I had finally realized what Jameson had been trying to tell me. Everyone had a choice. Nicky. Callie. Meriwether.

Even Jameson had a choice, and it was finally clear to me what the priest had planned.

Haagenti was the one who lacked free will.

And, because of the demon's control, so did Milford Barlow.

Meriwether glared at me. "I'm going to enjoy killing you, stupid little ape. Your talk of free will is worthless. Kill him, little beast."

"Free will," I said as Barlow wrapped his hands around my neck. "It's the one thing you'll never understand, you predictable smug bastard. Father Jameson!"

As Barlow began to throttle me, Jameson murmured the words I was betting he had been preparing since leaving the Kormans' farm, words that would hold a greater effect in a thin spot between worlds.

Jameson unmade the spell holding Milford Barlow captive.

Chapter Eighteen

There was a powerful buzzing against the back of my neck and the sensation of a million ants crawled over my skin as the spell collapsed. I grabbed Barlow and threw him like a sack of potatoes across the clearing, where he slammed into Meriwether. The blow sent them both staggering back against the stone altar.

There was a moment of complete silence as Barlow recovered. The little man spotted the blood at Dawn's neck and he went wild, shoving Nicky aside and going for the young woman's throat.

The matronly woman from Meriwether's house stood, threw off her hooded cloak, and grabbed for Meriwether to help him up. Barlow was busy lapping at the blood on Dawn's neck, but he sensed the movement, saw the woman helping Meriwether to his feet. The vampire sprang like a cat, crossing the distance between them in the wink of an eye, and shoved his fist through the woman's meaty chest.

The woman didn't even have time to scream. Barlow yanked his hand back and it made a sickly wet squelch. The vampire raised his handful of meat, fat, and blood to his face and smeared it over his lips in orgasmic delight.

Barlow's eyes went solid black, the way I'd seen vampire eyes do when they lost control.

Not good!

Everyone screamed as the reality of a ravenous vampire set in. Both covens looked on in shock, but I used the opportunity to rush to Jameson's side and fumble with the ropes that held him to the pole.

"Look out!" Jameson shouted as a ball of fire hurtled across the clearing. Lisa Doll was pointing at me and chanting, the hood of her cloak thrown back and her beautiful face screwed up with hate.

I ducked down and the flames washed over my trench coat. Jameson took the brunt of it. The flames only lasted a few seconds, but when I glanced up, Jameson's hair was burning. He yelped as I stood and beat at the fire with the sleeve of my trench coat, finally managing to untie him with my other hand.

The screaming continued behind me and I heard Jameson grunt a warning. I turned to see the stick man lumbering across the clearing, heading for us, its eyes glinting in the light from the fire. It was closing in on us when Lisa sent another fireball swooshing across the open space. The fire accidentally struck the stick man, setting it ablaze, and it fell to the ground as the fire consumed it.

My heart soared, but Jameson grunted again. I pulled him down just in time as Meriwether sent a bolt of lightning that buzzed over my head and made the hair on the back of my neck stand up.

People were crying out in fear and pain, but I tilted Jameson's head down and checked his scalp. Most of his hair was gone and the skin was either charred or waxy. The smell of burnt hair and skin made me gag.

"Don't worry about me," Jameson croaked. "Stop Haagenti."

I nodded and turned back to the clearing, only to watch in horror as Barlow slashed his claws across Rachel Warren's belly, gutting her in a spray of blood.

Meriwether waved his hands in the air, trying desperately to regain control of the vampire. Jodie was crouched on the dirt and she shouted something incomprehensible. Meriwether grimaced and I realized she was blocking his attempts.

Callie screamed as one of Meriwether's coven, a bald-headed fat man with deep hollow eyes, grabbed at her and started ramming her head against the wooden pole. I grabbed a tree branch from the ground near the fire. It was as thick as my wrist and nearly three feet long. I ran to Callie, swinging it like a bat. It connected with the man's head, and there was a sickening crunch that vibrated up my arms. The man fell to the ground, his head caved in. Gray brain matter covered the end of the branch and I dropped it in disgust.

I heard a whistling noise that grew louder, and then a sharp stinging erupted from my shoulder. I screamed and looked down to find a foot-long bone spear sticking out of my shoulder through my trench coat, right below the collarbone.

"Sam!" Callie screamed. "Untie me!"

There was another whistling sound, and I dropped to the

ground as something flew over my head. A tall young woman stood near the fire, holding a stack of bone spears and chanting, preparing to throw another my way.

It was lucky for me that Molly Gary tackled the woman and knocked her back into the bonfire. The woman's cloak caught on fire and she screamed and thrashed, sending huge clouds of embers soaring into the sky. She screamed bloody murder and almost managed to get up, but Molly stomped the woman's chest and sent her back into the fire. The woman fell still as the fire consumed her.

An old man with a shock of gray hair jumped on Molly and they went sprawling to the ground. I lost sight of them as the fighting in the clearing escalated. So much magic was flying about that it set my teeth on edge, giving me a splitting headache. I tried searching for Meriwether amid the chaos and found Jodie had made it to her knees and was screaming something at the demon. Barlow was ripping through coven members, sending sprays of blood arcing through the air, and I froze at the sight.

"Sam!" Callie yelled.

Her voice, so full of fear and anguish, brought me back to my senses. "*Right*," I yelled back. I made it to my feet and lurched toward her, working by the firelight to untie the knots that held her to the pole.

Jodie slumped to the ground, exhausted or dead, I couldn't tell which, and then Callie said, "Get down."

She pulled me to the ground and I felt a wave of something dark and slimy pass overhead. The sheer alien-ness of it made my stomach clench, and bile started to rise in the back of my throat. "What the—"

"It's Haagenti," Callie said. She looked exhausted, but her eyes were wide, and I saw an expression on her face I'd seen once before in Marshalltown.

She was furious.

I remembered the phone call with Henry.

It has to be exorcised.

Meriwether was preparing more magic when Barlow finished tearing a man I recognized as Del Doll in half, sending Doll's entrails spilling over the ground, then jumped ten feet into the air and landed next to Meriwether, slamming his hand down on Meriwether's right arm with a sickening crack.

The vampire was snarling and snapping at the man, but

Meriwether held his own, beating the vampire back with a ferocious assault using his remaining good hand.

Nicky held his hands over his eyes, stumbling away from the altar, repeating over and over, "I wanna go *home!*"

I ran to his side. "Get out of here, Nicky! Go!"

Nicky stopped and turned to me, his eyes wide. He was sniffling and sobbing. "I don't wanna play anymore."

Poor Nicky. He deserves better than this.

I scooped him up like a child, ran to the edge of the clearing, and deposited him in front of a giant fir tree. "Stay here."

"O—Okay."

Back near the fire, the vampire was a whirlwind of motion, trying to claw or gouge at Meriwether, but Meriwether was, impossibly, fending him off.

Two of Meriwether's coven, a younger man and woman, were attempting to strangle Karrie Showalter. They had their cloaks pulled back? And their faces were masks of fierce determination. Jameson had made it to Karrie's side and beat at the pair, trying to save the young woman.

The battle was useless if we didn't get rid of Haagenti. I hated to do it, but I ran to Jameson and pulled him from the two coven members, although I did manage to kick the older woman in the back near her kidneys, which made her scream and fall forward, clutching herself in agony. That earned me a look of hatred from the man, who growled, "I'm gonna kill you!"

"There's a lot of that going around," I said. The man's cloak had spread open, exposing his naked body, and Karrie kicked him in the balls. The man dropped to the ground and vomited, unable to make good on his threat. Karrie coughed and sputtered, but managed to give me a weak thumbs-up.

"You've got to exorcise the demon," I said to Jameson. "It's our only chance."

He struggled to break free, ready to go to the aid of Jaime Alcorn, who was being attacked by the same old man that had helped the matronly woman in Meriwether's basement. "We can't just—"

"We're all *dead* if you don't," I said.

He continued to struggle, then relaxed against me. "You're right."

I released him just as Meriwether used magic to send Barlow hurtling across the clearing like a cannonball, flying through the snow and smashing through the trees, knocking branches to the ground in a shower of snow and bark.

Jameson took that opportunity to stagger to Meriwether's side and said in a halting voice that grew stronger with each word, "St. Michael the Archangel, defend us in the battle against principalities and powers, against the rulers of the world of darkness and the spirit of wickedness in high places. Carry our prayers to God's throne, that the mercy of the Lord may quickly come and lay hold of the beast, the serpent of old, Satan, and his demons, casting him in chains into the abyss."

Meriwether froze, his mouth drawn back in a snarl. "You *can't.*"

Callie had threaded her way among those who still fought and those who lay dead or dying. "We can and we will," she said. Her voice was as hard as iron, and I shivered when she finished.

A woman in a cloak ran toward Callie, but I caught up with her as she neared the fire and clocked her in the back of the head with my fist. She dropped to the ground and slid through the thin coat of snow now covering the earth until she came to a stop next to the altar. Dawn, still tied to the stone, twisted her head, trying to catch a glimpse of what was happening.

Jameson and Callie stood to the right and left of Meriwether, only a handful of feet from the altar, and they made the sign of the cross, which drove Meriwether crazy. He tried to move, but his feet were rooted to the ground.

The sounds in the clearing died down as Jameson spoke.

"We cast you out in the name and by the power of our Lord Jesus Christ," Jameson thundered, his voice carrying a weight to it that I could actually feel pressing down on me. "We command you, begone and fly far from the Church of God, from the souls made by God in His image and redeemed by the blood of the Lamb."

Meriwether's face stretched, the skin turning white as something within pressed its way out, then he threw his head back and howled like an animal. Some … thing … emerged from his mouth, long and black and snakelike. It plopped on the ground and began squirming away through the snow and mud.

"God of Heaven and earth," Jameson continued, as the air around us crackled with energy, "God of the angels and archangels, God of the patriarchs and prophets, God of the apostles and martyrs, God of the confessors and virgins, God who has power to bestow life after death and rest after toil; we humbly entreat Thy glorious majesty to deliver us by Thy might from every influence of the accursed spirits, from their every evil snare and deception, and to keep us from all harm; through Christ our Lord."

"We beg thee to hear us," Callie said, and her voice rang out like a thousand trumpets. "Amen."

God must have heard.

Light appeared, as pure as the falling snow, and it filled the clearing with its radiance. It was beautiful and terrifying, full of love, but also anger and wrath at the one who dared interfere with God's work.

Ghostlike forms appeared around the edges of the clearing, beings of pure light, and they stared at the demon. I could make out flaming swords and steel-like armor, but the more I tried to see their faces, the less of them I could hold in my mind.

The snakelike form of Haagenti screeched and chittered, and then there was an explosion of sound and light that made Jodie's magic wand look like a firecracker. When I could see again, Haagenti was gone, banished from our earth.

The angels of light slowly faded from view once God's judgment had been passed until the clearing was once again illuminated by the roaring fire that made the snowflakes twinkle.

Jameson groaned in pain and fell to the muddy earth. Callie rushed to his side, but I had other concerns.

Meriwether stood alone, the remaining members of his coven either hurt or frozen with fear. His right arm dangled uselessly at his side. He stared at Nicky, who sat against the tree where I'd left him, still covering his eyes with his hands and mumbling to himself.

I made it to my feet, slipping and sliding in the fresh snow, and approached Meriwether. He looked up and shook his head. "I didn't *mean* for this to happen," he said softly.

I yanked my Kimber from his waist. "I'm sure you didn't."

"I just—just wanted to help my son."

I sighed. "I'm sure you did."

His eyes widened. "It wasn't my fault. The demon *made* me do it."

"I'm not a priest," I said. "I don't care about your conscience. Or your soul. God will judge you accordingly." I raised the Kimber and pointed it at his head.

"Father, tell him I'm not possessed," Meriwether said over

the crackling of the fire. "Tell him. You saw. *Tell him.*"

Those who still lived, including Father Jameson, watched in silence.

"But I'm free," Meriwether pleaded, his eyes fixed on mine. "I'm *free.*"

"You are," I acknowledged, then pulled the trigger and blew the back of Meriwether's head off in a spray of blood, bone, and brain.

* * *

I caught up to Barlow in a ravine not far from the clearing. The little man sat on a tree stump, as still as a statue, a light dusting of snow swirling around him.

He glanced up as I approached. Moonlight sparkled off the snowflakes that clung to the blood stains on his clothes.

Bloody tears ran from the corners of his eyes. "Hello, Samuel."

I stopped short and nodded. "Milford."

The portly little man shook his head. "It was … crazy back there."

"Yes, it was."

"I didn't mean to," he said. "You know that."

The tragic part was that I believed him. "I know."

Barlow sighed. "The blood. It made me crazy. I haven't killed like that in years. After all that time, to have it…"

"I understand now." I stood quietly, watching him, then asked the only question that came to mind. "How did this happen?"

"Eva was dying," Barlow said. His voice caught in his throat. "I brought her to Bement to be with family."

"Jodie?" I asked. "Randy?"

"Nieces and nephews. She wanted to die among them. And…"

"What?"

"It wasn't safe anymore," Barlow said. He wiped at the blood staining his arms. It smeared with snow and turned into scarlet slush against his ice-cold skin. "Do you remember Gloria?"

Gloria Freeman had been a nurse in the fifties before she was turned against her will. I had ventured into her underground lair in the catacombs of Indianapolis, begging her for help in finding Silas.

215

"Yes."

"She'd hidden for years, feeding on the homeless, but after Silas died she seized control of the Indianapolis packs."

"What?"

"Your visit … ignited something in her. She'd controlled her hunger for years, but after she met you, she became…"

"What?" I whispered.

"Wanton," Barlow said, watching me sadly. "She fed indiscriminately. She killed all rivals and named herself Queen. I tried to speak with her, but she demanded I kneel before her."

"You couldn't do it."

"I *wouldn't* do it. I vowed after escaping Silas's grasp that I would never bow to another. She promised I would be tortured if I didn't submit. I gathered Eva and fled that very night."

"Where is Eva now?" I asked.

"She passed in her sleep. Peacefully. We burned her body on the Kormans' farm. I spent the night in Monticello. Meriwether came for me there and caged me before I could escape. He forced me to feed. That was a week ago."

"You killed." It wasn't a question.

He nodded. "First a young man. Meriwether kidnapped him and brought him to me. I don't know how, but Meriwether called the hunger in me. I resisted, but in the end, it was futile. I fed for the first time in years."

I was horrified. "There were more?"

Barlow nodded. "*Many* more. As I fed on them, he … studied me. It was perverse. When he commanded, I obeyed. I didn't understand it then, but now it makes sense."

"He was possessed by a demon," I said.

"A demon," Barlow agreed. "Eighty years after my death and I'm still surprised by the utter stupidity of humanity. I felt it, you know. The demon. It rubbed against me. Even after all I've done, it still felt … *unclean*. Perhaps there's hope for me, Sam. Perhaps I still have some semblance of a soul."

The silence stretched between us and I finally shrugged. "Who knows?"

"I felt the light, Sam. I felt what you did … did you banish it?"

"The Father did."

"I heard a gunshot. You killed Meriwether?"

I shrugged. "He made a pact with a demon."

"Wasn't his soul clean once the demon was banished?"

I shook my head. "Maybe, but unlike the demon, I have free will and I'm not in the forgiveness business."

Barlow sighed. "So that's it, then?"

I thought about it for a moment. "I guess it is."

"I don't mind. I've outlived everything I loved. There's nothing in this world for me. I just pray I'll see Eva in the next."

I raised the Kimber, pointing it at Barlow's chest. "I pray you will, Barlow. If anyone deserves it, you do."

The little man blinked. "Thank you, Samuel. You've been kind. I wish you the best."

"I'm sorry—"

"It's alright. I'm ready."

I hesitated. "I—I don't know if I can do this."

Barlow laughed quietly, a whispered snicker among the trees. "Yes, you can. It might not have been who you were when we first met, but it's who you are now. Jack would be proud."

The gun began to shake and I blinked back tears. "I…"

"Do it," Barlow urged, so softly I could barely hear. "Please."

The Kimber barked and a hole appeared in Barlow's chest, right through his heart. He pitched forward, a peaceful expression on his face, and hit the ground. Nothing happened for a moment, then fire erupted from the back of his chest. The falling snow hissed and sizzled as the flames spread. The light beat against the darkness, illuminating the snow-covered trees.

A surge of black smoke snaked from the burning body and plunged inside me as Barlow's vampire essence joined the rest, burning all the way down to the bottom. A keening echoed against the trees and I realized it was coming from me.

Then it was done and I watched as the fire roared and consumed Barlow's body. In less than a minute, all that was left was a greasy pile of ash and smoldering leaves which I quickly stomped out.

A voice said from behind, "Sam?"

I turned and found Callie, bloody and bruised, leaning against a tree. She looked woozy. She trembled, barely able to stand. "How much did you see?" I asked.

"All of it."

"I had to do it."

"I know."

I approached her and held out my arm, which she gratefully accepted. Together we made our way back to the clearing, where the living and dead waited for us. "You still think I'm a good man?"

She stumbled against the root of a tree that blocked our path, then said, "He knows the choices you've made and why you've made them. I'm sure He will forgive you."

I helped her over the root and up the almost-invisible footpath. "He damned well better. I don't see anyone else rushing to do His dirty work."

* * *

The rest of the night was a blur as we loaded the living and the dead into the vehicles and left the park. Jodie was finally awake and moving around, barking out orders, having assumed control of Meriwether's coven.

I helped Callie and Jameson to my truck and followed the Durangos out of the park and through the country roads to the Kormans' farm.

I turned to Callie along the way and asked, "Are you guys okay?"

"You've already asked," Callie mumbled. "Twice."

I had?

I was exhausted and kept blinking, trying to focus my blurry vision. As an added bonus, my hunger came roaring back. I wanted a rare steak, and every time I thought of it, my stomach growled. Somewhere deep inside me, the vampire essence licked its lips and nodded in approval.

Jameson was leaning against the passenger-side door. He opened one eye and said, "I think I have third-degree burns."

"Sorry, Father. I'll get you some painkillers when we stop."

Jameson was quiet for a moment, then said, "You can call me Patrick. You've earned that right." He closed his eye and settled back into his seat.

I leaned closer to Callie. "Are you going to be okay?"

She stared at the taillights of the SUV in front of us. "The cuts aren't deep."

"They carved symbols over your body," I said. As I spoke, the image of her hanging from the beam in Meriwether's basement came to mind. I remembered how her nipples had stiffened in the cold and how her panties had barely covered her down there.

I pushed those memories deep inside, down where the vampire essence lurked, before my imagination could elaborate on them, and vowed to keep them from *ever* rising again.

Callie turned her head to look at me and said, "My body will heal."

In the darkened cab of the truck, I almost missed the tears in her eyes. "It's not your body I'm worried about."

"How's your shoulder?" she asked.

She had helped me yank the bone spear from my shoulder and had tossed it into the fire before we left the clearing. The wound had clotted, but it throbbed in time with my heartbeat, and I winced with every bump in the road. "My body will heal," I said.

We pulled into the Kormans' drive sometime around three in the morning. Everyone got out of their vehicles and stood looking at each other. Jaime Alcorn was glaring at Lisa Doll, who had somehow survived unscathed. Jodie put her hand on Alcorn's shoulder. Jaime shrugged it off, but he turned to Jodie and said, "You better do something about this. I don't trust them."

Jodie nodded. "Listen, people," she said, her voice ringing out. "What's done is done. The Goddess knows we've all made mistakes, but it ends tonight."

Lisa Doll was leaning against a young woman and she spoke up, "Who died and made you the coven leader?"

The young woman next to her, a pretty brunette with dirt rubbed into her face and leaves stuck in her hair, reeled back, almost spilling Lisa to the gravel driveway. "Don't—"

"Shut up, Kendra," Lisa said. "This doesn't concern—"

"Carlton died," Jodie said so softly that everyone leaned forward to hear. "And my husband died. And your husband, too, Lisa."

Lisa rocked back as if struck. "I didn't..." She searched the faces of those around her, but no one would meet her gaze. She began to cry, and squeaked out, "I'm sorry." She no longer looked like a self-assured sex kitten, but like a somewhat well-kept housewife who had just realized her husband was dead.

"We're all sorry," the girl, Kendra, said. "If it makes a difference—"

"It doesn't," Jodie said, her voice dripping with derision. "But, for the sake of the community, we're going to work through this and pull ourselves together." She reached out and pulled Molly Gary and Dawn close to her, hugging them tightly. "We're going to come together, and we won't *ever* let something like this happen again. Swear on it. Swear that you will help me make this coven whole again. Swear on your talents!"

A murmuring rose for the group as the witches joined in, vowing to help Jodie rebuild.

I glanced over to Callie and Jameson. Both appeared as skeptical as I felt, but I pulled Jodie aside and explained what I needed from her, and she got busy ordering her people to work.

The farm was a beehive of activity when the sun rose. The runes in the concrete outbuilding had been chiseled off by weary members of Meriwether's coven and the bodies arranged in the kitchen and living room.

Jodie was waiting for me outside. "You really think this will work?" she asked.

"You really think Meriwether's coven shouldn't be punished?" I countered.

"Honestly?" She paused, and for a moment the mask dropped. She wasn't a hard woman leading her coven anymore. She was just a tired, middle-aged secretary consumed by grief. Then her face hardened and she growled, "I want to kill every last one of them."

I nodded. There was a moment as I poured gasoline around the Kormans' house when I looked at all the dead and felt an insane desire to murder the remaining members of Meriwether's coven. "It's your choice. If you can keep them in check—"

"They'll do as they're told," she said. "After tonight, I think they finally understand the consequences."

"What about Dawn?"

"She's a mess, but she'll survive. I'm bringing her into the coven."

"Is that a good idea?"

"She has a talent," Jodie said. "Now that she knows about magic, she could head down a dark path, especially as she deals with … with Dorothy's death."

"And Nicky?"

She pointed to the SUV, where Nicky was sleeping, peacefully unaware of anything around him. "He's family, Mr. Harlan." She raised her hand before I could speak. "He didn't understand what he was doing when he killed Dorothy, but that kind of magic twists someone. I saw the way he looked at Dawn."

"Yeah," I conceded. "You better watch him. He's … not going to be so easy to control. He's smarter now."

"He also has a talent," Jodie said. "We need to control it."

"Control it?"

She lowered her voice. "Remember what Randy said? The sight is fickle. Sometimes it shows you the truth and sometimes it shows you one of many *possible* truths. Nicky isn't evil, and I'm going to make sure he stays that way."

I wanted to argue with her about free will, but I just shrugged, stroked a match against the matchbox in my hand, and tossed it into the kitchen. The gasoline caught immediately. "There might be people who question this fire, but in my experience, they'll let it go. Too much of it won't make any sense."

"A party gone wrong, and over a dozen men and women, including some of Monticello and Bement's most prominent members, burned beyond recognition." Jodie shook her head. "I'll have to smooth things over, but it's nothing a little magic can't fix."

"Yeah," I said, "about that. You saw what magic did to Meriwether."

"It *wasn't* the magic," Jodie said. "That was his twisted desire to help Nicky."

"Maybe," I said. "Maybe not. He played with forces he didn't understand. You catch my drift?"

Jodie frowned. "When I looked into you, I saw pain and death. Don't take this the wrong way, Mr. Harlan, but when you leave here, don't return."

I smiled. It wasn't friendly. "Yeah, I understand. But I need you to understand something. You so much as even say the word vampire, and I'll be back. And I'm going to get real mean." Jodie blanched and started to mumble something, but I raised my hand to silence her. "Take care, Mrs. Rexford. Take all the care in the world, but don't you ever, *ever* do something that will make me darken your doorstep."

I left her there, in front of the roaring fire that now consumed the Kormans' farmhouse, got into the truck with Jameson and Callie, and headed to Saint Michaels Church.

* * *

We cleaned ourselves as best we could in the church's bathroom, bandaging or gluing our wounds and changing into fresh clothes. I gave Jameson the last of the Tramadol from our medical pack and he collapsed on the couch.

I stopped and inspected his head. The stench of burnt hair and skin made my stomach turn. "You need a hospital."

"Not around here," he said, without opening his eyes. "Too suspicious."

"Can you make it back to St. Louis?" I asked.

He sat up woozily, blinked, and said, "I only have to make it to Springfield. There's a priest there who can help. He knows the truth. Thank you, Samuel. What you've done? It's more than most would."

"It's my job," I said.

"No," Jameson said softly. "A lesser man would have quit." He paused. "You didn't have to kill Meriwether."

"I didn't," I conceded. "I didn't take any pleasure in it."

"I don't believe you," Jameson said.

"You don't?"

The priest smiled sadly. "I think you took a *little* pleasure in it."

"Could be that you're right," I said.

"You shouldn't have killed him."

"You think he deserved to live?"

"It's not our place to judge," the priest said solemnly. "Murder is a mortal sin."

I clenched my fists. "I couldn't risk him making another deal with Haagenti."

The priest frowned. "Perhaps God will forgive you. I will pray for you."

I nodded and spoke from my heart. "I've never been faithful, but I've tried to do right. I've fought evil and I've sacrificed ... so much. I hope He understands."

"I believe He will," Jameson said. His gaze roamed around the office and he blinked again. "I miss Ethan."

I took the seat next to him. "Me, too." We waited for Callie to finish cleaning up and I finally said, "Patrick? Is Haagenti really gone?"

There was a long moment of silence before Jameson replied, "For now."

"It sounded like Haagenti held a grudge."

"It thought it had me all those years ago. After an eternity of tempting humans, it maddened it to think I slipped away."

"Will it try again?"

"It has all of eternity," Jameson said. "What do you think?"

I grunted. "It seemed awfully interested in vampires. What if I cross paths with it again?"

"I'll pray for you," Jameson repeated sincerely.

Callie entered the office looking more like her old self but was moving carefully and limping heavily.

An intense desire to protect her rose within me and I felt the anger returning. I pushed it back down and turned to the priest. "I'll take all the help I can get."

Chapter Nineteen

We headed north on US-105. When we passed the turnoff to the Kormans' farm, I looked to the west and saw a billowing cloud of smoke still rising to the sky from the burning farmhouse. We continued on to Monticello and I stopped long enough to do a quick search of Meriwether's house.

I found my toolbox inside his garage. I tossed it in the back of the truck and got in, only to find Callie fast asleep. She was hugging herself tightly and she snorted with every bump in the road. I headed south and pulled through the Hardee's drive-through, grabbing a cup of coffee and six bacon, egg, and cheese biscuits before taking I-72 to Decatur, wolfing down my breakfast as I drove.

The food was greasy, fattening, and delicious. The coffee was black ambrosia. I thought about waking Callie, but she was snoring softly and I didn't want to wake her.

I used the opportunity to make a phone call.

Henry answered on the first ring and said, "I'm halfway across South Dakota."

"Don't bother," I said. "It's done."

There was a long silence. "You took care of it?"

"Yep."

"That's—that's good, Sam. Jack would have been proud."

"About that. The demon said something about my family."

"Jack—"

"It *wasn't* about Jack," I said.

Henry sighed. "I don't think this is the time—"

"You're not going to tell me you're my distant grandfather?"

Henry laughed. "We are *not* related, I promise you. Look, it won't change anything, and—"

"What?" I demanded. "I'm sick of the lies."

There was a moment of silence before Henry said, "You've earned it, I guess. Jack's family wasn't targeted by a passing vampire."

"He wasn't?"

"Harlans have fought and killed vampires for as long as I've been ... well, you know. Since I turned."

After all I had seen and done, I didn't believe in coincidences anymore. "What makes us so special?"

"There's a stubborn streak in your family, Sam. The Harlans fight back."

"That's it?" I asked.

"Not what you were hoping for?"

"I just thought there was more to it."

"In all my years, I've never known anyone like your kin. Don't laugh that off. It makes you dangerous as hell."

There was a squeal of tires over the phone. "What's that?" I asked.

"That's me heading home," Henry said. "Alma's going to be mighty sore with me for taking off in the middle of the night. Call me when things settle down." The phone went dead as Henry hung up.

My next call was to Billy. "How's the spirit world?"

"Things are back to normal," Billy said. "What did you do?"

"Just cleaned up a mess. Killed a vampire. Exorcised a demon."

The silence on the phone stretched out. "A demon," Billy finally said. "I'm—I'm not sure I should be talking to you. You're going to get me killed."

"It's all fine now," I said. "Everything is back to normal."

"Demons aren't normal," Billy said loudly. "A demon that's powerful enough to disturb the spirit world is the kind of thing that gets people killed."

"I told you," I said, trying not to raise my voice, "everything is *fine.*"

Billy barked out a laugh. "I'm a coward, Sam. I know it. You know it. I can't—"

"You tried, Billy. You could have told me anything and I would have believed it. But you risked a spirit walk for me. You're *not* a coward."

When Billy spoke, he didn't sound quite so freaked out. "Flattery will get you nowhere, white man."

"Just keep working on your chips," I said.

"Go fuck yourself," Billy said, then ended the call.

I continued driving and Callie finally opened her eyes when we were on I-74, well past Bloomington. "Take the next exit," she said in a tired voice.

I gave her a quizzical glance. "Why?"

"Trust me," she said.

I took the Goodfield exit, and she directed me to a restaurant on the south edge of town. A few minutes later and she was eating a breaded cod sandwich and I was tearing into a grilled rib-eye sandwich as big as a plate.

"How did you know about this place?" I asked between mouthfuls of bloody rare beef.

"A few of us used to come here," she said, taking a delicate bite of her sandwich.

"The food's good," I said.

"Just wait," she said. "It's the pie that makes it all worthwhile."

She was right.

I'd owned a diner and I knew a thing or two about pie. It was *amazing*. The blueberries in the pie were fresh and large, not the usual sugary mush from a can. "Oh my God."

Callie licked banana cream from her spoon. "I told you."

We sat in the south section of the restaurant. The nearest customers, a pair of women in homespun dresses and blue bonnets, were at least twenty feet away. "I've been thinking..." I started.

Callie nodded. "I'm sure you have."

"This was my fault."

She frowned. "How was *any* of this your fault?"

I told her what Barlow had said, then finished with, "That's on me. If I hadn't begged Gloria for help..." I shook my head. "I've been fumbling about, making choices without understanding the stakes. I confronted Gloria. That sent Milford to Bement. That's probably what finally pushed Carlton over the edge. He thought Jodie had captured Milford and he made the pact with Haagenti. Action and reaction."

"You've lost everything," she said in an angry whisper, "and you've fought back. You've killed vampires and helped exorcise a demon. Carlton's deal with the demon was *his* choice. Not yours!"

"I got you kidnapped," I said, my voice breaking. "They ... did things to you."

"Don't worry about me. I have faith." She leaned back in her chair. She looked tired and had dark bags under her eyes, but she offered a small smile and it was like the sun shining on a warm summer day. "You saw the Powers."

"Powers?"

She nodded. "Those weren't just *any* angels, Sam. The Powers belong to the second hierarchy of angels. They are God's warriors, keeping the forces of darkness in check. That should be all the proof you need that you're following the righteous path."

* * *

Sister Beulah sat behind her desk at the rectory. She stood as we entered, taking note of Callie's limp with a raised eyebrow. She held up her hand. "Sister Callie—"

"What is it?" Callie asked.

"I have some bad news," Sister Beulah said. "Father Lewinheim passed away last night."

"H—how?" Callie asked.

My heart hammered in my chest. "What?"

Sister Beulah's eyes narrowed. "Follow me."

She led us up the stairs to the Father's room and closed the door behind us. "Edmund passed last night, shortly after supper."

I swallowed. "There wasn't anything ... funny about it?"

The Sister regarded me coolly, then she blinked and her face softened. "You've been through something horrible."

"There was a vampire," I started.

"The demon Haagenti," Callie finished.

Sister Beulah staggered back. "I see." She sat down heavily on Lewinheim's bed, an unreadable mix of emotions playing across her face.

"Did he ... die peacefully?" I asked.

The Sister raised her head and inspected me, then said softly, "He was an old man. It was his time. He'd seen much. Lived through much. But no, there was nothing 'funny' about his death. He died peacefully."

I let out the deep breath I hadn't realized I was holding. "It's just ... so many things have happened."

"He was *old*," Sister Beulah said. "Everyone grows old, boy. Everyone dies. It gives our life meaning." She stood and handed me the book from the table next to Lewinheim's recliner. "He wanted you to have this."

I took it gingerly from her hands. It was a well-worn and dog-eared copy of the Holy Bible. "I've never read it."

Sister Beulah snorted. "Why am I not surprised? Edmund prayed for you, you know. The both of you. Things are going to get harder."

"Harder?" I asked. "I don't know how much harder things can get."

"Things can always get harder, Harlan." The Sister's face fell and she said quietly, "It's the way of the world."

"What will you do?" Callie asked.

The Sister turned to her. "Does he know?"

"Know what?" I asked.

Callie shook her head. "No, but he can be trusted."

I glanced between the two of them. "What are you talking about?"

"The Church has fought against vampires for centuries," Sister Beulah said. "Men can be … weak of body and spirit. Sometimes they need help. The Order helps them when they falter and cares for them when they can no longer fight. I was assigned to watch over Edmund. Now that Edmund is gone, I'll be moving on to my next assignment."

"Wait," I said. "You belong to this Order?"

"As does Callie," Sister Beulah said.

"As did Katie," Callie said.

Sister Beulah said nothing and Callie finally broke eye contact.

"Take care of her," Sister Beulah said to me as she stood and made her way out of the room. "You'll need each other in the times to come."

She left us alone in Lewinheim's room. I sat in the recliner. Without Lewinheim, the room was cold and lifeless. "I can't believe he's gone."

As soon as I said it, I realized how dumb it sounded. Callie had known Lewinheim for most of her life. He was the one who had brought the Calahanes to Peoria.

Only, that wasn't *quite* the truth. Apparently, Katie and Callie were part of an order assigned to Lewinheim. That piece of knowledge cast everything in a different light.

"He was a good man," Callie said. She took a pad of paper

and wrote a note.

"What's that?" I asked.

"I'm having Father Lewinheim's journals sent to Toledo."

"*Smart,*" I said. I opened the Bible and fingered the pages. "I guess I should start reading this."

Callie laughed, and for a moment I forgot about my guilt and worries and all the bad things that had happened.

"It's your choice, Sam. You've got free will." She stood and nodded to the door. "Let's go home. It's a long drive back to Toledo."

ABOUT THE AUTHOR

Kevin Lee Swaim studied creative writing with David Foster Wallace at Illinois State University.

He's currently the Subject Matter Expert for Intrusion Prevention Systems for a Fortune 50 insurance company located in the Midwest. He holds the CISSP certification from ISC2.

When he's not writing, he's busy repairing guitars for the working bands of Central Illinois.

If you enjoyed this book, please leave a review at Amazon. Kevin loves to hear from his readers.

www.ingramcontent.com/pod-product-compliance
Lightning Source LLC
Chambersburg PA
CBHW020107180626
46812CB00006B/2504